COUNTDOWN

CAROLYN RIDDER ASPENSON

COUNTDOWN

Copyright © 2022 Carolyn Ridder Aspenson.

Severn River Publishing
www.SevernRiverBooks.com

ISBN: 978-1-64875-437-1 (Paperback)

ALSO BY CAROLYN RIDDER ASPENSON

To find out more about Carolyn Ridder Aspenson and her books, visit severnriverbooks.com

To Jack
LUMI

1

The smell of iron penetrated my nose. I knew before seeing the bodies there would be blood. There's always blood at a crime scene, and even the smallest amount can trigger the iron scent. I slipped into my booties and gloves, took a deep breath, and walked into the scene with an open mind and the door to my feelings slammed shut. Murder investigations didn't get solved with emotions, and I chose to protect myself emotionally from the nightmares I faced daily. If I didn't, I'd be institutionalized, as would most cops on the job.

The scene was tragic, a stunning house on a gorgeous summer night set up as the perfect home for wonderful lives, except those lives lay extinguished on the floor of the main room. Murder scenes were always tragic, but the level of tragedy varied. The couple should have been eating dinner, or watching the sun set, or having sex, not sitting lifeless on their wood floors, their last emotion fear.

The man's left side rested against the gray wall. He appeared to have been posed in a seated position on the dark wood floor, but experience told me he wasn't. There was a small bloodstain on his shirt and a hole in the center of his forehead. The woman was sitting also, but when the bullet entered her skull, she had fallen toward his side, landing with her right shoulder resting on his left hip. Based on the angle of her body, I assumed the shooter stood to her left. Best I could tell from a cursory overview, she'd been shot just once. There could be several reasons for that; this was about the man, the most common being the woman being in the wrong place at the wrong time, or the second most common, the killer wanted them both dead and wanted to make a statement. The extra shot was often a *just in case* trigger pull.

The room, what Hamby real estate agents would call the keeping room, located off the kitchen, was big enough to hold an orchestra and its audience, but it felt cold, and small, and empty from the loss of life. It wasn't designed for the coldness seeping from the walls. No decorating detail had been spared, with six-foot-tall, expensively framed oil paintings lining one wall and large print photos of mountains and beach scenery and a distant wedding photograph matching in size on the opposite wall. Tacky but still expensive figurines and other knickknacks my grandmother would have loved filled the built-in bookcases framing the stone fireplace. It was too much for my taste, but most everything about Hamby Georgia homes overwhelmed me. I quickly noticed there were no real photos of the couple other than the wedding prints.

I shook my head and sighed. "Homicide sucks."

I asked an officer on the scene to take photos of everything on the shelves. I'd have time to examine things more carefully once I addressed the victims, but small details like that usually gave clues to the more critical information we needed to solve a case, and I didn't want anything missed while my partner, Bishop, and I had more urgent things to handle.

"Strange that there's just the wedding photo of the couple. It's like they've had no life since the wedding. I wonder if they were newlyweds?" I studied the victims' positions carefully. "Backs against the wall says one shooter trying to maintain control. Could be panicked, unplanned, even."

Bishop was staring at something on the other side of the room. "If it's my doc, he wasn't a newlywed." He walked across the room at full stride, his arms swinging with determination and intent. He nodded as he dragged his fingers down his overgrown five o'clock shadow and stared at the male victim. "Damn, it's definitely him. That's too bad. He was a good doctor."

"He's an ortho, right? Was, I mean."

He nodded. "Specialized in back treatment. Pain management, that kind of thing."

"So, this could be a drug issue?"

"As in prescription drugs?"

"For starters."

"It's something to consider, but he never prescribed any opioids for me. We talked about it a few times, and he said he didn't want to contribute to the opioid crisis. He was a fan of nerve blockers like gabapentin and your standard NSAIDs."

I raised my brow. "How is it I had no idea you go to a back doctor?"

"Do you tell me when it's your time of the month?"

I laughed. "It's 2021, Bishop. You can say 'period,' and no." I smiled. "I figure you can tell, anyway."

"Damn straight I can. As I was trying to say, I'm not one to brag about my aches and pains." He rubbed his lower back as if just mentioning it triggered pain. "But this one is an old football injury. MVP on varsity two years in a row."

I smiled. "In what, the late 1800s?"

He narrowed his eyes and shot me a death glare. "You were probably the Fridge on powderpuff. Not in size, of course. I'm talking about power."

"I sure hope that's what you meant, and how do you even know about powderpuff? Was that a thing back in the golden years?" It was hard not to laugh at my own wit sometimes.

Bishop rolled his eyes. "Golden years, my ass. Of course I know about powderpuff. Girls pretending to play football so the guys can watch and pretend it's mud wrestling? Isn't that still a thing?"

I shrugged. "Probably a victim of cancel culture, and from the way you just described it, I can understand why, but kudos for the reference to William Perry from the Chicago Bears."

"I miss the good old days." He stared at the wall as if we weren't standing over two dead bodies.

"Surprised you still remember them." I couldn't help but smile again. I was on a snarky roll, and it was just what the mental health professionals ordered after such a tragic and complicated investigation. "You take anything now?"

"Still take gabapentin, but only when absolutely necessary." He patted his growing belly. "It causes rapid weight gain in some people, and I'm one of them."

I glanced at his belly and smiled. "I wasn't going to say anything, but…"

He shook his head. "Can we get back to the investigation, please, smart ass?"

If citizens saw how cops acted at murder scenes, they'd be angry and offended, but we had to keep things light to maintain our sanity. It's tough to compartmentalize, but we can't—and shouldn't—live inside the trauma of every murder. Those that do end up alcoholics or victims of suicide.

"Yes, sir." I mumbled, "Testy old man," under my breath.

"I heard that."

I laughed, then got back to business by crouching down and examining the man's entry wound. "One shot's perfectly centered just above the bridge of the nose. No need for the second one with that kind of hit." I studied the bloodstained wall. "Whoever did this has a steady hand and good aim."

Bishop nodded. "Shot the husband first. What's that say to you?"

"They wanted the wife to suffer more, which could blow the whole drug theory. What do you think?"

"Like I said, I'm not sure the drug theory works anyway. Could just be someone who was scared or desperate. That being said, it could be a tweaker could have shot the wrong person out of nervousness, but this really doesn't read drugs to me."

"Agree, and a tweaker doesn't normally have that kind of aim." Tweakers shook too much from either being high or being in withdrawal. A steady hand wasn't part of their playbook.

"Tell that to the families of deceased persons shot by them." He pointed to the coffee table and bookcases. "Look around. The place doesn't say a tweaker desperate for a hit. Nothing's been touched."

I studied the room again. "You're right." I pointed to an expensive-looking vase on the coffee table. "There's a lot of sellable stuff in this room alone, and none of it's out of place." I glanced behind me and checked the name tag of the officer standing nearby. He didn't look familiar. "Hey, Padget, you new?" I assumed so since I didn't recognize him.

He nodded. "Yes, ma'am. Just transferred from Johns Creek."

"Detective Rachel Ryder. Welcome to the department. Quick question.

Do you know how many LEOs are on scene?"

He raised an eyebrow. "Not sure, but it's a slow night, so I'd guess all patrol on shift has been by to check it out."

"Great. I need two officers searching the house. The male vic was a doctor. We need to make sure this isn't drug related. Look for anything that stands out and could be associated with why someone would want this couple dead, but definitely, say, a medical bag that appears rummaged through, prescription bottles with missing drugs, that kind of thing."

"We've got people doing a scene review already, Detective."

I smiled. "Then we'll have two more focused on those items in particular."

"Yes, ma'am," he said and took off running.

"Always Ms. Personality," Bishop said. He'd been studying the victims. "First assumption is an employee over a patient, but from my experience with him personally, I don't see either fitting."

"Why?"

"Rockman was well liked. Always got doctor of the year in the local papers, and getting an appointment was tough. He booked months in advance."

"That popularity could have been because he liked to screw his patients, and one of them decided she'd had enough." I exhaled. "Or he."

"Anything's possible," he said. "Call came from the office manager, so I guess that could be the case for an employee too, but I still don't see it."

"Did he talk about his wife much?"

He shook his head. "He focused more on me and my problems. I think he probably did, but honestly, I can't say."

I glanced at the victim's left hand. He wasn't wearing a wedding ring. "Did he wear a ring?"

He shrugged. "Not that I can recall."

I pointed to the victim's wedding finger. "Looks like he wasn't a ring wearer."

"I didn't wear one when I was married either."

"And we know how that ended." Bishop was divorced. His wife cheated on him, but it didn't make him bitter. For the most part, anyway.

"Back to the office manager," he said.

"It's not uncommon for the doer to make the call and stick around to watch. We'll talk to the employees. Odds are someone will have something to say about a patient and employee."

"Doctor's offices can't give patient information."

"Precedent is iffy on this," I said. "And besides, we're not asking for medical information. We're asking for information regarding the interpersonal relationships of a doctor and the people in his practice, patients, and employees. Medical history is entirely different."

He sighed. "Slippery slope, partner. And like I said, he's the number one ortho doc in metro Atlanta. You know how many patients he's got?"

"I'm guessing a lot."

"That's an understatement." He checked his watch. We'd just come off a large DEA task force case, literally a few hours ago, and we were exhausted. He'd worked triple duty as a football coach, history teacher, and DEA agent. "No rest for the weary, I guess."

"Sleep's overrated, anyway." I checked the bullet entry location on the woman. "Just off-center." I held my flashlight aimed at the hole for a more precise visual. "Look at this."

Bishop groaned as he crouched down and looked. "What am I looking at?"

"How perfectly round the hole is."

He grimaced. "You're not wrong." He stood up and brushed off his pants.

"Studying the wound is part of the job, Bishop. When you've seen as many as I have, you get numb."

"I hope I don't ever see as many as you."

I tightened the band around my ponytail as I stood. "It's going to be a long night."

"Puts a damper on that date you had planned." He winked at me.

"That'll have to wait." A sharp pain shot through my gut. The truth was, there wasn't always enough time for that stuff, and I needed to remind myself. My husband's murder was proof. We shouldn't live our lives thinking we have time later, because there isn't always a later. Tragedy could happen at any moment. I knew that from personal experience.

As for the date I'd had planned, it was just dinner with someone.

Someone I'd worked with and failed at having a one-night stand with. I say failed because that event led to more even though I'd tried to pretend it hadn't. Things were moving along with Agent Kyle Olsen, though slowly, and I had to figure out a way to come to terms with moving on while I still loved my dead husband.

Detective Michels walked up, and I asked him, "Where's the person who called 911? Office manager for the male vic?"

"Sitting in Officer Emmett's vehicle, ma'am," he said. "Name's Heather Maynor."

"Can you bring her over to the garage for questioning, please?"

Michels nodded. "Sure thing, Detective." He trotted away.

Michels was a relatively recent addition to the detective roster within the Hamby Police Department. Hamby is a suburb of Atlanta, a growing city with a nod to its former equestrian farms still largely intact, and a small-town feel. The residents were primarily wealthy, minus a few areas, and for reasons our chief hated, crime was increasing. Because of that, he'd begun adding detectives to the department.

Michels had been with HPD for some time and finally received a much-deserved promotion. His training lasted over a year, but it was on the job, and that was the best kind. A little green still, but he was kicking ass and taking names already.

Bishop swiped his finger over his iPhone's screen. "I have an appointment with him next week."

"Had," I said and turned to walk outside. "You got this, right?"

He nodded. "I'll toss out some markers, take some notes, do a little of the searching myself. Go interview. If you need me, you know where to find me."

I caught up to Michels as he went to tend to the office manager. "Change of plans. I got this," I told him. "Thanks for helping. Can you please assist Bishop?"

"But you just—"

"Like I said, change of plans, Detective." I decided I'd rather hit the office manager up before anyone else got to her. I didn't want her answers shaped by too many patrol officers' questions.

"Yes, ma'am," he said and smiled as he left. The smile was filled with snark and humor because Michels knew it yanked my chain to be called *ma'am.*

I understood the Southern politeness of the word, but it just made me feel old, and given my very recent work with teenagers, I felt old enough. I knew Michels's intentions were meant to be humorous, so I didn't give him a hard time about it, even though he was being a smartass.

A tall but slim woman somewhere north of fifty stood near the garage. A paramedic placed a mylar blanket across her shoulders as I walked over and introduced myself. "Heather Maynor, Detective Rachel Ryder. You're the one who called us, yes?"

She held the blanket tight as she nodded. "Yes. Is Steve...are...they're dead, aren't they?"

I nodded slowly. "Yes, ma'am." I waited to see if she'd respond. When she didn't, I said, "I'd like to ask you a few questions. Do you think you're capable of answering them?" I didn't usually ask that, but the distant look in her eyes and her constant shivering made me think she was going into shock. I glanced at the paramedic. He smiled and nodded, giving me the all-clear.

"I...I...where's Ryan? Is he okay?"

"Who's Ryan?"

"Oh my God! He's...he's their son! Where is he? I...I should have looked for him inside. I...I don't know what they'd planned to do with him tonight. The nanny. I...is she here?" Her lower lip trembled as she stared at the home from the yard.

"Ma'am." I used the term I hated unintentionally, trying to calm her. My mind went back to the photos on the wall. The distant shots of a wedding, lots of scenery, but no additional photos of the couple or a child, and nothing in the room to indicate a kid lived there. "Are you sure there's a child?"

"Yes, I'm sure! Ryan. He's...he's five, and..." She gasped as the panicked look on her face intensified. "He's diabetic. Type 1. Oh, God! Someone needs to find him. He'll get sick if he doesn't get his medicine."

"Okay, please, remain calm. Do you know who was supposed to have the boy during the dinner?"

"I...maybe the nanny or Mary. I'm not sure."

"Mary?"

"Melodie's mother."

I held up my finger to stop her from continuing, said, "Just a moment," and spoke into the radio immediately. "We've got a possible missing five-year-old boy with a medical condition. Type 1 diabetes. I need a check through the house for him or anything that might show a possible kidnapping, and I need a phone number for—" I asked Ms. Maynor the grandmother's name.

"Mary Hagerty."

I clicked on my radio's mic. "A Mary Hagerty, the female victim's mother." I clicked off the mic. "Do you know where she lives?"

"Hamby, I believe. I don't have her number, though, I'm sorry."

"It's okay," I said. I spoke into my radio again. "Grandmother resides in Hamby."

An officer responded immediately.

I added, "Let's get boots on the ground hitting the neighbors' doors stat. The kid might have been home and run off when he heard the shots. Make the ones nearby check their video cameras for any vehicles leaving the Rockmans' home or driving past. Get copies emailed to us ASAP." I clicked my radio button off and turned back to the woman. "Do you have a contact number for the nanny?"

Her chin trembled, and it took her a moment to get the words out. "The nanny? I...I don't recall her name, but I made Steve a family emergency binder, and I know their numbers are in it. It's in...it should be in the desk in the kitchen. Please, you need to find out who has Ryan. Something could happen if he doesn't get his insulin."

Wish she would have told me about the binder a minute ago, but she was stressed, and I understood. It just didn't make our jobs any easier. I sent an officer into the kitchen for the binder.

I held it out for the office manager to examine. "Is this the binder you're talking about?"

She nodded. "The...the numbers are in there."

"I found the number," I said to the team.

"Ten-four, Detective."

The nanny's number went straight to a store in Atlanta. It was closed. I called the female victim's mother.

She answered on the fourth ring. "I'm not interested," she said and disconnected.

"Dammit!" I hit the number again.

"I said I'm—"

I spoke before she could finish. "Mary Hagerty, this is Detective Rachel Ryder with the Hamby Police Department. I'm calling to see if you have your grandson, Ryan."

"What?" She coughed. "Where's Melodie? Is she okay?"

"Ms. Hagerty, please answer the question."

"No. No, I don't have Ryan. Why would I have—" She gasped. "Oh no!" And then she cried into the phone. "What's happened to my daughter? Was it a car accident?"

"Ms. Hagerty, there has been an incident at your daughter's home, and we currently are looking for your grandson. I need to know if there is someone he could be with. I called the nanny, but the number went to a store in Atlanta."

She struggled to breathe. Shit, was she hyperventilating on the phone?

"Ms. Hagerty, I know this is a lot to take in, especially over the phone, but I need your help." It wasn't protocol to deliver an end-of-life notice over the phone, but when a missing kid's involved, it's hard to follow homicide protocol, but I left out the details of the shooting and actual death.

"They fired the nanny a few weeks ago. I...I—where's Melodie? Is she okay?"

"Ma'am, who else could have Ryan? A neighbor, a babysitter, maybe?"

"No, there's no one. Melodie wouldn't do that. She's too protective of that boy. I...I live fifteen minutes away. I'll be right there."

"Is your husband with you?"

She laughed. "I'm divorced, and the bastard lives across the country," she said and then disconnected the call.

Ashley, our *soon-to-be-on-to-bigger-and-better-jobs* crime scene tech, walked over as I stuck my cell phone into my back pocket. "I was just coming to tell you the victims have a son when I heard you on the radio. Why are there no pictures of the kid anywhere?"

I pulled her away from the ambulance and out of Heather Maynor's earshot. "I was just asking myself the same thing. Did you notice there aren't any photos of the couple, either? Just the big presentation one of the wedding."

She nodded. "Strange."

"Very. We have LEOs searching the house. Why the hell didn't they tell me about the boy's room?"

She shrugged. "This place is massive. I don't think they've gotten to it yet, but I have."

"Of course you have." God, I was going to miss her. "How'd it look?"

"Untouched. Didn't notice anything out of order, and if we've got a kidnapper, they either made the bed before they left, or it was still made from this morning. I checked for prints right quick. I'll look at those first, but I also found a safe in the den."

"Was it open?"

She shook her head. "I checked it for prints too."

"Did you dust or use the light?"

"Used the light and took photos. Do you want me to dust?"

I shook my head. "Send the photos off to Bubba ASAP. He can run them. Let me know immediately if he gets anything, okay?"

She nodded. "Of course. Bubba can come and get that safe unlocked too. He's good at that."

"Not yet," I said. "The female vic's mother is on her way. Let me see if she knows the combo first."

"Gotcha."

Heather Maynor sat shaking on the back of the ambulance. "Did you find Ryan? Is he okay?"

"We're still looking, but Mary Hagerty is on her way. I need you to tell me what brought you here tonight and everything you saw when you arrived, okay? In the order it happened. But first, I need to know when you saw Dr. Rockman last. Do you understand?"

She nodded. "He was in the office this morning. We had a company dinner tonight. A company dinner," she repeated as if she was trying to come to terms with everything. "Steve—Dr. Rockman holds them once a quarter, but he…they didn't show, and I called him. He…he didn't answer. I tried Melodie too, but her phone went straight to voicemail."

"What made you decide to come to their home?"

"He was supposed to be there, and he wasn't. That's not like him. I just… it was strange. I got worried. He's been a little off lately."

"A little off, how?"

"It's hard to explain. Like something was distracting him. Sort of distant, not as, you know, in tune to what's going on at work. Mixed up patients. Nothing major, just not normal for him."

"What happened when you arrived?"

"I knew something wasn't right. The garage door was opened, and both cars were here. This is obviously a safe community, but it surprised me that the garage was open. Melodie is very protective of her family. She worries something will happen to Ryan all the time."

"What did you do next?"

"I, uh…I went to the front door and rang the bell. When no one answered, I checked the garage door into the house, and it was opened. I called out to Ste—Dr. Rockman and Melodie, and when they didn't answer, I walked in. I was in the middle of the kitchen when I saw them…" She began to cry again. "I saw them lying there with the blood. God, it was awful." She sobbed into her hands.

I placed my hand on her shoulder. "I know this is hard, and I'm sorry you have to go through this, but I need you to continue. Can you do that?"

She nodded, sucked in a breath of air, and continued. "I…I just froze, you know? I couldn't go to them. I wanted to, but I…it was just so awful, and I didn't know what to do. I just stood there for, I don't know how long, and then I just ran back to my car and called 911."

"You didn't see the boy anywhere?"

She shook her head. "I don't know why, but I just didn't think of him until you came up."

That wasn't unusual with someone in shock, and I was beginning to think Heather Maynor was in shock.

"I'm sorry. I should have—"

"It's not your fault, Ms. Maynor. You did the right thing." I removed the small flip spiral notebook from my pocket. I didn't keep them there all the time, but I did keep a stash in my car and grabbed them as needed. I had a feeling this one would fill up quickly. "You said there was a dinner tonight. Can you tell me more about that? Who was coming, where it was?"

She gazed off into the distance. As she spoke, she rubbed her arms under the mylar blanket. "We, uh, we had a reservation at Coalition in downtown Alpharetta. Steve, I mean, Dr. Rockman picked the location, but I made the reservation and set up everything. Dr. Rockman likes to show his staff appreciation and recognize their efforts."

I'd get the details on that in a moment. First, I needed to establish a time frame for what happened. "And the reservation time?"

"Eight o'clock."

I glanced at my watch. "When was the last time you spoke to Dr. Rockman?"

"When he left the office just before noon, but I also called him to let him know I'd arrived at the restaurant at about five thirty."

"Did you speak to him then?"

She shook her head. "I left a message."

"And you weren't concerned?"

"No. I leave him a lot of messages."

I nodded. "It's eleven now, and you called 911 at nine forty-five. Can you tell me why you waited?"

"I got busy with the party. I knew he wasn't there, but I just figured he was running late, or maybe he and Melodie had problems with Ryan's arrangements or something. She's always so particular about Ryan because of his diabetes."

"Did you try to contact him again to see why he was running late or if everything was okay before coming here?"

"You mean after I left the message before the dinner?"

"Yes."

She nodded. "He didn't answer. Oh, I texted him then too."

"What time was that?"

"I, uh...I'm not sure."

"May I see your phone?"

"Uh, yes." She stuck her hand in her purse and dug around in it until she pulled out her phone. She opened the text thread and handed the phone to me.

"So, you texted him at eight forty-five. When was the presentation?"

"A few minutes after I texted him. I don't know the time."

"It looks like you called him at nine thirty."

She nodded. "He didn't answer, so I decided to go by his place."

"Go on," I said. Sometimes those simple words kept people talking.

"Like I said, he hadn't been himself lately. I guess I was...I was worried."

"But you don't know why?"

"No, I don't. One day he was his normal self, and the next, he wasn't. I can't explain it."

"Do you know of anything that's happened in his personal life that could cause that change?"

She shook her head. "Not that I can think of, but Steve didn't really share personal things with me. Not in the past few years, anyway."

"Past few years? Did something happen then to cause him to change?"

She pressed her lips together. "When Ryan was diagnosed, he kind of closed up."

"I understand. Tonight, when he didn't show up or answer his phone, did you try calling his wife?"

"No. I only tried her cell when I arrived here."

"May I ask why?"

She shrugged. "I don't...I guess I just didn't think about it. I work for Dr. Rockman, and this was a business function. Besides, Melodie and I aren't really connected. We haven't been for a while."

Or she didn't like the wife. I'd dealt with many cases where a close employee to an authority figure developed feelings for their boss and despised the spouse out of contempt or jealousy. I couldn't rule that out with Heather Maynor. I'd hit on that later, though. "Can you tell me if Dr. Rockman's had any problems with patients or staff recently? Does he have any pending lawsuits against him or the practice? Has anyone been let go in the past few weeks or so?"

She took in a deep breath and exhaled. "I...I...everyone loved Dr. Rock-man. He...I...no, I don't know of any lawsuits, and why would someone want to sue him? He helps people." She shrugged off the blanket and stood.

"We have to find Ryan. He might need his insulin. When was the last time he got it? I...where is Steve? Is he okay?"

The paramedic and I made eye contact. He nodded and said, "She needs a break, Detective."

I'd gotten all I could from her. She'd begun the descent into full-blown shock asking for the dead victim. "Let the hospital know we'll send someone there to talk with her in a bit."

"Will do," the paramedic said and nudged her back into the ambulance.

I tossed on a fresh pair of gloves and booties and rushed toward the kitchen to check for insulin in the fridge. "Anything on the kid?" I asked a passing officer.

"Not that I'm aware of, ma'am."

There was no insulin in the refrigerator. A mother would never be without insulin for her diabetic child, which told me the person who had the kid probably took it. And that meant whoever took him knew him. I ran up the stairs to the second level. I wanted to see the boy's room for myself. I practically fell on top of Dr. Barron, the county coroner, on my way.

"Sorry," I said as I pushed past.

"Hold up, sweetheart, I've got some questions."

"You're going to have to wait, Doc. We've got an insulin-dependent kid we're trying to locate."

He stepped aside quickly. "Understood. I've got insulin in my truck if needed."

"Thank you."

Michels stopped me on my way upstairs.

"What?" I asked impatiently.

"There's an insulin pump in the child's bathroom," he said. "But no medicine."

"That would be in the fridge, but I just checked, and there's nothing there."

"What parent doesn't have insulin for their kid?" he asked.

"In this house, none." As I headed toward the bedroom, I added, "You're not asking the right question. You should be asking who took the insulin when they took the child."

"Shit."

"Now you're getting it." I knew nothing about insulin pumps or diabetes, but I had a feeling I'd learn a lot in the next few hours. "Are you sure what you saw was an insulin pump?"

"Google is my friend." He smiled. "It's probably an extra in case the one he's wearing breaks. Also, if the kid had a suitcase," he said as he led me to the room and over to the closet, "it's gone."

I exhaled. "Dammit. Search every bit of this house just in case. He could be a witness. He could have seen something, freaked, and hid. Basement storage. Attic. He could be hiding in a closet. Oh, by the way, Barron's here. He's got insulin in his truck if we need it." I got on the radio and spoke. "We need a team of officers outside. I want every single neighbor on the street and on the street behind the home questioned. Pronto. The child is insulin dependent, wears a pump, and there is no medicine in the refrigerator. Ask everyone you meet if they knew the boy was diabetic and if they knew who stayed with the kid when the parents were out. Get whatever info you can, and report back to Bishop or me if you get a hit."

I studied the room, amazed at the fact that in such a big house, the child had just the one space for his things. Granted, the space was the size of my townhome's main floor, but still. Other than the room, there wasn't anything in the home that showed a child lived there. Who the hell lives like that? No family photos, no school photos, nothing family oriented or personal. Something wasn't right. Everything that would show a loving, connected family was MIA in the home, and when that stuff was MIA, a happy family usually was too.

Thoughts raced through my mind. Possibilities of what could have happened to the boy and why the scene showed nothing of the child. Abuse. Neglect. Marital problems. Depression. It could have been anything. I exhaled and re-wrapped my long hair into a twist at the base of my neck, then spoke to Michels again. "We need a photo of the boy—" I glanced around the room. "Check the drawers in the parents' room. Maybe there's something in there. Check their closets and any storage. There's got to be a photo of this damn kid somewhere!"

"I'm on it," he said.

"Get the kid to Barron ASAP if you find him," I yelled as he left.

I checked the windows, all locked. I went through the closet, checking for something that might be missing, then ran my hands down the walls of it for a hidden door or break. I found nothing and went on to the next room.

If someone used the rooms, it wasn't anyone with stuff. The home felt staged, like a model home. Personal things were nowhere to be found. The next room was probably a guest room, unlived in, both literally and emotionally. The entire house felt filled with furniture yet void of family. The additional three bedrooms were the same. Even the master, with its grand fireplace, lush sitting area filled with comfy but elegant furniture, and a poster bed the size of Rhode Island, felt emotionally sparse. I picked through the nightstands filled with over-the-counter medicines, notepads, books, and two boxes of condoms. The boxes hadn't been opened. Not a good sign, I thought.

Michels entered the room breathless. "I found a photo in an office downstairs. In fact, there are several."

"I guess that's the photo room," I said.

"Mostly of the boy." He took a moment to catch his breath. "Sorry, those stairs are a bitch."

"Male or female office?"

"Looks like the man's, why?"

"Just processing. Strange that there's no photos of the kid in any room but the man's office. Any of the wife?"

"Nope."

I headed back downstairs and checked the built-in cabinets in the great room. I found several photo frames, but none with photos. Someone must have removed them from the frames, but why?

A woman's shrill scream followed by a boatload of swear words echoed from outside. I heard the commotion before I saw it, but I knew it was the victim's mother. The mothers always screamed. The fathers were usually too emotional to speak, even before they knew what happened.

The woman's voice shrieked loudly over the rush of law enforcement crowding the home's yard. "Where is my daughter? I demand you take me to my daughter now!"

Bishop tapped me on the shoulder. "Time to roll."

2

Bishop and I rushed over to Mary Hagerty before she drew any more unwanted rubberneckers to the street.

"My daughter! Where's my daughter? Is she okay?" Tears streamed down her face and the inevitable snot dribbled from her nose. It always happened, and it never ceased to gross me out.

"Ma'am," Bishop said. "Come with us, please." With a gentle hand to her elbow, he guided her toward the garage and away from the bustle of the scene outside.

She shoved him away near the garage door. "Tell me where my daughter is now!"

There are many victims to violent crimes, and people sometimes forget about the survivors. This poor woman lost her daughter, her son-in-law, and possibly her grandson, and we had no answers, nothing to tell her other than to inform her that her daughter and son-in-law were dead and her grandson missing. Nothing else would have mattered in that moment. Information wouldn't bring her daughter back, and until we found the boy, she'd never find peace. It was our job to do the work and keep her calm.

"Ms. Hagerty," Bishop said. "I am sorry. Your daughter and son-in-law were found deceased in the home. We need to know where your grandson is."

"We called the nanny, but the number goes to a store in Atlanta," I added. "Do you have a name and contact number?"

"I...the...Melodie fired the nanny. Wait." She shook her head as if it was all beginning to make sense. "Ryan's alive?" Her eyes widened.

"We don't know. He's not in the home, and his medicine is gone," Bishop said.

"And my daughter...my daughter is dead? Oh my God!" She dropped to her knees and bawled. "My baby!" She pounded her fists onto the garage's cement floor. "I need to see her! Please, let me see my baby."

Bishop placed a comforting hand on her shoulder but waited to help her up. "Ma'am, I'm sorry. We can't allow that, and believe me, this is not the last image you want of your child. It's important we find your grandson. Can you tell us who Melodie may have babysitting the child? She and Dr. Rockman were going out this evening."

"I..."

Bishop helped her up. I handed her a tissue, and then Bishop and I shared a look.

"I'll get on it," he said.

I knew he meant on starting the official process for a missing child. Even though we already had a team out canvassing the area, there was so much more to do, very specific steps to take, and timing was key.

"I...they didn't ask me. Why didn't they ask me? I always take Ryan." She gasped. "He's diabetic. He needs his medicine!" She stepped toward the door leading inside. "It's in the refrigerator."

I grabbed her arm tightly. "No. You cannot go inside. Not that way." I gently pulled her out of the garage and to the side of the home away from the buzz of police officers and firemen working the scene. I whipped her around toward me. "Ms. Hagerty, the medicine is missing." I needed her to listen, to understand my words. "Please, I need you to focus. Who could have your grandson?"

"I...I...no one. They would have left him with me."

My best guess was the nanny had the boy, and I needed something, anything, to lead us to her location. "Why did your daughter fire the nanny?"

She stared at me with a blank expression on her face.

I spoke clearly, enunciating each word carefully, hoping that would help it sink in. "Ms. Hagerty, tell me about the nanny. What's her name?"

"She...she fired the nanny."

I nodded. "Yes, I know." I worried she was going into shock too. I had to get my questions answered quickly before that happened. "Do you know where she lives? Why was she fired?"

"She...I...Melodie fired her. She...Oh my God!" She cried into her hands.

I was desperate and losing my patience, which never played out well in a murder investigation, but I didn't have time to coddle her. I gave her exactly five seconds before hitting her with questions. "Do you know where she lives? What is her name? Where can we find the nanny, Ms. Hagerty?"

She shook her head and dropped her jaw for a moment before I saw the focus come back in her eyes. "I think...Melodie said they paid her under the table. She's illegal, and she said...oh my God! She said Steve was having an affair with her. She said Ana was pregnant with Steve's child! She did it. She took my grandson, and she killed my daughter."

"What's Ana's last name?"

"Uh, Flores, I think. Ana Flores. I...I..."

"Do you have a current phone number for her?"

She stared at me.

Dammit. I needed her to stay with me. "In your phone. Do you have a contact number for her? The one in the binder isn't right."

"I...I deleted it when she was fired. It was the fourth nanny. I stopped keeping the nanny's phone numbers because my daughter was constantly hiring someone new, and I sure as hell wasn't going to keep the number of the whore who seduced my son-in-law."

News flash, granny: men weren't seduced into sex. They made a conscious decision to have it regardless of the efforts by the woman. In my experience in these situations, the husband was usually the aggressor, but it wasn't the time to have that conversation. "You deleted her number even though Melodie fired her because she thought she was having Steve's child?"

"That's exactly why, and she didn't think it. She knew it. Ana told her."

She cleared her throat. "Melodie wanted me to stay out of it. She said she was handling it."

"Have you ever called Ana?"

She shook her head. "Melodie didn't like me interfering in her life. I stayed out of her business relationships."

"Did you ever pick the boy up from Ana? Maybe somewhere in town or at her home?"

"I...not that I can recall."

"How long did Ana work for the Rockmans?"

"I'm...I'm not sure. A few months? Six, maybe?"

"Do you know if your daughter kept any records, maybe canceled checks showing payments to any of the nannies?"

"I...I don't know. Maybe that would be in the office or the safe? Please, I really need to see my daughter. Where is she?"

"You can see her in a bit," I said, meaning at the morgue once her daughter was processed and ready for formal identification. I guided her toward the ambulance, but she took off running, and faster than I'd expected. "Son of a bitch!" I bolted after her and was quickly knocked to the ground by two other officers running toward her. I stood up, gathered my senses, and shouted, "Seriously?" And then chased her down. But I was too late.

Again, I didn't need to see her to know what happened. Her screams echoed through the house as I rushed inside a few too many seconds behind her.

She stood in the keeping room, staring down at the victims. "No!" She collapsed into Bishop, who carefully moved her into the foyer.

"Melodie!"

Bishop sat her on a bench against the stairwell. I sat next to her.

Bishop handed me a tissue box, and I handed her a tissue. "Ms. Hagerty, it's imperative we find your grandson. I'm going to need you to—"

"Please, I...please let me see her again. Something's not right. I need to make sure that's my daughter."

Bishop and I shared a look. He raised an eyebrow, but we both knew the stress of seeing a dead loved one caused people to think and often act irrationally.

"Soon," I promised. "Right now, I need you to come upstairs and look at your grandson's room."

We all but carried her upstairs as she mumbled about her daughter not being right. She was in shock, and I felt bad for pushing her, but we needed to know if things were off in the boy's room. We needed everything we could get to find him. Once Barron got a look at her, he'd force us to get her assistance. So, our time was limited.

She wandered through the large room, running her hands along the Spiderman comforter and body pillow. "He loves Spiderman. Melodie just decorated the room a few months ago." She stared up at the string spider web draping from one side of the ceiling to the other. "The web was my idea. Ryan loves it." She formed her fingers and thumbs into the character's signature hand pose. "Pew, pew," she said. "He's always shooting imaginary silk from his fingers. He swears the real Spiderman made the web, so we don't tell him I picked it out. We don't want to dampen his spirit."

I glanced at Bishop.

"We're losing her," he mouthed.

I mouthed back, "A little help?" We didn't have time for a nostalgic trip down memory lane. Not with a missing kid.

"Ma'am, is anything missing or out of place?" he asked.

She took her time wandering the room again, examining everything with a careful eye. Bishop and I exchanged questioning looks. Was she intentionally stalling, or was she going into shock?

I walked over to the closet and opened the door. "Does this look like it normally does? Can you tell if anything's missing?"

She meandered over and stuck her head into the large walk-in closet. "The suitcase. Did you do something with it?"

"We didn't see a suitcase," I said. "Do you know for sure if he had one?"

She nodded. "I got him a Spiderman one for Christmas last year. Did you check the basement storage?"

I made a call on the radio and had an officer back there in a matter of seconds.

He responded quickly. "No sign of anything Spiderman, Detective."

"Could Melodie have gotten rid of it?" Bishop asked.

"No," she said, shaking her head repeatedly. "It's his favorite. He brings it everywhere. It's what he holds his superhero equipment in."

I'd kept the radio in talk mode so the officer could hear Mary's comments.

"I'll keep looking," the officer said.

"Does Ryan spend the night at friends' homes? Could he have left it there?"

She shook her head. "My daughter doesn't believe in child sharing."

"Child sharing?"

"When parents let other parents take their kids for a night or bring them on vacations. She thinks it's unhealthy for Ryan. She would never let him stay with a friend. She just started letting him have playdates at home a few weeks ago."

"Do you know which friend?"

"I..." She stared at the ground. "I don't think she told me. I'm sorry."

"Would he have taken the suitcase to school?"

"She homeschools him."

Of course she did. "Does he attend any group classes?"

She nodded. "He's part of a private program that gives the kids structured play time and physical education along with arts and music."

"What's it called?"

"I'm not sure." She thought for a moment. "Enhanced Learning Opportunities, maybe? Something like that."

"Ms. Hagerty, when was the last time you spoke to Melodie?"

"I speak to her almost daily. Text or on the phone."

I nodded. "Okay, what about his father's office? Could he have brought it there?"

"No. Melodie doesn't really go there much anymore. She's just too busy with Ryan and her clubs. Melodie's meticulous with everything, and that keeps her busy. The house is always immaculate. Everything has a place." Her eyes wandered toward the door. "May I see her now, please? I won't cry, I promise."

I steered her toward the bedroom door. "Not quite yet. I'd like you to wait outside with an officer and have a paramedic examine you first."

"Why? I'm fine."

"I'm sure you are, but this is a terrible situation, and I'd like to make sure you're not going into shock." Which I knew she was.

"Oh, okay."

"I'm going to have more questions for you in a bit, okay?"

"Sure. I just really need to see her. Something's not right."

"What do you mean?"

"Melodie would never leave her child. That's just not who she is."

"We're going to find him, Ms. Hagerty."

Jimmy Abernathy, Hamby's Chief of Police, Bishop, Michels, and I congregated in the den with Dr. Barron.

"I've handled a lot of missing children's cases, and most of them don't turn out well," I said. "Ms. Hagerty claims Melodie wouldn't send the child to a friend's house—or anywhere, for that matter. Child sharing, she called it. Said the vic didn't believe in it. Sounds like she wouldn't let him out of her sight. Homeschooled him and everything. We need to get the boy into NCIC right away."

"We're on it," Jimmy said.

"What about other family members?" Michels asked. "Maybe the mother and grandmother had a fight, and the mother didn't want the kid with her mom for a while. Does she have a sister, father? Husband's family, maybe?"

"Good point," Jimmy said. "We need a list of family members. Can you get on that and make the calls?"

"Yes, sir," Michels said.

"Check the family binder in the kitchen. I left it on the desk. There are numbers in there."

Jimmy added, "Don't provide any death notifications. We don't need another family member crashing the scene."

"Yes, sir," Michels said and headed toward the kitchen.

The large landscape painting hanging on the wall to hide the safe swung back toward the wall and caught our attention.

"Did you get the code?" Jimmy asked.

"Not yet," I said. "I'll ask the mother now." I walked outside to the mother sitting in a patrol car. "How's she doing?" I asked the officer.

"Paramedics gave her a clean bill of health but want us to tread carefully."

"Got it."

"She wants to see the victims."

"I know. I don't want to tell her that's not going to happen again and that she has to wait until her daughter's body is in the morgue."

"Understood."

I approached the vehicle's window. "Ms. Hagerty, do you happen to know the combination to the safe?"

"The safe? No, I...I...she was planning to give it to me, but she hasn't yet."

"Has she mentioned what's inside?"

"We discussed it once a few months ago, but I don't know what's in there now."

"What did she tell you two months ago?"

"She said there's just about ten thousand in cash, some important papers, and some jewelry."

"Has she kept you in the loop with what's in there before?"

"She..." She tilted her head to the side. "Funny, she told me she wanted me to know in case anything happened to her. She thought I should know where the insurance papers were, I assume."

"Did she think something was going to happen to her?"

"I..." She twisted her hands together. "I don't know. She'd been acting strange for a while, and I just wrote it off as her paranoia."

"Melodie suffered from a mental disorder?"

"Oh, I don't mean that. She's just struggled because of Ryan's diagnosis. She's very overprotective."

"When was he diagnosed?"

"Sometime after she came back from Mexico."

"And when was that?"

"When Ryan was two, so three years ago."

"How many children do you have?"

"Just the twins."

"Melodie is a twin? Identical or fraternal?"

"Identical. They have different hairstyles now, or last I knew, but otherwise, they're hard to tell apart."

"Where is her twin?"

"Still in Mexico. They, uh...they went together. Emily stayed on after their trip. Fell in love with the area and a man, of course. Emily is all about her romantic relationships. She's always doing something for a man."

The hairs on the back of my neck stood up. I knew something was coming, I just wasn't sure what. "Okay, I'll be back in a bit." I asked the officer staying by the vehicle to get her a glass of water.

I walked back to the office manager. She'd been moved from the ambulance to the back of the squad car next to it to wait for further instructions. "How you holding up?"

"Have you found Ryan?"

"We're working on it."

"I'm worried for him."

I tried to pacify her. "We have insulin ready to go at any moment."

"That's good. May I go home now? I'm tired."

I looked at the paramedic standing between the ambulance and squad car. He nodded and mouthed, "She's okay."

"Ms. Maynor, I have a few more questions, and then you can go."

"Okay."

"Do you know anything about the financial state of the medical office?"

"What do you mean?"

"Is it turning a profit? Struggling?"

"The accountant handles all of that, but we have standard bill collection procedures that I oversee."

"Do you have a lot of accounts in collections?"

"We always have a lot of accounts in collections."

"More than normal now?"

She shook her head. "And as far as I know, things are going well financially. Several staff members just received raises, including me."

"You said Dr. Rockman was acting different. Can you give me some examples?"

She sipped a bottled water. "Examples?"

I nodded. "Did he yell at staff or was he different with patients?"

"Oh, no. Nothing like that. He was just off. Distant at times. It wasn't a memory issue or anything. I think he just had a lot on his mind, and it distracted him. He's a very busy man."

I tried a different angle. People often left out details, intentionally or not, and usually didn't think straight in traumatic situations. Repetitive questioning was key to getting what we needed. "What was he like on a normal day?"

She smiled, her eyes wandering off into the distance. "He's kind. He loves the staff. Many of us have been there since he first opened the practice. And he's always good with his patients. He does so much for them, listens to their problems, and not just their medical problems. I'm always getting on him because he's only supposed to spend fifteen minutes with each patient, but he always goes longer. It sets us back every day, but the patients don't seem to mind. They appreciate the care he provides, the attention he gives them."

Rockman sounded like a saint, so I knew there was a story somewhere. No one was a saint, and usually, the people portrayed as saintly were anything but. "And lately he's been that way?"

"Not as much. He's been rushing patients, canceling appointments. He's even left early a few times."

"Did he say why?"

"Just family stuff. I assume it's Ryan's illness. Melodie was very particular on how they handled Ryan's diabetes."

I nodded. "And you said you weren't particularly close to his wife. Did you ever have a relationship with her?"

"I threw an office shower for them when she was pregnant. She was beautiful pregnant. Stunning, really, and she was so grateful for the shower. After Ryan was born, she would come in, and we'd all love on him. He was such a pretty baby. Perfectly round brown eyes, and a pile of thick dark hair you wouldn't believe. We all loved seeing him."

That didn't quite match the Melodie Mary Hagerty described. "When was the last time she brought him in?"

"Oh, it's been a few years now. Steve, I mean Dr. Rockman, said she worried coming here would compromise his immune system, and she didn't like bringing him around sick people."

That was probably why she chose to homeschool him too. I reiterated a question I'd already asked to see if she'd give the same answer. "When was he diagnosed with diabetes?"

"He just turned five, so it's been about three years now."

"And she stopped bringing him around a few years ago?"

She nodded. "Yes."

"Do you know why?"

"I never really thought about it. I just assumed it was his diagnosis, but I just realized she stopped before that. I assume it was because he was sick a lot, or that was what Steve said."

"Did Dr. Rockman agree with her about her concerns?"

She shook her head. "It didn't seem to bother him, but he was very respectful of her concerns."

"Do you know if the couple had an active social life?"

"They used to. Once the baby came, it lessened, of course, but they've had nannies for a long time, and Melodie was fine with going out again a few months after he was born. She even told me once she needed to go out more often so she could stay Melodie while being a wife and mother."

I addressed her comments separately. "Do you mean the recent nanny?"

She shook her head. "No. They had one for two years, but shortly after Melodie got home from Mexico, she fired her. She said she didn't like the way she handled things when she was gone. Since then, they've had several. Melodie is probably very concerned because of Ryan's condition. Everything revolves around his condition, which, of course, I understand."

"Do you know the nannies' names?"

"No, but I think I mentioned that the most recent one is in the current draft of the family binder, and I'm sure I can locate the others in previous versions. I can check if you'd like."

"That would be great," I said. "When did she tell you she needed to go out more?"

"About a year after Ryan was born. I think that's why she finally decided to go to Mexico with Emily."

People always knew more than they thought, but extracting that information from them was always a challenge. "Did she tell you about the trip?"

"Beforehand, yes. When she got back, she stopped coming around as much."

"What did she tell you beforehand?"

"Just that she was nervous about going but excited too. She didn't spend a lot of time with her sister, and her mother had been pressuring her to, so when Emily suggested they go together, she felt obligated in a sense, but I think she really wanted to get away. She even said she needed the break. Eventually, she was cautiously optimistic about spending time with her sister."

"So, the twins weren't close?"

"Not that I know of, but like I've said, I wasn't that close to Melodie."

"What about the sister? Did you know her?"

"Not really. She came into the office a few times, but I wouldn't say we talked, other than normal courtesies, obviously. I can say they seem to be very different. Or were, I mean." Her eyes filled with tears.

"How do you mean?"

"Melodie is very determined, very structured. Her sister appeared opposite."

∾

I left Heather Maynor with the go-ahead to send her home knowing we'd meet again for additional questioning and further information, and then I made a quick call to Bubba, who'd gone home for the night long before. "I'm sorry to bother you, but I need a check on some finances stat."

"No worries. Ashley's been sending me stuff since y'all got to the scene. I came back to the office after her first text."

"Sorry about that."

"Murder investigations don't stop so the tech dude can sleep."

"Or the detective."

He chuckled. "What do you need again?"

"Some financial info."

"On whom?"

"I'll text you everything I have. I'm looking for any changes in spending, debt, et cetera, over the past few months but going back at least three years."

"I'm on it."

We disconnected the call, and I walked inside and found Jimmy and Bishop. "I'm starting to think this is about the parents, not the child."

"Explain, please," Jimmy said.

"I will, but first, here's an interesting tidbit for you." I tipped my head back and sighed.

"Don't keep us waiting," Bishop said.

"Melodie was a twin."

Bishop's eyes widened. "Shit, really?"

I nodded. "And I should have said something earlier. My bad."

Jimmy pressed his lips together. He was mad, but he did his best to stay calm. "Jesus H. Christ, Ryder, when did you find out?"

I shrugged. "About a half hour ago?"

"Are you serious?" he asked. "You should have told us immediately."

"I know, and I said I'm sorry." Sort of. I really needed to be a better team player.

"Are we sure we've got the right one, then?" Bishop asked.

"Don't jinx us like that. That shit happens more often than you think," I said.

"That's what I'm afraid of," Jimmy said. "And why you should have said something right away."

I moved on. Jimmy was right, but I wouldn't continue to waste our time addressing it. "According to the office manager, Dr. Rockman's been acting differently lately, and Melodie made a strange shift in personality toward the people at his office. Could be an affair, but I've not dug into that yet."

"Then why is the boy missing?" Bishop asked.

"It's possible he witnessed the murders go down," I said.

"My guess is the person who killed them didn't know the kid was here and took him, or he wasn't here to begin with," Jimmy added.

"If it's an employee, they knew the parents were going to the party. They probably expected the boy to be with a sitter or his grandmother and panicked when they saw him. They took the kid because they didn't have any other options," I said. I pressed my palms in a praying position and touched the sides of my index fingers to my mouth. "The party started over five hours ago, and the last time the office manager heard from Rockman was around noon when he left work. He never responded to any of her text messages. Each one said delivered, not read. The kid could have been gone for hours already, which puts us way behind in finding him."

"Let's hope they didn't kill him too," Bishop said.

"I doubt they did, or his body would be here," I said. "Besides, it doesn't fit the scene. Best case scenario is the kid witnessed the shootings, and the shooter panicked, took the kid, and dumped him somewhere."

"I'll get someone on all the gas stations and convenience stores within a ten-mile radius," Jimmy said.

Bishop struggled to make sense of my theory. "It's possible they could have taken the kid and then killed him."

"Killers take what they see as the easiest, most effective action. Putting a bullet in the kid's head is easier than transporting him somewhere else and then doing the same thing, and if it's a disgruntled employee or someone who knew the victims personally, I doubt that's the case. They're going to have a harder time killing a kid they know."

"I don't see this as someone they knew. The insulin pump is here. If it was an employee, wouldn't he or she know the kid is diabetic? Why would they leave the pump?"

"Because they have two."

"How do you know?"

"I'm assuming. Rockman's a doctor. He would get two just in case."

He nodded. "I can see that."

I shouted to an officer to come over.

"Yes, Detective?"

"The female vic's mother is in a squad car. Can you ask her how many insulin pumps the boy has?"

"Yes, ma'am." He rushed to locate her.

"Michels did some research and said a lot of people have two. Stands to reason a five-year-old would need an extra in case he breaks his while playing or something."

The officer returned. "Yes, two, and she wants to see her daughter."

"Please tell her soon," I said.

"Yes, ma'am."

Jimmy sighed. "Great. So, at least it's possible the kid has a pump on him already, but that doesn't mean the person who has him understands how to replace the insulin." He pinched the bridge of his nose. "Shit. This is bad. The mayor's going to be all over my ass with this one. I'll get someone on the local pharmacies and urgent care facilities for any reported thefts or requests for emergency insulin."

"Shelters and vet clinics too," I added. "They usually have insulin available. And Chief, we need to look at the other possibility too."

"The parents were murdered because someone wanted the kid," he said.

I nodded.

"Shit," Jimmy said.

"What the chief said," Bishop replied.

Before I could say anything else, Mary Hagerty ran screaming through the house. "I told you something wasn't right! Oh my God! I can't believe this is happening!"

Bishop and I stepped in front of her as she ran toward us. I stepped quickly to the side when I realized she was staring through us, but Bishop took the bull by the horns and stood his ground. She hit him with extreme force, but Bishop had at least fifty pounds on her and stopped her with a full body slam. She dropped to the ground with a thud.

She rolled and clutched her stomach. Bishop crouched down to help her up, remaining respectful. "Ma'am, please—" He gently grabbed her arm, but she shook away.

"Don't touch me!" She bounced up and screamed, "I told you that's not Melodie! That's Emily!"

3

Dr. Barron's face was so red I worried he would stroke out right over the victims' bodies. "What in the hell is going on here?" He crouched down and re-covered Melodie Rockman's remains with the white sheet. "And why the fuck are these bodies not already on their way to the morgue? I released them an hour ago."

"We're on it, Doc," one of the paramedics said.

I rushed over as Bishop dealt with Mary Hagerty. "It's my fault. I wanted to examine them again. I'm sorry, Doc."

He tipped his head back after rolling his eyes at me. "These victims deserve respect, Ryder. And now that image will be burned in that poor mother's brain for the rest of her life. The rest of her goddamned life! Do you get that? You can't erase that kind of thing, Detective."

I knew that better than he understood, but Barron was angry, and I wasn't about to use guilt to make my case. I'd never seen him angry before. It wasn't pretty.

Bishop rushed over. "Doc," he said. "Enough."

Doc glared at him. "It is not enough. I gave a direct order to remove the bodies, and your partner didn't comply. These bodies belong to my department, not yours. Am I clear? They are my responsibility. And now I have to deal with the mother—"

"Enough," Bishop said. "We get it."

Barron's eyes bulged as he leaned in toward my partner. "What did you just say to me?"

I stepped between the men and held out my hands to keep them separated. "Stop it! Now's not the time for this bullshit. Set your egos aside. I screwed up. I admit that, and I'm sorry. It won't happen again, but we have an investigation we have to handle." I stepped back and glared at them. "Right now!"

Jimmy walked over and stood between them. I chose to keep my mouth shut even though I could have said a hell of a lot more. Their tempers were as hot as lava flowing quickly down an explosive volcano, and I didn't have the time or desire to be in the thick of that.

As I walked away, I heard Bishop say, "She saw her husband get shot in the head."

"Shit," Barron said. "I knew that. I'm a dumbass."

"There is that," Bishop said.

I caught my breath, gathered my resolve, and sped up my walk toward Mary Hagerty with a heart full of gratefulness toward my partner. He was protective, and I appreciated it.

The paramedics had her set up in an ambulance with an oxygen mask to her mouth. Her skin color was normal, the paramedic said her heart rate was fine, and the panic in her eyes had subsided. For a woman who had just lost her daughter and son-in-law, whose grandson was MIA, and who thought her dead daughter was the twin, she was holding up well. A little too well.

A chill crept up my spine. That wasn't right. Anyone would be panicked, in shock, devastated, and definitely not adjusting to it all so quickly. I stepped to the other side of the ambulance and sent a text to Bubba with the victims' details as well as what little I knew about Mary Hagerty.

Check on the mother too, please. Mary Hagerty is all I've got on her now, but I'll work on more details. Something's up with her. Send.

I watched the three dots on my iPhone as Bubba typed his response.
Will do, boss.

I stuffed my phone back into my back pocket and approached the back of the unit again. "Is she okay to chat?" I asked the paramedic.

He nodded. "Seems to be fine, and she's definitely in the mood to talk."

"She tell you anything?"

"Insists the vic is her daughter's twin. How cool is that?"

"Probably not cool to her."

"Oh, dang. That was shitty of me."

"Just a bit," I said. "But don't worry, I've said a hell of a lot worse." Before talking with Hagerty again, I glanced at the growing crowd behind the yellow crime scene tape. They stood on the road, men, women, and children, all hoping for a glimpse of something, anything that would hint to the drama unfolding inside. Regardless of what happened, what was happening, they'd make up their own stories, with their own biases, and the media would find one to latch onto, making this a hate crime or a murder-turned-suicide, anything to get it online and in print quickly. By the time we got to the truth, the rest of the world will have forgotten about it, and those assumptions first reported would be their truth.

I hated the media, and I didn't really like people in general.

I looked up at the sky. The dark of night had settled in even quicker than just two weeks ago. It was after midnight already and pitch black out except for the lights of emergency vehicles. Fall was coming, and people would be thrilled for the cooler temperatures, but even the cool night air wouldn't help to hide the death secreting from the home. I admired the sky, remembering that the ambient light cut the true view by half, but knowing it was far better than the city lights hogging the sky over Chicago. It wasn't cloudy, but there were enough clouds to hit the moon at just the right angle and cast its shadow over the large, heavily landscaped yard.

I studied the people, noting the women dressed in the expensive outfits with more bling than the grandmother who lived across the street from my parents. My neck hurt thinking about the number of chains weighing on her spine. I'd learned that fashion was fluid and its success depended on who wore it.

I told the paramedic I'd be back in a minute and walked over toward the crowd to speak with an officer keeping them behind the tape. "How many reporters?"

"Three so far."

"Okay. I'm sure the chief will be out here soon."

"They're asking a lot of questions."

I offered him a piece of gum from my pocket.

"Thanks, but I'm good."

"Let me tell you a little Chicago cop secret."

He moved closer, and I leaned my head toward his ear. "We chew gum to keep our mouths busy. It's an excuse, but it works."

He laughed. "Got it."

I handed him the gum, and he took it.

I walked back to the ambulance and climbed inside. I sat in the small seat beside Mary. I'd hoped she'd had enough time to relax and think about the incident. Not in a regretful way but one that allowed her to explain her claim and, hopefully, back it up. "Ms. Hagerty, can you please explain to me why you think that's Emily and not Melodie?"

She sat up and removed the oxygen mask from her mouth. "The scar. I saw the scar on her neck."

"A scar?" I asked as I opened my notepad.

Mary Hagerty began to hyperventilate. She wasn't close to calm, and I was stupid to think it was possible. I grabbed the oxygen mask and stuck it toward her mouth. "Please, keep this on."

The paramedic climbed in and raised an eyebrow. "Everything okay here?"

Mary nodded. "I...I...it's hard to breathe."

I got another raised eyebrow, and then he checked her vitals.

"Your pulse and BP are fine. Just keep calm."

A good pulse and blood pressure meant she wasn't in shock, which I would expect in this situation. She was either a tough woman or full of shit. I teetered on the *full of shit* side.

He shined the little light into her eyes. "Her pupils aren't dilated." He clasped her hands, flipped them over, and rubbed her palms. He then checked her heart rate, straightened his posture, and asked her a series of questions. "Are you feeling dizzy or nauseous?"

She shook her head.

"Light-headed?"

Another headshake.

"Is your mouth dry? Are you thirsty?"

She dropped the oxygen mask. "No. I'm not in shock, dammit! I'm confused. Why is my Emily in there on the ground with her sister's husband, and where the hell is my grandson and his mother?"

The paramedic twisted around and smiled. "I think she's good to question."

I couldn't help but smile. "Ms. Hagerty," I said as I took over the chair from the paramedic.

He stepped off the ambulance, turned around, and said, "Good luck."

She sat up and shifted her legs off the gurney. "I need to go. I need to find Melodie and Ryan."

"Ms. Hagerty, that's our job, but we can't do it if you don't help. I have questions, and I need you to stay and answer them, please. You mentioned a scar. What scar?"

She nodded. "Yes, I'm sure. I know my children. I know that scar."

"Tell me about the scar."

She swallowed a sip of water from a bottle the paramedic had given her. "It's from a scuba diving accident in Mexico."

"Are you sure Emily got it and not Melodie?"

She narrowed her eyes at me. "Of course I'm sure. Why would you ask that? Do you think I can't recognize my own children?"

My cousins were identical twins, and they'd made it their life's purpose to mess with people and switch identities all the time. My aunt once told me they had to put markings on their feet as babies to distinguish between the two. I tried not to feed into her growing frustration and didn't suggest they could have switched lives as a joke that turned tragic. "When was the last time you saw Emily?"

"Before they went to Mexico."

"And that was?" I had a general idea, but hearing it from the mother would help confirm what Heather Maynor said.

She stared at the side of the vehicle as if she was doing math in her head. "June of 2018. She and Melodie went together. It was their first trip together in years."

"You haven't seen Emily since before they went to Mexico, where you say she got a scar from a scuba diving incident. If you haven't seen her, how do you know she has a scar?"

"Because she...I...she told me what happened and sent me a photo. Melodie didn't have a scar. Not on her neck." Her eyes widened. "But Emily also has one on the back of her left knee. It's faded, but I'm sure it's still there. She fell off her bike at the greenway when she was younger." She stood. "Let me see if I can—"

"No. You can't go back to your daughter. They're preparing to take her remains to the morgue now."

"But I can tell you—"

I stopped her. "I'll have someone check."

I hammered out a text to Bishop asking him to please have Barron check the back of her left knee for a faded scar. A minute later he responded and said there was one.

Great, I thought. A twin-switch double homicide with a missing kid. Just what the doctor ordered after a multiple overdose task force investigation that drained us all emotionally and physically. "Okay. Tell me more about your daughters. Were they close?"

"Not like you'd expect from twins. They are so different. Emily is the spontaneous one, she never had a plan, but she was always doing something. Melodie's different. She plans everything from her hourly schedule up to the entire year. You couldn't even talk to her the week between Christmas and New Year's Eve because she was busy setting up that planner of hers."

"Planner?"

"She's into that monthly planner with all those stickers." She pressed her lips together. "I can't remember what it's called. I've never understood it, but she said it keeps her life organized, and she couldn't live without it."

I got on my radio and asked someone to look for a planner with stickers. "Ms. Hagerty," I said. "When was the last time you spoke to Melodie?"

She twisted her hands together, then rubbed them on her expensive-looking pants. "I told you we talk daily."

"You talked today, then?"

"We texted today."

"What did you text about?"

"We're supposed to go shopping tomorrow. We were discussing where we planned to go."

"What time did you receive the texts?"

"Sometime early this morning. She's an early riser. Always has been."

"Did you notice anything different in her messages?"

She blinked. "Different? I don't understand."

"Text speech is similar to normal speech patterns. It's our own personal vernacular. Some people punctuate, some use acronyms like LOL or TTYL. Some write paragraphs. Did you notice her pattern changed recently?"

She shook her head. "Not that I can recall." She removed her phone from her large purse beside her. "I have my phone. Would you like to see?"

"That would be great."

She handed me the phone, and I studied the texts over the past few days. There were only three, which seemed odd to me. "I thought you said you talked often?"

"We only text when she has something quick to say, but yes, I do talk to her often, like I said. She knows I prefer talking. Those phones are so confusing."

"Did you notice your daughter acting different lately?" I kept that vague so I wouldn't lead her any particular direction.

"Not any more than usual. I know she and Steve were going through a rough patch, but I didn't think it was anything they couldn't overcome. Then again, it's not Melodie in there, so of course they'd be experiencing problems." She paused. "I wonder if that's what caused this? Could her husband have killed her and then himself?"

"We're investigating all possibilities, Ms. Hagerty. Can you explain what you mean by rough patch? Did your daughter tell you anything?"

"I don't want to make a mountain out of a molehill, but Melodie, or I guess Emily, has been frustrated with Steve recently. She's complained of the normal marriage things. Which now, looking back, seems surreal."

I ignored her additional commentary and kept to my intended script. "Normal marriage things such as?"

She chuckled. "Obviously you're single."

I didn't bother giving her my backstory, but I was worried about her seemingly nonchalant attitude toward the murders, and the casualness of her emotions regarding her missing grandson raised a red flag. Sure, people reacted differently under stress, but three big hits were a hell of a lot more stressful than just one in most people's books. And coupled with the fact that she believed her dead daughter was the twin, she should be freaking out. I sent Bubba another text asking him to dig as deep as possible on her info. Something didn't sit right with me. My mother and I weren't close, at all, but if something like this happened to one of her children, she'd be off the wall, how I'd expect most mothers to react.

"Married couples struggle with finances, decisions on how to raise their children, things like that. Melodie wanted to be more involved in their financial decisions, and the way she explained it, Steve didn't think that was necessary. He considered it an inconvenience to have to report his financial information to his wife."

"His financial information?"

She nodded. "That was her issue. She considered them a team, but apparently, Steve felt different."

She talked as if the victim in the house was the real Melodie. I made note of that. It could be because up until a little while ago, she thought she was, or it could be manipulation on her part. The back-and-forth struck me as odd, but I continued on without correcting her. "Were things always separate between them?"

She shook her head. "Not in the beginning. Things seemed to change over the past year or so." She looked down at her hands. "I can't say for sure. All I know is that Melodie's been frustrated for a while now." She stared up at me. "Could that be because she wasn't actually Melodie?"

Well, so much for letting the theory of hers go for now. "When was the last time you were in contact with your daughter in Mexico?"

"I just spoke to her yesterday."

"On the phone?"

She shook her head. "She texted me."

"What did she say?"

"That she's loving Mexico and her life there."

"Do you still have the text?"

She nodded and showed me a text from an unknown number.

"Why is her number listed as unknown?"

"Oh, since she's in Mexico, she uses an application that is less expensive than a traditional phone service. Mexico rapes their citizens every way they can, she said, and this way, she can text or call and use numbers that Mexico can't track."

I nodded. "Do you know the name of the app?"

She shook her head. "It's called CoverUp, I think?" She tilted her head to the side. "Or CoverIt? I'm not sure. She asked me to download the app, but I couldn't get it to work. Or Charles couldn't."

"Charles?"

She smiled and blushed. "My significant other. He's an up-and-coming jewelry designer."

Bishop and Michels peeked into the vehicle.

"A minute?" Bishop asked.

I excused myself from the ambulance and walked with them away from people.

"We've got movement on locating the son," Bishop said.

Michels added, "As requested, patrol is hitting the neighbors, but word got out about the boy, and a few have joined the search. We're working on a two-mile radius with several citizens, ten patrol, and two DEA dogs. Forsyth County is en route to assist with the search."

Bishop smiled when he caught my expression flip at the mention of the DEA K9s. "Kyle's got his dogs," he said.

"Good to know." I tried hard not to show any emotion about my new and awkward personal relationship with the DEA agent. "I've got Bubba looking into the grandmother, and I'll have him check to see if Melodie's access to their financials changed recently." I hammered out another text to Bubba asking for that additional information.

"Why?" Bishop asked.

"Mother said she was frustrated about it."

"A mother would know."

Not always. "I can't put my finger on it, but something's not right. I don't trust her."

"Then I don't either," Michels said.

Bishop chuckled. "Suck-up."

"She's rarely wrong."

"Regardless, still a suck-up."

My cell phone rang. I held up the screen to show them Bubba's contact and then clicked answer and made sure it was on speaker. "Shoot."

"There's been no activity on any of the Rockmans' personal accounts in the past twenty-four hours, and regarding your recent text, Melodie was on all the accounts except one, a high-yield CD."

"How much?"

"The max. Two hundred fifty thousand."

"That's not small," Bishop said.

"Any idea if it matured?" I asked.

"Yes, five years ago."

"Was she on it then?"

"Nope."

"Anything on the other accounts?"

"There's a monthly withdrawal of two thousand from their savings for the last three months. It goes straight to a diamond jeweler in Cumming."

"Okay, that's probably the significant other Hagerty mentioned. Hagerty probably introduced them and the vic bought something from him on a payment plan. Anything on Hagerty?"

"Working my magic takes time, boss," Bubba said.

"And it's well worth it, but we're pressed for time on this."

"Understood."

"I appreciate you getting on this so quickly."

"Who needs sleep?" he asked, then disconnected the call.

"Nikki's doing well," Bishop said. "Ashley said she's already on her own going through the finer details of the scene."

"Hopefully, they'll find something that'll lead us to the kid," I said.

Ashley was training her replacement, and it just so happened she was getting on-the-job training during this investigation. According to Jimmy and Ashley, she was well skilled in forensic technology and has worked for two other departments, but she would need to prove herself to me before I trusted her like I trusted Ashley. Ashley's one of a kind.

Jimmy walked over. "Jesus H. Christ. This is a fucking shit show. Barron's on my ass and just a few steps behind the mayor who's already up it. Where are we? Who's the suspect?"

Bishop pressed his lips together as Michels tiptoed away to manage the search for the kid.

"Here's where we are," I said. I kept my tone professional. Jimmy didn't stress often, but from the sweat on his forehead and the tone of his voice, I knew he was ready to blow a gasket. And that wouldn't be pretty. He'd already been informed about Hagerty's theory, but I reiterated it. "As you know, the mother claims the dead daughter isn't Melodie but rather the identical twin, Emily, who's supposedly been living in Mexico for the past three years. She's back and forth in how she talks about the victim, saying Melodie, then correcting it some of the time. She doesn't appear as upset as I would expect someone in this situation to be, which makes me think she knew it wasn't Melodie in there in the first place."

"She's in shock," Bishop said.

"Not according to the paramedic," I offered.

Jimmy tipped his head back and sighed. "We're fucked. DNA is the same in identical twins. How are we going to tell the difference without delaying the investigation?"

Investigations take as long as they take, and though he was right, we didn't need this one delayed, not with a missing kid, but we couldn't control how long it took. "We can get a rush on dental records. If they've had any work done, it's unlikely it's the same work. We'll compare them to previous records, and that should be all the confirmation we'll need."

"That could take a week," he said as he nodded to himself. I nearly saw the wheels in his brain turning. "Yeah, a rush on them should work. I'll have Doc get X-rays and molds of the vic."

"And I'll get Bubba on dental records," Bishop added.

Jimmy hadn't stopped nodding. "Good. Good."

"In the meantime," I said. "We should continue our investigation with the possibility of the vic being Emily, not Melodie." I flipped my small notepad to a blank page. "My cousins are identical twins, and they used to switch places all the time. It pissed everyone off, especially the guys they dated. This could be a similar situation." I shook my head. "Also, about a year after I joined the Chicago PD, we had a twin steal her sister's identity and rack up about seventy-five K in debt."

"How'd you find out it was the twin?" Bishop asked.

"The vic swore it wasn't her and proved it through medical records. Took a year to get them from the sister, though."

"We don't have a year," Jimmy said, exasperated.

"Technically, we don't have a twin yet, either," I added. "If Hagerty's right, and that's Emily in there, where's Melodie? Is she the twin in Mexico? Why the switch? Was it a mutual decision, or did Emily somehow force the change?"

"You think the wife is dead?" Bishop asked.

Nikki walked up but didn't interrupt. Point for her.

"It's possible. The mother showed me a text from Emily, but apparently she uses an app to send them so that Mexico doesn't charge her."

"Is it CoverUp?" Nikki asked.

"Something like that."

"That's not good news. CoverUp uses random cell numbers to send texts, documents, even photos from various countries so there's no way to know where the call or text originated from. It's the current favorite for cheaters."

"Damn, people are assholes," Bishop said.

"Surprised it took you that long to think that," I added. "The way I see it, we've got three theories to work from, but without further investigation, I can't guess which is the hottest."

Jimmy shook his head. "Shit. That's three too many for a quick close."

"And we need a quick close or the kid could die," Bishop added.

"Here's my theories," Jimmy said. "Twin steals sibling's life, sibling gets revenge. Twins switch lives, but one here in Hamby likes it too much and won't switch back, so sibling gets revenge. The sisters could have planned this. Melodie could have wanted to sow her oats or have her freedom and asked for the switch. I've read stories of this happening and—"

"So have I," Bishop said. "Husband finds out, gets pissed, and kills the twin."

"But the husband is dead, and we all know he didn't shoot himself twice," I said. "Don't discount the mother. She could have found out and killed them."

"The mother?" Bishop asked. "Killing her daughter and son-in-law, then what, taking the kid?" He shook his head. "I don't see it. Sure, maybe if they didn't have a kid, but the grandchild makes that a tough one for me."

"It's the ultimate punk scenario," I said. "Switch lives and don't tell the person who gave birth to you. That could have been too much for Hagerty, especially if it took her a while to figure out, and if the husband knew and she didn't."

"You think the husband would stick around after learning something like that?" Bishop asked. "Again, don't see it."

"Maybe he didn't know, or he found out, and that's how the mother found out."

"Explain," Jimmy said.

"Mary Hagerty said Melodie had been complaining about her husband limiting their financial information from her. I had Bubba do a quick check, and he has a two-hundred-and-fifty-K CD without her on it."

"How many other accounts?" Jimmy asked.

"The rest include Melodie."

"Life insurance policies?" Bishop asked.

"Bubba's getting back to me."

"Okay, but," Jimmy added. "What if Melodie wanted to leave, and she's the one that pushed for the switch, and Emily goes along with it but decides she doesn't want to be a wife and mother. She calls her sister home, they fight, and Melodie kills her, then the husband comes home and she has to kill him too?"

"This is a damn soap opera," Bishop said. He sighed.

I pointed at Bishop and smiled. "Could be worse."

"Don't suggest how," he said. "I don't want to know."

"It doesn't matter," I said. "The theory doesn't fit the scene. There's little blood, and the blood on the wall is consistent with the bodies being shot where they were. Science would point to the husband being shot first. But that doesn't mean the twins didn't switch lives. It's possible they did, and it could be for a number of reasons."

"Maybe," Bishop said, finally getting into the swing of theorizing. "Maybe the real wife didn't want the husband in the first place but decided she wanted the kid, so she kills the sister and the husband and takes off with the kid."

"There are several sub-scenarios under the main ones," Jimmy said. "But the case probably boils down to one of the twins for the kills, or someone closely involved with the family."

"I agree, but we can't rule out other options," I said. "It could be someone who knew about the switch, someone who was blackmailing the twin living in the house. Bubba said money was leaving one of the accounts monthly and going to a jeweler. Hagerty's significant other is the jeweler."

"Like you said," Bishop added. "That could just be a layaway deal."

"Right. Our priority is confirming which twin is on the way to the morgue. Once we have that, we can get moving on the rest."

"First, we need to find the kid," Bishop said.

"Best way to do that is to find the killer."

"I was a twin," Jimmy added. "And I can't imagine having any desire to kill someone that connected to me."

Bishop and I both blinked. "You're a twin?" I asked.

"Was. For about sixteen weeks, but my mother miscarried my brother."

"Damn," Bishop said.

"None of us can imagine it, but that doesn't mean it's not happening," I said.

"What if we're not looking at it right?" Jimmy asked. "What if Melodie disappeared or died in Mexico, and Emily took the opportunity to take her identity?"

I nodded. "Let's hope that's not the case. We won't get shit from Mexico."

"Unfortunately, that's true," he said.

"Shit," Bishop said. "This isn't going to close soon. We've got a shit ton of work to do."

"Then let's get started," Jimmy replied. "I'll move with Barron on the dental molds. I'm officially giving you two the murder investigation."

"What about the missing kid?" Bishop asked.

"I'm putting Michels on it with you two overseeing."

"That works," Bishop said.

I agreed.

"Let them finish up here. You two need to head back to the department and make use of that elaborate investigation room our taxpayers bought."

"Yes, sir," we said collectively as he walked away.

"Time to get to work," Bishop said.

"I don't know what you've been doing the last few hours, but I've been working my ass off."

He smirked. "Edit, then. Time to solve this case."

"I can get behind that."

4

Bubba left us a list of social media connections with regular contact for both victims. He'd also contacted the carrier and finagled their contact lists. I'd checked out Melodie's planner from evidence at the scene and wrote down my top five based on her appointments and notes. I chugged a strong coffee made from the Keurig in the investigation room, then tipped my chair back and stretched. "Why is this coffee so nasty? I thought that machine wasn't supposed to do that."

"It's not the machine," Bishop said. "It's you. When was the last time you brushed your teeth?"

I cringed. "I didn't think of that. We did just eat tacos from a Hispanic stand inside the gas station."

"That's my point."

I grabbed a mint from my bag. I'd given away or chewed the two packs of gum I had with me on scene. "I have two left. Want one?"

"No, thanks. It screws up the taste of my cigarettes." He smiled. "In fact," he said as he stood. "It's smoke time."

"You suck."

"You're just jealous." He waved at me from behind his head as the door closed behind him.

I didn't miss smoking, but I missed the stress release it provided. It's a double-edged sword, being a non-smoker, but I'd made the final, no-going-back decision to quit too long ago to turn around and start again. But damn, there were days when that stress relief was much needed, and in my field, it was just about every day.

I stared at the clock. It was a little past three a.m., and soon Hamby would wake up and start their day while ours just bled into the next. I closed my file, slipped into my jacket, and gathered my things. The door opened as I reached for it.

"Leaving so soon?" Kyle Olsen leaned against the doorframe wearing a DEA polo shirt and a pair of tight-fitting khaki pants.

If I was the type of woman that swooned over a man, I would have definitely swooned. We'd only recently officially stated our interest in seeing where this attraction could go, which was then immediately and abruptly interrupted by the Rockman murders. Of course, we'd had a one-night stand a while back, though I tried not to think about that. And it wasn't easy to forget, especially while he stood there in those pants smiling from ear to ear like he knew my deepest secrets.

Damn.

"I'm checking in with Michels on the search and if he's done all the paperwork. You know," I said, blushing uncontrollably as I stared at his pants. "Cop stuff."

I would have kissed Bishop if he'd chosen that moment to walk in and save me from embarrassing myself further, but my partner always had bad timing.

"We switched groups and told the citizens to go home and get some rest, though I believe there are still some out looking."

"No one found anything?"

He shook his head. "Dogs lost the scent just past the driveway. Which is surprising, but not impossible."

I sighed. "So much they can't control determines their success."

"There's no wind, so that's on their side, but it's a high-density area, and that works against them. It's nothing like the city, but there are a lot of objects to decrease the scent. They're bringing them out right around sunrise to go at it again. We want them out before the weather destroys the scent completely."

"How hot is it supposed to get today?"

"Just eighty, but it's supposed to rain."

"Great."

"We'll find the kid. It might not be tomorrow, but we'll find him."

"We need to find him alive."

"Unfortunately, I can't guarantee that, and neither can you." He popped himself up from the doorframe and walked over to my side. "Are you going home to get some sleep?"

Bishop walked in then and turned right back around to leave.

"You!" I pointed at him. "Stay."

"Yes, ma'am." He turned around with a big smile plastered on his face. "Olsen," he said and nodded at my...my...oh hell, Kyle. I still hadn't figured out what to call him.

"Any news?" Bishop asked.

Kyle repeated what he'd told me, then asked Bishop his take on the investigation.

"We have a few different theories, but nothing that says easy solve, and no amount of coffee is capable of keeping me awake any longer. I need at least a few hours of shut-eye, and so does my partner here."

"I agree," Kyle said. "I was just going to offer to make sure she gets home okay."

I rolled my eyes. I'm a detective. Getting home okay doesn't require any specialized skill above my paygrade. "I think I've got it."

"I'll feel better following you."

Bishop's eyebrows shot up, and I glared at him, silently threatening him to keep his mouth shut.

"Let's regroup at eight. That'll give us a good few hours of sleep," he said.

"That's five hours. We can't be away from this that long," I said. "Six. Regroup at six."

"I'm still catching up from the DEA task force case." He looked at Kyle. "Feels like that ended a year ago already."

Kyle checked his watch. "About nine hours ago."

"And we're not solving anything if we can't think straight."

"I was already on my way out after I touched base with Michels," I admitted. "But I'm coming back in three hours, if not sooner."

"Fine, I will too," Bishop said. "But I've already spoken with Michels. Ryan Rockman is already on an AMBER Alert across the Southeast. We have a BOLO for him and a woman fitting the twins' descriptions, and Michels has a team of patrol officers working the hospitals and shelters for any diabetic kids."

"What about urgent care centers?"

"It's three in the morning," Bishop responded. "There are two in Alpharetta that are open twenty-four hours. They've already checked them and the emergency vets, which there are only two of also. One in Alpharetta, and one in Roswell. We need to go home and sleep, Ryder, or neither of us will be any good for this case. Don't make me pull rank here."

"You're my peer."

"But I have seniority."

I groaned. "I'm leaving."

"Good," they said collectively.

We walked out together.

∾

I agreed to let Kyle follow me home under duress. Having him in my home felt strange. He'd been there before, but not in the nine or so hours since we decided to move forward with our feelings, and I felt guilty about betraying my deceased husband.

He leaned against the kitchen counter. "You haven't eaten in hours. Would you like me to make you something? I'm a pretty decent cook."

I smiled but declined. "I'm just really tired. Listen, I appreciate you wanting to...to be here, but I need to get some sleep, and I'm not...I can't—"

"I'm not here for sex, if that's what you're concerned about. I'm here because I care about you. How about if you get showered or whatever your normal bedtime routine is, and I'll toss something together for you to eat in a few hours? That way you don't have to eat donuts on the way to the station."

"I don't have much," I said as I opened the refrigerator. "I don't think you can make something."

"Watch me." He smiled, then pulled me into a hug. He didn't try to kiss me, and given my stale breath, I appreciated that. He knew he had to tread carefully, and I assumed he sensed my discomfort. Our one-night stand months ago wasn't at my place, so it wasn't in the bed I'd shared with Tommy. If this budding relationship turned into something, which I couldn't fathom, I'd need a new bed. Even though this had never been Tommy's house, it felt like cheating having Kyle there, and I couldn't imagine the guilt I'd feel if I had him in my bed.

He detached from the hug and sent me off to my bedroom. I closed the door behind me, stripped off my clothes and tossed them into the hamper, brushed my teeth, splashed hot water onto my face, and ran a comb through my hair, then hopped into the shower. After I finished, I threw on my favorite pair of Tommy's old boxer shorts and a tank top and fell into bed. I stared at the photo of me and Tommy on my nightstand and fell asleep almost the moment I closed my eyes.

I wrapped my hair into a low bun on my neck, tossed on a pair of jeans, a black T-shirt, my work boots, and a light jacket as I breathed in the smell of eggs and spices seeping under my door. When I walked out, Kyle was on the couch, freshly showered and changed into a clean outfit similar to the one he'd worn yesterday.

"Good morning, sunshine," he said with a smile.

"Who are you?" I asked, also with a smile. "Had I not smelled that heaven from the kitchen, I wouldn't have known you were here. You're very stealth-like."

"I'm DEA. I'm specially trained to be stealth-like."

"Or else I'm a really bad detective."

"Not even close. Just tired, and deservedly so." He stood and walked into the kitchen, used a mitt to remove a cast iron skillet from the oven, and set it on the stove. "Egg, ham, potato, and mushroom casserole, fresh out of the oven."

I was starving even more from the smell and could shovel it in quick enough to still make it to the department on time. I should have never left. The department is small, and when we have a case, it's all hands on deck. But after literally just closing a case and then being handed another one, we needed the rest. Bishop was right. We couldn't function well exhausted, and a detective needs to be quick and clear minded to get the job done.

I waxed on about Kyle's generosity as I stuffed food into my mouth, then caught a glimpse of my fish, Herman, swimming himself into the side of his glass bowl. "Oh, crap!" I rushed over and dropped a few pellets into his water, begging for his forgiveness. "Sorry, buddy. I was so tired last night, I didn't even think to say hi, let alone feed you."

Kyle laughed.

A tinge of anger swept through my mind. "What? He's family."

"I know. He's also a master manipulator. I fed him when you went to bed last night. He just knows how to work you."

I blinked and crouched down to study my fish as he munched on his food. "Did you do that? Did you just manipulate me, Herman?"

Kyle laughed. "I'm heading to work. We have a case working in Atlanta, and as of ten minutes ago, I'm on the team at least for the short term."

I flipped around, already uncomfortable about how we'd say goodbye. "Okay. Keep in touch."

He raised his eyebrows and smiled. "Keep in touch." He nodded once. "The romance is big in you, Ryder."

"I'm...it's—"

He held up his hand. "Baby steps. I'm good with that." He added, "Call you tonight," as he walked out the door.

Well, that wasn't at all awkward.

～

Hamby's small-town reputation had changed over time, and those changes were showing. The city's master plan never included high-density housing, things like apartments, townhomes, and lot lines of less than an acre, but the new mayor, who wasn't all that new anymore, pushed back on the master plan and bullied the council members into voting his way. Why?

Money.

It's always about money.

It might sound hypocritical of me given that I live in a high-density community, but in my defense, it's not in direct view of the McMansions nearby. I live behind an equestrian farm, and the entrance to my community looks like a small farm road for the property. It appears more secure than it is. Anyone paying attention can figure out where the road leads, but my point is my community isn't easily accessible or visible to the community.

But because of other communities like mine popping up around town, we've seen an increase in traffic and the need for better functioning intersections. Lights are old-school, and Hamby has fallen victim to the roundabout trap like so many other small, wealthy communities. The problem with roundabouts is no one can figure out how to use them. I spend half my time cussing out drivers who stop at the yield sign, knowing full well they roll right on through most stop signs. We've worked to educate them with traffic notices, public service events, and Jimmy's even put traffic officers on them to direct traffic, but people don't get it.

I waited impatiently behind a line of seven cars as they stopped and allowed a total of twenty-six vehicles to go before them. If it was Chicago, someone would have ended up in a fist fight. At least it would have made the wait interesting.

I arrived late, passing blame of my lateness to those ridiculous roundabouts as I rushed in bitching to myself, loudly, about Hamby residents and their inability to understand simple physics.

"Good morning," Bishop said. He handed me a Dunkin' cup. "Just how you like it."

"Thank you. I would have stopped, but the damn—"

"Roundabouts and the idiots that don't know how to use them made you late."

I cringed.

He smiled. "Yes, the entire department heard."

"Well, they're completely idiotic. What's the point of controlling traffic when people don't know what the hell they're doing?"

"These things take time."

Jimmy stuck his head in the kitchen. "Investigation room. Now."

We followed him.

"Okay," he said. "No news on the kid, but we've been back on the search full swing for an hour now. Some other things have come to light in the past hour. Barron completed the initial steps of the autopsy of the female vic about fifteen minutes ago. As we all assumed, all signs lead to the bullet wound as the cause of death."

We all collectively nodded.

"At this time, I'd like Doc to give us a report on the scar, which, as we all know, is possibly key to the identification of the female victim." He pulled Doc's live feed up, and we all said hello.

Doc adjusted his wrinkled button-down shirt. Clearly, he hadn't gone home yet. I felt bad for the guy. I could see he was tired. Barron is smart and very Southern, but when he's all business, he loses the casualness of his Southern accent. I've never heard anything like it.

"The process of determining the age of a scar, even in the most experienced and expert hands such as mine, is inexact for a variety of reasons. The healing process from acute wound to a static scar involves the actions of several cells and requires a coordinated—"

I stopped him. "Doc, with all due respect, please dumb it down to detective speak."

Bishop chuckled.

"The neck is thin skinned, and since there is a rich amount of blood flow to the wound area, the healing process of any scar there is quicker than, say, a bullet wound to the shin. Aging a scar requires mostly a visual determination, and based on my initial exam, and this, by the way, is all subject to change once the autopsy is complete, and given the fact there are no signs of crusting, redness, infection, or increased blood supply to the wound, and considering the fact that the skin is minimally thickened around the scar area, my best guess is the victim acquired the scar several years ago."

I thought I got the gist of his incredibly long run-on sentence, but I wasn't sure.

"Can you be any more specific?" Bishop asked. "With less words?"

I smirked. "Yes, please dumb it down further, and give us a time frame,"

I added. "Would several years before be more than two, less than ten? How do you define that?"

"At this point we can reasonably assume the injury occurred sometime in the last ten years, but likely not less than two."

"That's in the time frame," Bishop said.

I nodded. "Were you able to get the dental molds?"

"Those are setting now. I've completed the mouth X-rays, and I am waiting for the dental records of both twins as we speak."

"I'll see if we can put a rush on those," Jimmy said.

"Doc," Bishop said. "What are the odds of the victim being the twin?"

"I can't confirm that without dental records."

Bishop glanced at me. I knew he was looking for a magical answer, but we both knew magic wasn't real.

"I can say this," Barron added. "A mother usually knows her child, and if she's certain the scar is the sibling's, then I wouldn't doubt her. Not professionally speaking, obviously."

Once Doc signed off, we discussed the missing child and created a more complete plan of action.

"Michels and his team," Jimmy said.

I glanced at Michels and smiled. He beamed with pride at Jimmy's words: *his team.*

Jimmy looked at Michels. "Can you update the team?"

"Yes, sir." He stood and coughed. "We have done a complete search of the community, including knocking on every door. Unfortunately, many of those people didn't answer, but we had over one hundred community volunteers on the search, and we are matching their addresses to the surrounding area. We'll get back out there starting at about seven thirty and hopefully catch people before they leave for work."

"Last night it was what, twenty?" Bishop asked. "Good job."

"Word got out, and more people showed up. I've been on this all night. Haven't been home since we arrived at the scene last night."

Bishop and I snuck a look at each other. I felt immediately guilty for going home, but Michels's involvement in the recent DEA investigation wasn't as big as ours, and he wasn't as exhausted. Plus, he was about ten years younger than me and thirty years younger than Bishop. He had the energy.

"I'm assuming NCIC is updated?" Bishop asked.

The National Crime Information Center, NCIC, is a criminal records database available to every criminal justice agency for communication about stolen property and, most importantly, missing or wanted persons.

Michels had already sat back down. As he began to answer, he stood again. "Yes, sir. We also, as you know, have an AMBER Alert out, and the phones are manned for the tip line calls."

"How many calls are coming in?" I asked.

"We're at five thousand messages already." He smiled. "I've pulled a few hundred, and Bubba did a key phrase search on them. Seems the top tip is alien abduction. There was some bright light in the sky last night, and people seem to think he's going to see ET."

I laughed.

Jimmy wasn't as humored. "Jesus. The bright light was the fucking helicopter searching for the kid. What the hell is wrong with people? Why are they wasting our time like that?"

I understood his frustration, but those tip lines were buried treasures for detectives, and even though the weed-through was daunting, that golden egg we often received was always worth it. "Something will come through on those. Who's taking the calls?"

"I've got three men on them."

"Any update on the local medical facilities?"

"Nothing," he said. "No requests for insulin or diabetic supplies. No boys matching Ryan Rockman's description were brought into any urgent cares— that were open—or hospitals. No homeless shelters throughout the tri-county area have seen the boy, and no vets have been contacted for insulin."

"Okay, Bubba is running the former nanny's info. As soon as we know where to find her, we'll interview her. Bishop and I are heading to the doctor's office this morning to interview the staff as well as talk with friends. We'll find out something today."

"We'd better," Jimmy said. "The mayor wants an update for his five o'clock press meeting."

"Great," Bishop said.

"We need to focus on the woman victim, regardless of which twin she is," I said. "My gut tells me she's key to this, whether it's her identity or something else."

Jimmy agreed. "I'll be in touch as soon as I hear back from Doc on the dental records."

"Thanks, Chief," I said. As Jimmy walked out, I eyed Michels. "We need any updates or credible tips you get on the boy, even if they seem insignificant." A knock on the door interrupted my train of thought.

Bubba walked in. "I've found something."

5

The three of us jumped to attention.

"Let me rephrase," he said with an embarrassed look on his face. "I haven't located the nanny yet, and there's no activity on any bank or credit cards for Melodie or Steve Rockman in the past forty-eight hours."

Bishop raised a brow. "Didn't we already know that?"

Bubba nodded. "But I analyzed their activity for the month prior, and it was a steady stream of purchases, especially by the female victim. She liked to shop."

I tapped a pencil eraser onto the tabletop. "So, the husband was at work until about noon. We don't know where the wife was. The killer could have come to the house and been there with the wife and kid when the husband returned home."

"Or the wife just didn't go out that day," Bishop said.

"It's inconsistent activity on her end," Bubba said. "Doesn't fit her recent pattern of shopping and lunching daily."

"But she had an event that evening, so she could have chosen to stay home with the kid," Bishop said. He made a good point.

"Mary Hagerty said she heard from her daughter yesterday morning, but it was through text, not a call, and Heather Maynor said she hadn't heard from the husband since he left work. He never responded to her texts," I added.

"So, they could have been dead since just after twelve hundred hours," Bishop said.

I nodded.

Bubba handed us copies of their credit card and bank statements. As Bishop flipped through them, I glared at him and then read them carefully. "Our female vic either ate out or shopped every single day in the last month. Every day, Bishop. And look at some of these places. It's not Amazon. It's Tiffany & Co. Valentino. She was going to Phipps Plaza and the perimeter as well as stores in Avalon in Alpharetta. She lunched at Marlow's and Kona Grill." I shook my head in envious disbelief. "Girl liked to eat. And she worked out almost daily except for the past forty-eight hours."

Bishop furrowed his brow. "How do you know that?"

"I checked her planner. She was definitely anal retentive."

Bubba said, "I also checked her computer and saw she keeps an additional calendar in there."

Bishop's eyes widened. "Holy shit, you're good."

"It's not hard. She used her son's birthday as her password."

He wasn't my guy Joey in Chicago, but everyone in Chicago *knew a guy*, and those guys usually did things cops pretended not to see. Bubba followed the rules of investigation, and that would be important to the district attorney handling the evidence in court.

Bishop looked at me. "Wouldn't the sister change that if she posed as her twin?"

"The password? Maybe not. If she was trying to maintain her sister's identity, she would have kept everything as original as possible."

"Which means she could have another laptop or something somewhere."

"For what?" I asked him. "If she's decided to steal her sister's life, why would she keep anything from her former one? Unless, of course, she's stupid."

"Aren't most criminals?"

I couldn't disagree wholly, but given this was a possible identity theft with a big ol' twin twist, the rules of the game were different. "Identity theft to this degree takes a sociopath to pull off, and if it's been happening for the past three years, Emily wasn't stupid. Far from it, actually."

"Shit," Bishop said as he dragged his hand down his stubble. He'd grown it out a bit more over the past few months, and especially since our stint on the DEA task force. He very likely chose sleep over shaving, and I couldn't fault him for that. "We gotta get our priorities straight on this case and quick."

"Our first priority is the child, and our job is to find the killer, because, as I said, that will lead us to the child," I said. "That said, Michels, can you make sure Ryan Rockman is listed as *endangered* in NCIC due to his diabetes? And update the AMBER Alert with it also? Whoever's got him has to have his medicine, but we have no idea how much."

"His medical condition is already on both," Michels said. "I'm sorry, I thought I made that clear."

"Are you okay?" Bishop asked. "Did you get any sleep this morning?"

I knew by his tone he was referring to Kyle going home with me. "Yes, I slept, but as I suspect is also the case with you, not enough to recover from the lack of sleep over the past few days, smartass."

He held up his hands. "I meant no disrespect."

"Right." I directed my attention to Michels. "My apologies."

He smiled. "Understood."

Bubba said, "I'm assuming you want to know the script deets. I've already got a call into the doc already."

Impressive. "Great. Let me know what he says."

"She."

"She," I replied.

"What're deets?" Bishop asked.

Michels and Bubba laughed.

"Did you learn nothing with the teenagers recently, partner?"

"Too much," he said with a sigh. "But nothing about deets. Is it a new slang term for some drug or something?"

"It's details," I said with a headshake. "Deets. Details."

"Then why not just say details?"

"Because youth," I said.

The department phone rang in the investigation room. I hit the speaker button. "Detective Ryder."

"Detective, it's Officer Mannie at the front desk. I have a Dr. Finklestein on the line for someone regarding the missing Rockman child?"

"Send it through, please." I heard the click and said, "Dr. Finklestein, this is Detective Rachel Ryder with the Hamby PD. Thank you for returning our call. We have some—"

"I've seen the news," she said. "I can tell you what you're looking for since the boy is considering endangered."

Bishop and Michels took notes.

"Thank you, Doctor."

"Ryan Rockman just turned five about three weeks ago. He was diagnosed with Type I diabetes at twenty-seven months. Are you familiar with Type I diabetes and how it's treated?"

"Not as well as I should be with this type of investigation. Would you mind explaining?"

"Very well. I'll make it brief. In Type I diabetes, generally, point-five to point-eight units of insulin is needed per kilogram of body weight daily. Keep in mind that approximately half of that is needed for food intake, while the other half is the basal rate. Do you know what basal rate means?"

"No."

"Most people don't. First things first. The daily adjustment for normal eating, or DAFNE portion for food intake, is taken as long-acting insulin, while the other is a continuous supply and is divided into two injections of Levemir insulin. That would be the basal rate."

"Does Ryan Rockman receive both through a pump?" I wanted to make sure we weren't somehow being duped by the unsub, the unknown suspect.

"Yes."

"How long before a pump runs out?"

"Ryan's cartridge is changed every three days along with his site change. But his body may need more insulin at any given time depending on his diet and levels, which could require the site be changed earlier. It's a constant and detailed management, especially at his age."

I glanced at Bishop. "So, unless Ryan's got an additional cartridge, he's got approximately three days of insulin?"

"That would depend on when his site was last changed. Typically, parents of Type I children keep track of these changes on a calendar. Given Mrs. Rockman's personality, I would assume she kept detailed records."

Bubba handed me her planner. I swept through the pages to August and saw *C* marked every three days. I'd noticed it before and noted to find out what it meant, and it now made sense. It was changed yesterday morning. She also had a family calendar in the back of the family binder, so I checked that too, and it was the same. How and why someone kept so many calendars was unknown to me. "Thank you, Dr. Finklestein. Do you have to call these prescriptions in?"

"I have done so until the end of the year. It should be easy to get the medicine when needed."

"And do you know where they're called in to?"

"CVS in the older section of Alpharetta, off Alpharetta Highway."

I thanked her and said we may be calling back with additional questions.

"You're very welcome. May I add that Mrs. Rockman is a good mother, and I can assure you she would not let someone take her child without a fight."

"As I hope would most mothers," I said and disconnected the call.

"I'll call the CVS," Bubba said.

"If the unsub who's got the kid knows where to get the meds, this should be easy," Bishop said.

"Unless the script was refilled recently," I said.

"Two days," Bishop said. "We have two days. At least we know it was changed before this all started."

"Unless she was told to mark it incorrectly by someone holding her captive."

He pressed his lips together. "There are so many veins from this case. How the hell can we solve it?"

"Hard work," I said. "And fast, which is exactly what the mayor wants."

Bishop's expression changed from concerned to angry. "You know what I think about him."

"One hundred percent."

"The biological mother definitely did it," Bishop said.

"In the library with the candlestick?" I responded.

He rolled his eyes. "You have gut feelings. Why can't I?"

"Not saying you can't," I said as I studied every bit of the investigation to date laid out in front of us on the conference table. "But can you give me any evidence to corroborate that feeling?"

"I can give you theories."

"Please do," I said and sat down to listen as he paced circles around the large table.

"Emily and Melodie weren't close, at least according to the mother. Let's say they go on this trip to try and reestablish the twin connection, at Emily's urging, mind you. To save their relationship. But that's a lie," he said as he pointed his finger at me like a prosecuting attorney in a nighttime drama series. "Emily took her sister to Mexico so she could steal her identity. She brings her there, kills her, then pays someone to hide the body, and comes back as Melodie. Only she screwed up and forgot about the scar. So, she hides it from her mother, the only person we know of who knew Emily got hurt on that trip until her sister comes back and—"

"The sister she murdered in Mexico? Who else is tired?"

"*Thought* she murdered in Mexico, only she didn't, and Melodie returns to avenge her death and kill her sister for stealing her identity."

"Sounds like a soap opera from my childhood." I hated to think he could be right, but he could be.

He furrowed his brow. "Don't tell me it's not plausible. You said yourself this is a possibility."

"It's definitely plausible, but your storytelling is a bit over the top."

He sat across from me. "Then what do you think?"

"I think we find the kid, we'll find our killer."

"You can say that all you want," Bishop said. "But we can't sit on our asses wishing and praying for it to happen."

"Agree," Michels said.

I stared at him.

He said to me, "With you."

"Right," I said.

Bubba had returned to let us know the prescription had been picked up three weeks ago, and they agreed to inform us if someone tried to pick up another one, noting that in their system for other stores also. He left again to dig into his tech skills and hopefully give us something that would solve the case.

"I believe the child was taken in a car," I said. "Even Agent Olsen said the dogs lost track in the driveway." I looked at Michels. "What about the neighbors' cameras? Anything on those?"

"We got nothing from video cameras. I can't believe these rich people don't pay for recorded eyes on their homes."

"They live in a bubble," Bishop said.

"Michels," I said. "Did you run a pattern check for the kid?"

"Pattern check?"

"Yes, when you listed him as endangered, did you run his deets"—I glanced at Bishop—"through NCIC and see if there are any matches to other cases?"

"Oh, yeah, of course. But no. There are no endangered kids with a double homicide currently active in the system statewide. There are several missing children, but none nearby."

"Kids with diabetes?"

"Not within a three-state radius."

"And what were the finals of those cases in other states?" Bishop asked.

"Meaning who did it?" Michels asked.

Bishop nodded.

"A family member. Usually a spouse, but one is still missing."

"See, the biological mother," Bishop said.

If only it were that easy.

"What about past missing children from a more expanded area? The area's population has exploded over the past few years. Someone who lived in the city or south of it could have moved this way."

"We located two hundred and seventy-one known child abductors and child sex offenders in a fifty-mile radius," Michels said. "We're currently checking the status on those and comparing it with abductors not in prison."

"How many is that?" Bishop asked.

"About two hundred forty-three."

Bishop sighed and rubbed his chin. "Son of a bitch. That's a lot of parole officers to contact. That could take days."

"It won't take as long as you think," I said. "But you should have officers going to each offender personally."

Michels nodded. "That's the plan. Nikki's getting the list organized in a spreadsheet with a pinpoint map and should have it done in an hour or so."

Points for Nikki. "Good for her."

Michels nodded. "Apparently, she's a tech wiz too."

"Damn," Bishop smirked. "We've leveled up in Hamby."

"Jimmy would appreciate that," I said. But I still felt a strong attachment to Ashley.

I asked an officer to go gather as much intel on Type 1 children as possible. "Anything you can get about the symptoms when they run out of insulin, that kind of thing."

"Yes, ma'am, but I don't need to research to tell you. My sister is Type 1."

My eyes widened. "That's great!" I felt instantly awful and backpedaled. "I mean, that's not great. It's—"

"Helpful to the investigation?"

I nodded. "Yes, and I'm sorry for being an ass."

He laughed. "No worries, ma'am. You're an important ass to this team."

I smiled. "Is your sister on a pump?"

He nodded. "Changes the cartridge every three days religiously. Did you know, if you don't keep the pump clean, it can cause all kinds of problems?"

"Like infections?"

"If the insertion site isn't clean, yes."

"Anything life-threatening?"

"Doctors pretty much scare the shit out of you and your family when someone has diabetes. Whatever you think is the worst that can happen, can happen, and they make sure you know it. But the odds of something happening are slim unless the person responsible is just completely negligent."

"Okay, and are the pumps easily maintained?"

He shrugged. "You get used to dealing with them. When my sister was seven, she was changing it on her own, but if you're not trained on how to do it, it's kind of intimidating. Not hard, really, but intimidating."

"What happens if your sister doesn't get insulin?"

"The usual stuff. She gets dizzy and tired, definitely thirsty, and she gets sweaty and shaky."

"That's all?"

"In the beginning. She was five when she was diagnosed. My parents just thought she was a fussy kid, at first. Turns out when these things happen for too long, it's a bad sign."

"What's the worst thing that can happen to this missing child?"

"Like I said, death, but he'd have to be without his meds for a while."

"I guess that's good to know."

"There are other issues to consider, ma'am."

"Such as?"

"Like if the person that's taken him doesn't understand his diabetes, or if they break the pump, they can possibly give him too much insulin, which would cause a diabetic coma."

"Shit."

"It's rare. The pump is pretty self-regulated. Your bigger risk is if they break the pump and then have to give him shots. Unless they've done it before, they won't know how much to give."

"Unless they can get a hold of the script."

He nodded. "Anyone with any reasonable intelligence can usually figure it out."

I thanked him and headed to Bishop's cubby. He'd recently hung a banner from the high school we'd just finished our task force work for on his wall. His school pride was adorable. He absolutely loved being a coach, and I knew he'd been trying to figure out how to stay involved without overloading his schedule. I smiled and pointed to the banner. "I still love this so much."

He raised his eyes from his cell phone and shot daggers from them straight into mine.

"I'm serious. I know you loved that experience. Hopefully, you can find a way to stay connected."

"If we close this case, I'll have time to at least watch the games."

"We'll close it."

"Mary Hagerty is on her way here for her interview. You ready?"

"Definitely. I contacted the DA and asked how much I need for a warrant for Melodie Rockman."

"Would be nice to know if she's the dead twin first and maybe some evidence to show she killed her husband and sister?"

"Yeah, that's what the DA said." I shook my head. "She doesn't think a judge will go for it, but we've got both siblings on a person of interest list and a BOLO for each, so maybe we'll get a hit on those. FYI, I added a countdown for Ryan Rockman's medicine to the whiteboard in the investigation room."

"A countdown?"

I nodded. "We have to assume the worst-case scenario. If the kid doesn't get his next dose, we're going to have a sick child, one who'll get sicker as time passes, and if that happens, hopefully whoever took him brings him in for treatment."

"Let's hope it doesn't come to that."

"Right."

"If he's still alive and local, we have a shot of finding him soon, but if Melodie is the killer, I don't see her sticking around."

"Probably not, but we've got to start somewhere. She can't go far without cash."

"You're assuming she doesn't have any," he said.

"You're assuming she does," I replied.

"Hagerty said there was ten K in the safe. If the combo on that hasn't been changed, and Melodie's the killer, then she could have taken that cash."

"Do you tell your mother things about your personal finances?"

"My mother's dead," he said.

"Sorry."

"If Emily was posing as her sister, she'd keep things as superficial as possible. It's hard enough to remember lies. Add minute details, and that's a lot to keep track of."

Bishop made a solid point. "Bubba's keeping track of the finances. We'll know if there's any movement on them," I said.

He stood. "In the meantime, I'm going to hit the mother right in the feels."

Michels stepped into the cubby. "Barron's on the phone. Wants us all in the room."

"Investigation room it is," I said.

Barron coughed into the phone. I glanced at Bishop, who mouthed, "COPD?"

I shrugged. I'd never seen the doctor smoke, but that didn't mean he wasn't a closet puffer. People always hid the ugly parts of their lives from people. It was only in their worst moments that the ugly parts were revealed, and usually, I was there for the showing.

"I've determined the time of death to be approximately eighteen hours ago, which would be approximately one p.m. yesterday."

"That lines up with after the doctor left work," Bishop said.

"Did you expect otherwise?" Barron asked.

I smirked.

"Now for the good news. I've received the dental records for the twins, and I can confirm the deceased is not Melodie Rockman but Emily Hagerty."

Bishop fist-pumped the air. "I knew it."

"Once the autopsies are complete, I'll have more information."

"Thank you," I said.

The team all added their thanks, and we disconnected the call.

"Time to talk to Hagerty," Bishop said.

I followed Bishop to the interrogation room. "You want to start, or should I?"

"Let me. This woman just lost her family and discovered one daughter impersonating the other. She's probably an emotional wreck."

"Are you saying I won't be sensitive?"

"That's exactly what I'm saying. You think she's involved. I don't. Let me start and see if we can get something before you get all hardass on her."

"Aw, you think I'm a hardass. I love that."

"Of course you do."

"Give me five. I've got to take care of something first."

"You want to make her sweat it out and wait longer, don't you?"

"Never hurts when you're trying to get the truth from someone."

6

I tapped out a text message to my guy Joey Angelini while we headed to the room. Joey could find out anything and everything, albeit sometimes not exactly legally, with the tap of a keyboard, and even though we couldn't use the information in court, those skills were very important to an investigation. It was a fine line, though, getting information that way and finding a way to close a case without that information coming to light. Most of the time I could walk that line, but there were many I'd fallen over and messed up a trial because of it.

He responded quickly and said he'd get back to me as soon as possible.

Mary Hagerty sat in the interrogation room. Her eyes were bloodshot and swollen, her nose red and, from the sound of her voice, stuffed to the hilt. She sipped from a Starbucks to-go cup as we walked into the room.

I closed the door behind me and sat next to Bishop, directly across from Mary Hagerty.

"Ms. Hagerty," Bishop said. He used his compassionate voice, the one that sometimes cracked when he pretended, but it didn't crack this time, and he didn't appear to be acting. "We are truly sorry for your loss."

"Thank you," she said, sniffling. "The doctor won't tell me anything. I called this morning on my way here, and he said I have to talk to you. What's going on?"

"Doctor?" I asked.

"The one at the house last night. The coroner, I guess."

Bishop responded. "Dr. Barron can't release information to anyone during an active investigation, ma'am. That's our job, and we can tell you that based on dental records of both Emily Hagerty and Melodie Rockman, you were correct. The female victim is your daughter Emily."

She gasped, then sobbed into her tissue. "Oh my God! I knew it!" She wiped her nose carefully. "Then where's Melodie?"

"We aren't sure, ma'am. We're hoping you can help answer that."

"I...she was...I don't know." She gasped again. "Did she kill her sister? What's going on? Why was Emily posing as Melodie?" She shook her head and through sobs, said, "I don't understand what's going on."

"We're trying to figure that out, ma'am," Bishop said. "There are many tentacles to this investigation, and we've got a team of law enforcement professionals working them diligently. We have some questions for you, and your answers may help us figure out what's going on."

I paid attention to the woman's emotional state and watched to match it to her physical appearance and body language. She put on a good show. The sobbing, the gasping, all an Emmy-worthy performance, but they, along with her stuffy nose and swollen eyes, didn't coordinate well with her tailored suit and freshly styled hair.

Sure, there were women, especially rich women, who maintained an excellent appearance in times of angst, but a triple whammy of a double homicide, a missing grandson, and a switched twin were three hard hits, but there she was, looking like she'd prepared for a special event. I watched her carefully and took notes. I caught her staring at me for a moment, and I hoped I'd thrown her off-balance.

She nodded. "Okay."

"When exactly was the last time you physically saw your daughter?"

"Which one?"

"The daughter you thought was Melodie."

"I...I spoke to her via text yesterday. I...I haven't seen her for a week or so."

"Do you feel like your daughter has been avoiding you of late?" he asked.

"No. We…it's not…it wasn't like that. Melodie and I were close. She would never avoid me."

"But this wasn't Melodie, it was Emily," I said. "Were you two close also?"

She stared at the table. "Not as much as I would have liked, but Emily wasn't the type to be close to anyone. She did her own thing, lived by her own set of rules."

Did those set of rules include harming her twin and stealing her life?

"So, you didn't know she was pretending to be your other daughter?" I asked.

"You don't know that," Hagerty said. "Just because she was there doesn't mean she's been posing as her sister. She could have returned from Mexico to surprise us and was just there at the wrong time. Maybe someone else thought she was Melodie, like the rest of us." She wiped her nose again. "How dare you accuse my daughter of impersonating her sister for her own personal benefit."

Interesting how she made that connection, I thought.

Bishop glared at me. I decided to keep my mouth shut for the time being. It was fine. I'd succeeded in my goal, which was to throw her off-balance.

"Tell us about her relationship with her sister," Bishop said. "You said they weren't close like typical twins, but were they close like siblings in general?"

"I can't say. I only have twin daughters, so I don't want to compare them to other siblings and their relationships. But I can say that for the most part, they were very different, even though Emily liked to think they were the same."

"How do you mean?" he asked.

"Before I continue," she said, staring at me, "I want to make it clear that I am not at all assuming there was any negativity between my daughters, nor am I assuming Emily stole her sister's identity at any time in the recent or distant past."

"You've made it clear," I said. "But the fact is, we have reason to believe that is the case."

"Please, Ms. Hagerty, go on."

"My girls are different, yes, but I didn't see it as negative. Emily was always the one to jump on her sister's success train, if you will, and Melodie didn't like it. Melodie was homecoming queen, prom queen, she was a cheerleader, and everyone loved her. Emily was well liked in her social circle, but she wanted to be as popular as her sister."

"And did that continue as they aged?" he asked.

"In part. They didn't have the same goals or the same dreams. Like I said, Emily lived by her own rules. She was the adventurer. Melodie liked structure and consistency." She stared at the wall for a few seconds before speaking again. "Always a plan, and everything had its place. I think Emily wanted to be that way but couldn't. I think that was a bone of contention for them."

"I can see why they weren't close," I said.

"I didn't say they weren't close. I said they weren't close like other twins, but they did have a relationship, it was just..." She paused. "Injured for a while."

"Why was that?" I asked.

She let out a frustrated sigh. "Melodie met Steve at a charity event in Alpharetta several years ago. They immediately clicked, and things moved quickly for them, but when their engagement appeared in the paper, Melodie learned from a college friend that Emily and Steve were previously involved."

I made quick eye contact with Bishop. He nodded once.

"Melodie didn't know?" I asked.

She shook her head. "Neither Emily nor Steve mentioned it. I don't believe it was serious, and they made the decision not to disrupt Steve and Melodie's relationship. I thought that was best at the time, but now I'm not so sure."

Bishop adjusted his position in his seat. "You knew?"

She nodded. "Not at first, of course. I ran into Emily and Steve together at Avalon one evening. It didn't seem like they were serious, and honestly, I wasn't paying that much attention, but when Melodie and Steve began dating, and she introduced me, I remembered him."

"But you didn't say anything?" I asked.

"I didn't feel it was my place."

"How long did Emily and Steve date?"

She shrugged. "I don't know, a year, maybe? I'm not exactly sure."

My eyes widened. "They dated a year, and Melodie never knew? She never met Steve?"

"As I said, they weren't in the same social circle. I can't say why she wouldn't introduce them except that she was always the child who everyone talked about, and at some point, she decided to stop giving them things to judge, and I supported that."

"But Melodie was her sister," Bishop said. "They never double-dated or anything like that?"

"Not when Steve and Emily were together. Melodie was working a lot, focused on her career, and dating wasn't something that mattered to her. Emily was a social butterfly. She loved being out and about."

"What made Emily decide to maintain a more private life?" I asked. "Was it a specific situation, or was she just tired of the talk?"

"A little of both," she said. She twisted a ring with a large square diamond around the ring finger of her right hand. "She was accused of an affair, which she swore never happened, and the wife made sure to drag her through the mud for months after."

"Who was the couple?"

She tapped her chin as if she struggled to remember. What mother would forget a woman who dragged her daughter through the mud?

"Oh, Sara Reilly. She was married to Sam Reilly on the TV."

"Was this before or after Emily dated Steve?"

"Before."

"Sam Reilly, the news anchor?" Bishop asked.

She nodded.

"He had a pretty public divorce a while back."

"Yes, I'm well aware."

I jotted down the names and made a note to contact the couple, separately of course, as soon as possible. "What was Melodie's job?" I asked.

"She was a professional organizer." She smiled. "And she was excellent at it too."

"Do you happen to know any of her clients?"

"You could check her blog. They're on there, but she hasn't really updated it much or worked, even, since...oh, I didn't realize. She's not done any of it since she returned from Mexico. She said she just wanted to spend more time with Ryan. She'd been working part-time anyway since he was born because she felt she needed to focus on her child."

"What's the blog?"

"I don't remember. Something Strategic Organization or something."

"I'll look for it," I said. "Thank you." I quickly sent a message to Bubba.

He responded immediately. *Blog hasn't been active in three years and two months. I included the info in my notes earlier.*

I hadn't had the time to read through the pages of notes in detail. *Thank you*, I responded.

Bishop tapped his pencil on the table. "Can you tell me about Melodie's relationships?"

"How do you mean?"

"Did she have a best friend?"

"Oh, yes, of course. Though they both have children and haven't had the chance to spend as much time together."

"Her name?"

"Leah Marx. She's local."

She was on my list. Based on her daughter's calendar, they'd spent more time together than Mary knew.

"How long were they friends?" Bishop asked.

"Since high school."

"Was she friends with Emily also?" I asked.

She shook her head. "The girls didn't have the same social circle. I think I already mentioned that twice now."

I nodded. "Ms. Hagerty, you said your ex-husband is across the country. Is he away on business? Have you contacted him?"

Her eyes hardened, and her tone had a bite. "He's not away on business. He lives in Seattle with his bimbo."

Well, okay. "How long have you been divorced?"

"Why does that matter?"

"I'm just gathering information," I said.

"We divorced when the girls were eighteen. The day they went to college, the bastard served me with divorce papers. Said he was marrying the woman who worked at the front desk of his law firm. So typical for a man in the throes of a midlife crisis."

"We'll need to contact him," I said.

"Go ahead." She crossed her arms over her chest. "It'll be a cold day in hell before I do."

Bishop changed the subject, though I had additional questions about the twins' relationship with their father. "Where did the girls go to college?"

"Melodie went to Georgia, and Emily to Georgia Southern, but she only made it a year before dropping out."

I saw a pattern with Emily, with both twins, in fact, and the patterns were very opposite. These twins might have been identical, but they weren't similar at all, and as much as the mother tried to say they got along, it appeared otherwise. "Ms. Hagerty, can you tell me your ex-husband's contact information?"

"I don't have it, but it should be easy to find. Hagerty and Anderson, Attorneys at Law. The whore he left me for became an attorney, and they started a firm together. Leland, my ex, has had no relationship with his children other than to line their pockets with cash and expensive gifts. It's pathetic. To the best of my knowledge, he hasn't spoken to Emily since she left for Mexico."

"So, you're saying your ex has no idea about the death of his daughter?" Bishop asked.

"Not unless someone's called him, but like I said, it'll be a cold day in hell before I call that bastard."

"Thank you," I said. I opted to leave while Bishop finished interviewing her to check on the rest of the investigation, primarily any updates on the missing child. And most importantly, contact the father.

"Nothing at this time," Michels said. "I've double-checked NCIC to make sure everything's listed correctly. I've got a team of LEOs on the homes we couldn't connect with last night, three working the tip line, and two supervising the volunteers out looking for him in the community."

"Nice job. What about the hospitals and urgent cares? Any update?"

"Not yet. The Fulton County Sheriff's Office is assisting since we don't have the manpower for everything."

"Got it. You're doing great, Michels. I really appreciate it."

"Learned from the best, ma'am."

I rolled my eyes at the *ma'am* reference.

He smiled. "Just a Southern form of respect, *ma'am*."

"Bite me, Detective."

He laughed as I walked away.

I headed back to the investigation room and called Bubba to request he look up Leland Hagerty. I could do it, but he was much faster in the system than I was.

"I'm on it," he said before hanging up.

I added some notes to the whiteboard as I worked through my thoughts. I couldn't pinpoint specifically what bothered me, but I didn't trust Mary Hagerty. She was involved somehow. I knew it in my gut. I had nothing to back that up, no evidence, not even anything she'd said specifically. I just knew.

To verify my budding thoughts and hopefully encourage them forward, I pulled up both Emily's and Melodie's driver's license images and printed out copies. When Bubba texted the information on their father, I made the call.

"Mr. Hagerty is in a meeting," a woman said. "May I take a message?"

"This is Detective Rachel Ryder with the Hamby Police Department in Georgia. I'm calling about his daughter, Melodie Rockman. It's important that I talk to him immediately."

"Please hold."

I didn't have to hold long.

"Leland Hagerty. This is about my daughter?"

"Mr. Hagerty, I'm Detective Rach—"

"I know that already. What's going on? Is Melodie okay?"

"Sir, have you spoken to your daughters recently?"

"I...I...please, is my daughter okay?"

"I'm sorry to inform you that your daughter Emily Hagerty and your son-in-law, Dr. Steve Rockman, were found dead yesterday evening."

"What? How...Emily's in Mexico. Where's Ryan?"

"Mr. Hagerty, we are still working through the details and aren't yet clear as to why Emily was with your son-in-law, and we're currently looking for Melodie and your grandson, so I'll ask again. When was the last time you spoke to your daughters?"

He broke down. "Emily's dead? I...that...no. That can't be."

"I'm sorry for your loss, sir." I gave him a minute to get control of his emotions.

"I...my God. This is awful. My poor daughter."

"Mr. Hagerty, again, I'm sorry for your loss, but it's very important that you work with me and answer my questions. We are working hard to locate your daughter and grandson. Do you think you can answer my questions now?"

"Yes, I...I'm sorry. I'm fine."

I repeated, "When was the last time you spoke to either of your children?"

"I...I haven't spoken to either of them in a few months. Melodie sent me a photo of Ryan just last week and we talked over text, but that's it. They respect that I'm busy."

That was a great way to pass the buck for his crappy parenting skills. "Have you seen either of your children since 2018, specifically since their trip to Mexico?"

"I...no."

"Do you have any knowledge of Emily returning back to the States?"

"No."

"What can you tell me about their relationship?"

"Are you saying you think Emily stole Melodie's identity? Is that why she's dead?"

"What makes you suggest that?" I asked.

"Because she was the type to do just that."

It struck me as odd that Emily and Steve had a previous relationship, yet no one told Melodie, especially her mother. Deciding to stay out of her daughters' business seemed like a weak excuse as well as a sign that, like her ex-husband, Mary wasn't all that interested in parenting. I didn't have the best examples of parents, but I knew enough to know that dating the same guy should have been something Mary Hagerty at least pushed Emily to tell her sister.

Bishop walked in and broke my train of thought. He sighed. "That poor woman. She's a hot mess right now. Can you imagine? Losing your child and then coming to find it was the other one the entire time?"

"Can't imagine." I stared at the whiteboard. The twin switch, however it happened, was key to this situation, and I was beginning to think Bishop was onto something. But my gut told me Mary knew more than she was saying. "I'm beginning to think you're heading the right direction."

"How so?"

"That Melodie's possibly good for the killings, but Mary's involved, Bishop, or at the very least, she knows more than she's saying."

"I'll take knows more than she's saying first. Tell me how."

"Do you think a mother can really be duped by her children for that long and in that type of situation?"

"You're assuming the switch happened in Mexico. We don't know that for sure."

"You're right, but regardless, a mother knows her children." Most, anyway.

He handed me a photo. "She gave me this before she left. They're identical. It would be hard for anyone to tell them apart."

I studied the photo. He was right, there were many features the two shared, as is normal with identical twins, but I could pick at least two, maybe three things I noticed right away. "Check out their cheekbones. Yes, they're identical, but it looks like Emily had some work done on hers. And her eyebrow shape is different."

"That's cosmetic, isn't it?"

"Yes, but it's a significant difference and something her mother should have noticed. Emily could have done hers to look like her sister's."

"It's only significant if you're looking closely," he said. "It's possible Mary Hagerty didn't notice."

"Possible, yes, but likely? Not to me. I'll have Bubba check social media and see what they both looked like prior to their trip to Mexico." I tapped my pencil on the table. "You know how there's no photos of Melodie in the house? That could be so people didn't catch the differences. Emily could have removed them when she took over her sister's life."

"We don't know when that was," he said. "Emily could have returned a week ago, told her sister she'd slept with her husband years before, and Melodie lost it. Until we can find something showing when and if Emily came back from Mexico, we can't say if or when the switch happened."

"It happened in Mexico, Bishop. It's the easiest answer, and the easiest answers are usually the right answers. We need to get with a US consulate in Mexico. We need a team of people on the lookout for Melodie just in case she's alive and isn't the killer."

"If Melodie didn't kill them, and she's still alive, why wouldn't she have returned to her family already?"

"It's like we said before, maybe she wanted the switch?"

"That doesn't match the personalities."

"Actually, it does. Type A mother with a seemingly perfect life who caves to the stress and can't handle the pressure to maintain that lifestyle and wants to run, but she's guilt-ridden because of her child. Twin sister admits to always loving the husband, and they conjure up a plan to switch lives. It's like some twisted Lifetime version of *The Parent Trap*."

"*The Parent Trap*?"

I blinked. "Did you ever watch TV with your daughter?"

"Yeah, all the time. College football."

"Dear God. It's a movie about twins switching lives. And Bishop, I know I said it's possible Melodie's the killer, but there's something else to consider."

"And that is?"

"Maybe Melodie didn't come back because she couldn't."

"Because she's dead."

"Or being sex-trafficked, or in prison, or God only knows what."

"And let me guess. You think the mother is somehow involved in that."

"Yes."

He shook his head and blew out a breath. "I think she's in distress over the fact that her children are dead and missing, and her grandson is missing too. She doesn't strike me as the type of person to keep something from the police."

"She's exactly the type for that very reason. She's manipulative. Did you see her clothing and her hair? She didn't look like a damsel in distress to me."

"She'd been crying. Maybe you didn't look close enough. Her nose was red and stuffy. You can't pretend that."

I stared at the wall, kept myself from blinking, and in my head replayed the night my husband was murdered in front of me. I didn't force back or try to hide my feelings. I just let them consume me, and it was awful. Tears fell from my eyes, and my nose began to drip.

Bishop stared at me like I'd lost my mind. "Ryder? You okay? I...I didn't mean to upset you."

I grabbed a tissue and blew my nose. "You didn't. I'm fine. Chicks can cry, Bishop, even ones like me. All it takes is a little effort." Before he could say anything, I added, "Again, I stand by my thought that a mother knows her children and can identify one twin from the other, and I'm going to figure out a way to prove that." I immediately sent a text message to my best friend, Savannah Abernathy, who happened to be the wife of our chief, Jimmy. I would have contacted my cousins, but I hadn't spoken to them in years, and I wasn't about to call my mother.

Do you know any twins? I hit send and waited for a response. When I saw the three little dots pop onto the thread, I knew she was responding.

Interesting question. I know several. Fraternal and identical, males and females. Twins are big where I'm from. I swear it's something in the water. Are you asking for information for male or female? They're very different.

I responded with, *Either, though I'd prefer female.*

I know a set of female twins back in Macon. Would you like me to contact them for you? she asked.

Not them. Their mother.

Interesting. Is this about the Rockman murders?

I'm not able to discuss an active investigation.

No worries. I have a relationship with the chief, and I know how to get him to talk.

Information I don't need. I set my phone down. "Savannah knows twins. She's having the mother call me."

"For what, a scientific study on the identification of twins by parents?"

"Yup."

Bishop's face reddened. "This is a waste of time, Ryder. We need to be out there finding that boy!"

"We have a dedicated team searching for him, *Bishop*." I knew he was annoyed, but so was I, so I gave him a taste of his own medicine and used a similar tone. "What we need to do is find the killer, and whether you're right about it being Melodie or someone else, we find the killer, and we'll find the kid. Can we just roll with that, or are we going to continue to debate it every few hours?"

"You're an asshole sometimes, you know?"

"I know, and I'm going to be one again right now. You can doubt me all you want, but I'm confident Mary Hagerty is involved."

"You think she's the killer?"

"I'm not prepared to say that yet."

"You shouldn't be, because there's no evidence. How do you think she's involved, then?"

"I'm still thinking it through, but I think she's lying to us."

"Why would she lie to the police when her grandson is missing?" He sighed. "You think she's got the kid, don't you?"

"I think she knows he's safe."

His lips formed into a straight line. "No. I saw that woman in there. She doesn't know anything, and she's not lying."

"Did you and I see the same woman? She started off devastated, but that disappeared in seconds, and I'll repeat what I said before, because apparently you didn't listen. Her hair and her clothing, Bishop. She took the time to do her hair and put on nice clothes. She wanted to present herself well. A grandmother whose grandchild is missing and who's just lost her daughter doesn't give a damn what she looks like to the cops."

"You don't know Southern women very well. Ask your best friend. She'll tell you women will fancy up the day their spouse dies. It's just what they do."

My cell phone rang. "Detective Ryder."

"Hello, I just received a call from Savannah Abernathy about my twins? Is everything okay? Are they wanted by the law?" She dragged out *law* with her deep Southern accent.

I put the call on speaker for Bishop to listen. "No, ma'am. This is purely informational. We are currently talking with the parents of identical twins, specifically women, to gather information about an investigation, but it has nothing to do with your children. I'm assuming yours are identical?"

"Yes."

"Okay, as a mother, do you have trouble identifying which is which?"

She laughed. "Detective, I know my daughters, and I know them well. I can tell them apart the minute they walk in the room. Stephanie has a little hop when she's excited, and she walks with her right shoulder hitched up from carrying an oversized purse. You would not believe the stuff she puts in that thing. Lordy bee, it's heavier than a bowling ball. I told her to carry clutches, they're better on the shoulder, but she just loves those big purses. And—"

I didn't have time for a Southern fashion report. "Ms.—I'm sorry, I didn't catch your name."

"Lee. We're descendants of Robert E. Lee. He was—"

With Southerners, everything is a story, and they always want to take the time to tell it. It's been an adjustment for me, and I was still adjusting. "Ms. Lee, I don't mean to cut you off, but we have a short window for this investigation."

"Oh, bless. I'm sorry. Go on."

"Thanks. What about facial features? Could you tell the difference from those?"

"Sure. Stella has a little bump on her nose, had it since the day she was born, but regardless, they just look different to a mother, does that make sense? A mother knows her children."

I thanked her and said goodbye.

"Okay, fine, I can see that," Bishop said. "But you didn't see her after you left. I asked her about her children, about her grandson, and she bawled her eyes out."

"Then she's a good actor, and you've been duped. I'm telling you, Bishop, she's involved."

"I appreciate your gut, and I'll admit it's pretty damn good, but I've got a gut too, and mine is saying you're wrong on this one."

"Fine. We'll agree to disagree until I'm proven right."

He shook his head. "You're fucking unbelievable sometimes, you know that?"

"And I'm usually fucking right, you know that?"

He yanked the door open and stormed out, bumping into poor skinny-as-a-stick Bubba in the process.

"What's up with him?" he asked.

"It's that time of the month."

He cringed. "I'd be fired if I made that kind of comment."

"I'd stick up for you," I said with a wink. "You got the information I asked for?"

He nodded. "A few things. First," he said as he handed me a file. "Your Mary Hagerty has been receiving monthly alimony checks from her ex-husband for a long time. Dude's making bank."

I studied the information. "Twenty-two thousand bucks a month?" I looked at him. "Damn."

"I know, and if you look further down the page, she's also been making cash deposits of one to two thousand a month into another checking account. Guess which one."

I reviewed the information. "The jewelry store. It could be a layaway thing, but I'd bet it's not." I grabbed a highlighter and marked those deposits, then tapped out a quick text to Joey. I wanted him to handle this one in his special Joey way. If he could find something that would push the investigation forward, I'd figure out how to scrub it out of the investigation later. "How far did you go back?" I found the last page of those deposits and compared the dates on the first and last papers from that account. "Two years?"

"And four months."

"This is good, Bubba, thank you."

"You think this has something to do with the murders?"

"It's a pattern of behavior, and we'll have to determine if it does."

"Can I ask how it might be involved?"

"You can ask anything you want. It might be involved because she either has some serious debt or a shopping addiction for which she pays under the table, or she's paying someone off. And since the daughter's been paying cash to the same place, and that place happens to be owned by

Hagerty's significant other, it's something we have to look into further. If I'm right, someone at that jewelry store, maybe her boy toy, has them both by the balls, and I intend to find out why." I waved the file at him. "Can you make three more copies of this, please?"

"Already done, but there's something else you need to see." He held up the last sheet, which was a summary of another account.

I scanned the paper, then glanced up at him. "Interesting. The puzzle just keeps getting bigger, doesn't it?"

"Yes, ma'am."

"Do you know who that account belongs to?"

He shook his head. "I'm working on it."

"Let me know if you can't get it. I know a guy who might be able to help."

"I can get this to Bishop if you'd like," he said.

He held the sheet out, and I snatched it from him. "I'll take that to him. Thank you, Bubba. Great work."

He smiled as I walked out.

I charged to Bishop's cubby and dropped the file detailing the questionable bank account onto his desk in front of him. "Aside from a hefty alimony check, Mary's been receiving cash to the tune of a few thousand bucks a month since eight months after her daughter returned from Mexico." I plopped into the chair feeling validated. "And oddly, she's also been paying her boy toy a couple thousand a month, too, for about the same amount of time."

He studied the file. "Who's the account holder giving her the money?"

"Bubba's trying to find out."

"It could mean a number of things."

"Yes, like for example, it could mean Hagerty was aware of the twin switch and was blackmailing her daughter Emily to keep her secret. Or it could be money Melodie is filtering through her to keep herself MIA."

"It could just as easily be someone who owes her money. Bubba will find out, but in the meantime, we shouldn't waste our time on it."

"What about the money to the jewelry store? It's not a coincidence that she and her daughter have been paying them for months now."

"Ms. Hagerty is a classy-looking woman. She wears nice jewelry. She's probably paying the store on a layaway program, hooked her daughter up with the boyfriend to purchase something, and he gave her the same direct deposit information. It doesn't have to be something illegal. Attractive women like to wear nice jewelry."

"Oh my God. You've got the hots for Hagerty! How did I miss that?"

His face reddened. "What? No."

I pointed at him. "Yes, you do, and you can't see her clearly because of it!" I adjusted my position in the chair and laughed. "You're crushing on a possible murder suspect. Un-freaking-believable!"

"I am not crushing on any possible suspect. Whatever that means. I just said she's attractive and likes nice jewelry."

"Trust me, she is not the woman for you."

"Never said she was."

I laughed again. Since we became partners, I've never known Bishop to be interested in someone. Sure, I wanted him to be happy, but she was not the person for him. Not in the least. "Do me a favor, block that attraction until further notice, please."

"It's not an attraction, Ryder. Now, can we drop it and get back to the case? I'd like to get a good night's sleep sometime before October."

"Fine, but I'll be watching you."

"Watching for what?"

"Flirting and gross shit like that."

He rolled his eyes. "Can we head out for interviews now, or are we going to continue this ridiculous conversation?"

"I say we hit the jewelry store first and then the doctor's office to re-interview Heather Maynor."

"Agreed. I'll drive, but I'm getting caffeine first."

"Works for me," I said and followed him out the door.

When we got to the car, Michels rushed out. "Wait! The dogs found something."

7

Ashley handed me a photo from Steve Rockman's office. "It was buried in a drawer. It's the same blanket from the park."

Bishop examined it with me. "It's footballs," he said. "There could be a hundred local boys with football blankets."

"The dogs found it because it smelled like him, Bishop. You know that." This missing boy was hitting him hard, and he needed to get his emotions in check.

"I know that."

Ashley added, "There's no other signs of the child. No shoes, no blood, no footprints, no signs of a traumatic event. Nothing. Just the blanket."

"What about drag marks?"

She shook her head. "Nikki and I have combed the scene until our eyes hurt. If the kid was here, they carried him in and out."

Bishop dragged his hand down his stubbled chin. "Son of a bitch!"

I studied the area, taking in the location of the park, the traffic, the lights. "It's a setup."

A tall man with a freshly shaven face and short dark hair walked over. He was built like a brick wall. All muscle, but not the bulky, *I-spend-my-whole-day-at-the-gym-and-downing-testosterone* kind. Just real, honest-togoodness muscle. "That's what I suspect too." He nodded once. "Deputy Wilson, Field Operations, Fulton County Sheriff's Office."

I smiled. "Detectives Ryder and Bishop, Hamby PD. Thank you for participating in the investigation."

"We're here to assist, ma'am."

Bishop coughed.

"We came upon the blanket with Hampton, one of the county's K9s. He specializes in search and discovery of missing children."

"Can you tell us what happened?" Bishop asked.

"Yes, sir. Your department received an anonymous tip that the boy was seen at this park. We were called out, but there were no signs and nothing to lead us to the child or the blanket. When Hampton arrived, he went straight to the blanket, which had been left right there." He pointed to the edge of the park near a wooded area along the entrance road. "If I was to guess, I'd say someone drove in, tossed the blanket, and left. There are no other indications of him, and the dogs found nothing but the blanket. The smell disappeared much like it would if a vehicle were involved. I don't believe the child was here."

"We'll run the blanket for any DNA from the mother or father and see if it's a match just in case." I pointed to the lights. "No cameras on the park?"

Bishop shook his head. "We're the only town with them in the county."

"That's what a wealthy community will get you," Deputy Wilson said.

"Ain't that the truth," I said. Chicago had cameras in the wealthier areas, like the parks along the northern area of Lake Shore Drive or in smaller communities like Lincoln Park or the Gold Coast, but most of the city itself didn't have them. "Since we're in Alpharetta, can you assist in boots on the ground for the homes across the street? Someone's bound to have a Ring camera. Maybe they caught something."

"Happy to help."

I handed him my card, as did Bishop. "Please keep us informed," Bishop said.

"Will do."

As he walked away, Bishop sighed. "I'm torn between happy it's not the kid himself and pissed off it appears planned."

"I feel ya."

"It could be a sign the kid's dead," he said.

"I don't think so. A killer doesn't take the time to set up a scene miles away from the crime. Whoever did this thinks we're dumb enough to think the kid was here, or stupid enough to think he's dead. This is an amateur move."

"Who would benefit from the kid being dead?" he asked.

He already knew the answer. He just wanted me to say it. "Melodie Rockman."

"Told you."

"Or Mary Hagerty."

"Why? Why would she want him dead?"

"I don't know. Maybe she's not getting enough cash from her ex-husband and she's looking for more plastic surgery, so she wants to cash in on the kid's life insurance policy? That crap happens all the time."

"Then what's she going to do with the kid after she gets the cash? She can't keep him."

"No, but she can give him back to his biological mother."

"You think they're in on this together?"

"I think it's looking more and more like they are."

"Shit."

The jewelry store was located off Peachtree Road in Atlanta. Bishop drove, of course.

"Why don't I ever get to drive?" I asked.

"It's polite for the man to drive."

"You're kidding, right?"

"No."

"Bishop, we're partners. Equal partners. Just because you have a penis doesn't mean you should drive the vehicle all the time. People with vaginas are perfectly capable of driving, you know."

"Okay, fine. The truth is, I don't like driving with you."

I blinked. "What? Why not? I'm an excellent driver."

"You drive like a NASCAR driver. I take a risk every time I get in the car with you behind the wheel, and I'd prefer to die any other way but from your driving."

"I am a defensive driver, like I was taught in the academy."

"No, you're an aggressive driver. You always have to be first. Even when we're not going anywhere important, you have to be first."

"You drive like a turtle." I shifted to the side and stared out the window. "And it's these roads that make my driving seem aggressive. It amazes me the city didn't create a grid road system like Chicago."

"The highways and expressways were built after the war and without thought to city growth, but the city roads, like Peachtree, were designed back before the Civil War. Dirt roads became real roads, and no one took the time to think it through."

"Obviously. There's, what, at least ten Peachtree somethings. That's ridiculous. And I'm sure I can drive down them without killing anyone any time I try."

He ignored my sassy comment. "There are fifteen inside city limits. More in the surrounding area."

"That just to piss people off?"

"Probably."

We parked near the store but across the street.

"It's open," I said. "You lead. I'll play good cop."

"For like thirty seconds," he said.

"Probably."

We stepped inside and were instantly hit with bright lights that were meant to make the jewelry pop. A tall man with a scraggly, dark beard that didn't at all match his business suit walked up to the counter from the back room. "Good afternoon. Charles Haus. How can I help you today?" His stiff back and pushed-backed shoulders coupled with the fake smile plastered on his face and bogus politeness told me he was a fraud. A decent person doesn't dress that nicely and keep his beard untrimmed. They're too classy for that. I'd just have to figure out if that fraudulence was a business thing or an overall character issue.

"Good afternoon, sir," Bishop said. He showed him his badge. "Detectives Bishop and Ryder. Hamby Police Department." Bishop angled his body toward me. I chose to move my jacket slightly to the right and let

Haus glance at my badge attached to my belt next to my weapon. "We're here regarding both Melodie Rockman and Mary Hagerty."

He must have superglued that smile onto his face because it didn't appear to be going anywhere. "Detectives, I have thousands of customers through my store and website annually. I'm afraid I don't always remember them."

"Mary Hagerty claims you're her boyfriend," I said. "That not true?"

"Oh, Mary!" He scrubbed his beard with his hand. "I'm sorry, I guess I didn't hear you well. Of course I know Mary. We're friendly."

"Good, then maybe you'll remember the monthly deposits she and her daughter make into your bank account?" I showed him the photos of the deposits on my cell.

"I'm not aware of any monthly deposits, but it's probably a credit program I offer from time to time. Much like layaway, only they pay interest and get the handmade designs with the first payment."

I raised an eyebrow. "You're not aware of monthly deposits to the tune of three to five thousand bucks coming into your business? I think you need to find a better money management software or learn to balance a checkbook."

Bishop cleared his throat. "Sir, deposits are evidence and may be used in a murder investigation. If you'd like, we can discuss this at the Hamby Police Department."

He shook his head. "May I see the photos again?"

I showed them to him one more time.

"Oh, yes, well, now it makes sense." He stared into my eyes as he spoke, and the anger building in them was obvious. "I transferred the program's deposits to my main business account and must have missed those two. I have kept a small amount of cash in it for several years, but I don't actively use the account, and I don't check the statements online for it either, which is why it's obviously escaped me."

Bishop furrowed his brow. "When was the last time you viewed the account?"

He considered that for a moment. "When I switched to the other one, three years ago, I think? I'm not exactly sure."

"You have an account that clearly is receiving deposits and you don't pay attention?" Bishop asked.

"As I said, it's not the account for my business anymore."

I scanned the information. Other than some small interest earned and a monthly fee, as well as the activity from Rockman and Hagerty, there wasn't any other activity, and it struck me as strange. "Why keep the account if you don't use it?"

He shrugged. "I guess I just never got around to closing it." He shifted his position, and I noticed he was completely barefoot, the tops of his dress slacks giving away the casualness of his in-need-of-a-trim toenails. "I switched to Bank of America when BB&T merged with SunTrust. I'm not a SunTrust fan."

"Yet you kept the account open?" Bishop asked.

"Again, I had intended to close it but never got around to it. To do so, I need to go to a SunTrust location, and I guess it's just not a priority for me."

I wondered what it would be like to have the kind of cash that I didn't worry about closing an account. Cops didn't have that kind of income.

"When was the last time you ran that special layaway program?"

"Oh, a year or so ago? I don't recall. I'll do it for some of my regulars when asked because I trust they'll pay me."

"Like Mary Hagerty and Melodie Rockman?"

A tall woman dressed in a business suit with a short skirt and spiked heels walked in. She flipped her long blond hair back and smiled like she'd just left a meeting and had bitten the head off a business competitor. "Charlie, dear. Is my necklace ready? I can hardly stand waiting a minute longer."

Bishop's eyes nearly popped out of his head. His mouth dropped as he stared at the woman. Sure, she was pretty, but as Lenny always says, she wasn't anything to write home about. I elbowed him in the arm and whispered, "Keep it in your pants, partner."

He cleared his throat again.

"Alexandra, lovely to see you," the man said. "I'll be with you in a moment."

She flicked her hand and stared into the glass jewelry case, mumbling something. All I heard was "glorious" and "stunning" when I stopped paying attention.

"If you'd like, I can check the account and see what's going on. How can I get in touch with you?"

Bishop handed him a business card. "Today would be good."

"I'm not sure I can do it today. I've got several pieces to complete."

"Mr. Haus," I said. "We have a double homicide to solve and a missing child to locate. As soon as possible, but today, please."

He nodded. "Very well, I'll do my best. Now, I must get to my customer."

I purposefully let Bishop walk out first. Then as I walked through the door, I stopped, turned my neck back, and stared at the man. I knew his type well, and I didn't like him.

In the car, Bishop patted the sweat on his forehead with a Dunkin' napkin.

"Are you sweating because you thought the chick was hot?"

"Chick? Talk about classy, partner."

"Just keepin' it real. That woman's ninety-percent airbrushed and silicone."

"You think?"

"I know."

He started the car. "What's your take on Haus?"

"No one deposits money into an account without a reason, and no one keeps an account with money being deposited into it without a reason and pretends to have forgotten about it."

"My thought too. Wouldn't he have a layaway contract with them?"

"Not if he wasn't paying taxes on the income."

"But the money's just sitting in the account. If he hasn't touched it, what's the point of having it?"

"Maybe it's part of a slow-build plan."

"Such as?"

"That's the part I'm trying to figure out."

"Money laundering?" Bishop asked. He pulled out of the parking lot and headed toward our next stop.

"If so, they're really stupid criminals."

"Aren't most?"

"In general, white-collar criminals are smarter, but typically laundering doesn't come through personal accounts first."

"I know, but what's the reason, then? No one's touching the money."

"I don't know, but whatever it is is key to this case."

He sighed. "Dammit. I think you're right."

I laughed. "Which means you think I'm right about Granny Hagerty, then, too."

"You're a pain my ass."

Heather Maynor sat us in a small conference room off the employee kitchen. "Have you found Ryan?"

"Not yet, but we've got a dedicated team out searching for him," I said.

"Has anyone requested any ransom?"

Interesting question. I glanced at Bishop. He pressed his lips together.

"Oh, right," she said when we didn't respond. "That's probably not something you'd discuss if they had." She stood at the door and closed it. "Help yourself to coffee from the station in the corner." She handed us each a piece of paper with a list of employees and their information typed on it. "I assumed you'd be here this morning, so I've put together a schedule of employees and their contact information for your interviews. I've let them know you'll be calling them in at your leisure. There's no particular order to the list, but the top six do see patients, so we'll need to get to them when they're free."

Bishop asked, "How many are doctors?"

"Three of the six. The other three are nurses or physician assistants. We have four other doctors and nurses, but they're on rotation or have surgeries today."

I nodded. "Thank you, Heather. This is very kind of you."

She attempted to smile but failed. "Aside from ransom, is there anything on Ryan you can share?"

"Not at this time, ma'am," Bishop said. His reply sat on the line between lying and truth, but Heather Maynor didn't need to know that.

It was important to keep those close to the victims calm, especially with a missing child and a possible family abduction. The goal was to respect the fact that they're worried while keeping their mind clear and focused on the end game. And the end game was Ryan returned safe, the murders solved, and the unsubs caught and convicted.

"We'd like to ask you a few more questions," Bishop said. He motioned for her to sit. We'd hit the same questions as the night before, but stories changed, and it was important to find the consistent and inconsistent answers. Usually something led us closer to the truth.

"Oh, okay," she said uncomfortably.

"Were you aware of any tension or problems Dr. Rockman might have been experiencing here?" Bishop asked.

She shook her head. "No. Steve, er, Dr. Rockman was well liked. He helped people. They were grateful."

She continually corrected using a personal name for the doctor to a professional one.

"No discord with any patients or staff?"

"Not that I'm aware of."

"What about his personal life? Did he ever mention any struggles or conflicts?" I asked.

She bit her lip. "Not that I can recall."

Bishop continued. "How's the practice doing financially?"

Her eyes lit up. "It's great. We're seeing an increase in patients but also a cut in their care model, which means they're recovering or healing quite well and quickly. Which is what we want, of course."

Dr. Rockman sounded like a saint, which led me to believe he was the exact opposite. "Was Dr. Rockman having an affair?"

She blinked. "What? I...no, I don't...why would you ask that?"

She was genuinely surprised, which was good. "We were told he may have gotten a nanny pregnant. Do you know anything about that?"

"What? Do you mean Ana? No." She shook her head. "I don't believe it. Steve was committed to Melodie and Ryan. He would never do anything like that."

"I'm sorry," I said. "I'm confused. Is it Steve or Dr. Rockman?"

She blushed. "He preferred I call him Steve, but I try to maintain a sense of professionalism around others. Sometimes I slip."

I nodded.

"Tell us a little about your relationship with Melodie again, please," Bishop said.

"As I said, we don't really have a relationship. She was so focused on Ryan and his diabetes, and she didn't like to bring him here with sick people."

"To an orthopedic doctors' practice," I said. "Did that strike you as odd?"

"Moms are extremely overprotective of their children. I've seen that in my daily work here. It makes sense that Melodie would be protective of Ryan. He was a very small, sickly boy for a long time, and when they learned he had diabetes, she just stopped bringing him here."

"What about before his diagnosis?" I asked. "Did you spend time with her or talk to her more before that?"

She thought about that for a moment. "Initially, yes. She was here often. She'd leave Ryan with the nanny and bring lunch for the office a few times a month. It was really very sweet. She said it was her way of thanking us for working so hard."

"And that stopped when he was diagnosed?"

She shook her head. "I don't recall when it stopped, but I guess after he was diagnosed, yes."

"Did something happen to make her stop coming by? Maybe a confrontation with a patient or something?"

She chewed on a very short fingernail. "Not that I can think of, I mean, other than Ryan being sick all the time."

"So, he was often sick before he was diagnosed?"

"Yes and no. He always had a stuffy nose and wasn't exactly healthy. Like I said, he was a sickly boy, but not in the sense that she was taking him to the doctor all the time. Just regular toddler kind of sick."

I had no idea what that meant, but from Bishop's nodding, I assumed he did.

"Most everyone thought she was being a little too protective, and there were rumors, of course, but those died down eventually."

Bishop raised an eyebrow. "Rumors?"

She sighed. "That's all they were. People talk, and in a medical office, there's a lot to talk about, so the gossip train is always in motion."

"What were the rumors about?" Bishop asked.

"That the marriage was in jeopardy." She blushed.

I pressed my lips together. "Did these rumors include you? Were you two intimately involved?"

If we caught her in a lie, she'd go straight to the top of the suspect list. A part of me hoped that would be the case.

She shook her head. "No. No, of course not. I swear. We were friends, that's all, but I'm the office manager, and we spent a lot of time working together to grow the business. When we first started, it was just him, and we worked hard to get it where it is today."

I studied her body language. She'd set her hands down on the table, leaned in a bit but kept her shoulders back, and spoke with confidence as she looked me in the eyes. She wasn't lying. This woman was dedicated to her boss and the practice, but the more she spoke, the more I realized there wasn't a romantic element between her and the doctor.

"Did Rockman cheat on his wife?" Bishop asked.

That was us driving the point home. There weren't many other ways to ask it, but if we got a yes to any of them, we'd have another suspect to consider, and at that moment, we were SOL in the suspect category.

"I...not that I'm aware of, but I don't know. We are friendly, but he wouldn't share something like that with me. We had a common goal for the office, and that was the primary focus of our relationship."

"Did the rumors coincide with Melodie's growing absence from the office?"

She chewed the nail again. "I'm not sure. It was some time ago."

"Do you recall her trip to Mexico with her sister?"

She nodded. "I recall she didn't want to go but felt pressured. She didn't want to leave her son, and from what she told me, she wasn't that close to her sister. Steve confirmed that."

"How so?" I asked.

"He wasn't thrilled with her going either. He wasn't a fan of Emily, but I know he encouraged her regardless of his feelings about it."

"Did he tell you that?" Bishop asked.

"Not in so many words. He kept his personal life out of the office as much as possible, but Emily came by a few times, and he was visibly uncomfortable. He did tell me he wanted Melodie to go if that would make her happy. I took him at his word regardless of his feelings for her sister."

"So, you've met her? Emily?" I asked.

She nodded. "Yes, like I said, she came by, but for scheduled appointments. She had some issues with her hips, and she wanted him to treat her. He saw her initially, but he's a spinal specialist and referred her to our hip doctor."

"When was the last time she had an appointment?" I asked.

"Oh, that was years ago, just after Ryan was born. I remember because the nurse who initially saw her was confused when she went into the exam room. She saw a very skinny post-pregnant Melodie and couldn't understand."

"Meaning?" Bishop asked.

"Melodie gained quite a bit of weight during her pregnancy. It took her a bit to lose it. Most of the office didn't pay attention to the fact that she was a twin, so seeing her skinny so fast was a surprise."

"When did you find out she was a twin?" I asked.

"When Emily came in for her appointment. I didn't get the impression they were close, and later, when Melodie expressed her reservations about going to Mexico, I realized they weren't."

We thanked her and moved on to the staff on the list. Collectively, we gathered generally the same information from them all. Melodie's personality changed, but no one could quite say when or why. One minute she was social and involved and the next she wasn't. That trend bled into the rest of our interviews outside of the medical office.

Bishop stopped for a caffeine boost en route to Leah Marx's place. "Looks like Rockman was a saint."

"No one's a saint."

"He is if you're a guy."

"How?"

"Most men would kill for a chance with twins." He handed the Dunkin' drive-through person a ten. "If you get my drift."

I rolled my eyes. "I'm not sure what's worse, the fact that you're sharing your sexual fantasies with me or that you're channeling J.J. from *Good Times* with that seventies slang."

"You know J.J. and *Good Times*?"

"I watch late-night TV. And isn't it supposed to be twins together for sex, not separate relationships?"

"You gotta take what you can get."

"Gross."

He smirked. "Think the office manager's got a thing for the vic and we're dealing with a passion killing?"

I shook my head. "Don't see it."

"Good. I don't either."

8

In Chicago, unless you're in the wealthier spots, like the Magnificent Mile or Lincoln Park, the neighborhoods tend to bleed into one another. Most of the time the only way to tell the difference is by the street names. In North Fulton County, Georgia, there is no bleed. Roswell hits all income levels, and they all intermix like a bowl of Chex party mix. On one side of a street is a McMansion and across the street, apartments that resemble public housing. Leah Marx's realty office was securely tucked away in downtown Roswell next to an antique store and a Mexican restaurant and across the street from a set of run-down townhomes that should have been demo'd years ago.

She stood at the reception desk and greeted us with a smile. She was a tall, fit woman who spent a lot of time in front of the mirror and with a spray tan gun aimed at her. Her blond hair was bleached, but tastefully, and I liked the hint of lowlights wisping through her bangs. I couldn't imagine wearing stilettos to work every day, but a real estate agent's job required a certain look. Mine required pants my weapon wouldn't fall out of and that I could run in.

She motioned for us to follow her toward the hallway. "Please, let's talk privately in my office."

Bishop looked at me, and I knew it was because of her speech pattern.

Very confident and mature, almost elitist. Bishop knew I took issue with elitism because in my experience, elitism usually equaled criminal.

"So," she said as she sat behind her large oak desk. "Is it true?"

"Is what true?" I asked.

"Was it really Emily and not Melodie?"

"And you heard this how?" I asked. We hadn't exactly made that public.

She blinked. "I spoke to Mary. She was upset. She needed to talk to someone. Of course, I'll keep the details of the investigation private."

Right, and I'm a virgin, I thought. "Ms. Marx, can you tell me how you met Melodie Rockman?"

"I've known Mel since we were in high school. We were like sisters. More so than she was with Emily, definitely."

"And how was your relationship recently?"

"Of late, my relationship with Melodie has been waning, though I think more as an emotional connection than time spent together, and in retrospect, I should have known it wasn't actually Melodie but her bitch of a sister."

"You didn't like Emily?" Bishop asked. We already knew the answer to that. Mary Hagerty had filled us in, but we wanted to hear it from her.

"Most people didn't like Emily, but..." She shook her head. "Those of us who cared for Melodie knew how Emily treated her, knew the things she'd done, and we just couldn't tolerate it. I feel bad for Mary. Knowing one twin is a lovely person and the other scum must be taxing."

Bishop raised an eyebrow. "Why did you consider Emily scum?"

She drummed her French-manicured nail against her desk. "Let's just say Emily lacked class. She was rather flirtatious and craved attention. She'd hit on every man in a room regardless of their marital status just to make herself look good. What she didn't realize is it always made her look like a slut. The way to attract a man isn't by throwing it in his face." She cringed and shook her head. "That's so basic. Men like a woman with a bit of a challenge. Emily didn't know how to challenge anyone. Her emotions drove her, and that's all that mattered. Her feelings were more important than anyone else's."

"Did you know about Dr. Rockman's relationship with Emily before his relationship with Melodie?"

"Not until after the fact. It was very disturbing to Melodie when she found out. It was natural for her to turn to me for advice."

"And what advice did you give her?"

"Well, considering the circumstances surrounding their relationship— Steve and Emily's, I mean—I thought she shouldn't hold it against him. He was manipulated. That was Emily's calling card. Manipulation."

Bishop raised his brow. "What do you mean he was manipulated?"

She snickered. "You don't know? When Emily met Steve, she pretended she was Melodie. Apparently, Steve approached her and introduced himself. He'd seen Melodie at another event the week before. They weren't introduced, but he asked about her and was told her name. So, naturally, when he saw her twin, he thought it was Melodie. She eventually told him, but I don't know how long into their relationship that was."

"And he stayed with her?"

"From what I was told, only because she claimed to be pregnant, though that's more of a rumor, and Melodie never confirmed it. I'm assuming, if it's true, then he learned the truth, and of course he dumped her. Funny, I would have thought Mary would have told you all this? She knows the situation well."

Nope. Mary left out a lot of the juicy, important details.

"How did Melodie react when she learned the truth?"

"How you would expect. She was angry with Steve but forgave him because of Emily's trickery, obviously."

"And were she and Emily okay?"

She laughed. "Oh, hell no! If your sister posed as you and manipulated a man like that, would you maintain a relationship with her?"

"Thankfully, I don't have a sister," I said.

"Doesn't seem like a question I can answer," Bishop said.

Leah Marx rolled her eyes. "Melodie was heartbroken, but she expected it from Emily, and she was prepared. She wrote her off. Emily wasn't even invited to the wedding. They were not close."

"But she went to Mexico with her," I said.

"Because Mary guilted Melodie into going. She wanted her daughters to work on their relationship, but I can promise you, Melodie wanted nothing to do with her sister. She went for her mother. It was a very hard decision for her to make, and it would appear she shouldn't have."

"How was Melodie when she returned?"

"Different, now that I think about it. But not in obvious ways. It was little things. She changed the way she drank her coffee, did her hair differently, that kind of thing. Honestly, I didn't even think about it at all until Mary called me. At the time, she was just off. I thought it was just from spending the time with her sister." She drummed her nails against the desk one more time. I wanted to reach over and flatten them on the desktop. "Oh, but she was more private. Before, we'd talk about Steve and Dan—my ex—but she didn't do that as much over the past few years. Looking back, I can't believe I didn't notice Melodie wasn't Melodie. I should have known, if for no other reason than the coffee switch."

"Why the coffee switch?"

"Because she never put sugar in her coffee. She always thought it was disgusting."

"Did you ask her about it?" Bishop asked.

She nodded. "She claimed she'd been given the wrong drink once and that changed everything, but Melodie was a creature of habit. A wrong drink would have been immediately returned. She liked what she liked and never felt the need to stray from those likes."

In retrospect, Leah Marx believed Melodie didn't return from Mexico and that Emily had been posing as her sister for three years.

"Is anyone searching for Melodie in Mexico?" she asked.

"We're looking into what may have happened," Bishop said.

"I'll tell you what happened. Emily did something to force Melodie to stay, and she stole her life." She sniffled and grabbed a tissue from the table behind her.

"Do you think Melodie would return and seek revenge? Is she that kind of person?" Bishop asked.

"I think a person is capable of anything when pushed, Detective, but if she returned, why wouldn't she contact me? We were best friends. I would have done anything for her, and she knew it. No, she's not here. Something bad has happened to Melodie. I just know it."

"Do you think Emily would harm her sister?" I asked.

"Absolutely. She desperately wanted Mel's life. She probably killed her herself."

"You think she's capable of that?" Bishop asked.

"As sure as the day is light."

"Ms. Marx," I said. "Which twin do you think Mary was closest to?"

"Mary's not the traditional mother. Not since her divorce. And honestly, probably not for a while before that. She's more about perception and appearances than genuine love. Whatever twin fit her need at the moment was who she was closest to."

"So, how would you define her relationship with Melodie?"

"A better opportunity than one with Emily."

Ouch.

"Do you think she might have known Emily was acting as her sister?" I asked.

"I don't know. Part of me thinks that's just too insane. She was genuinely upset when she called me, but then the other part of me wonders if it isn't all an act."

"Why would you think that?" Bishop asked.

"Because Emily gets a lot of her personality traits from her mother."

We walked to Bishop's car. I smiled as he swept his hand down the driver's side doors and grinned. He'd traded in his personal vehicle some time ago, but because he'd purchased a luxury vehicle, he drove only work vehicles while working these days. I suspected he was imagining leaving work in his new one, thinking how awesome he would feel.

Boys will be boys, just with bigger toys.

I climbed into the Chevy SUV. "If I'd been a twin, I guarantee my best friend would have known if my twin stole my life."

He blew out a big breath. "I can't even imagine that."

"A twin stealing their sibling's life?"

"No." He laughed. "You being a twin."

I whacked his arm. "Asshole."

He laughed.

"I'm putting someone on her. She's right. If your girl is in town, she's going to need someone. Who better than your best friend who hates your sibling as much as you?" I made a call to the department and had eyes on Leah Marx twenty minutes later.

~

"Three hundred calls on the tip line in the past hour," Michels said. He guzzled back a sixteen-ounce bottle of water. "Guess the most common tip."

Bishop looked puzzled, but I smiled. "Alien abduction still?"

He held up the empty bottle and squeezed it. It made popping sounds like small bullets firing. "Bingo!"

"Still? With how many calls total?"

"Over six thousand."

"Are you serious?" Bishop asked. "And alien abduction is still the top tip? That's pathetic."

I laughed. "Pathetic, yes, but it's a common theme for missing persons tips."

"What the ever-loving—"

Jimmy walked into the pit and stopped Bishop flat. "Language, Bishop. We're trying to remain professional here."

I coughed and said, "Bullshit," while doing so, which made everyone laugh out loud.

"Alien abduction," Bishop said as he shook his head. "What the fuck is wrong with people?"

"That's a conversation that needs beer and wings," I said.

"Hell yeah," Michels said. "I have three—"

Jimmy interrupted him, and his tone turned serious. "We've got a missing kid. Until he's located and returned to his family, we're twenty-four-seven work, people. Wings and beer have to wait." He had a way of killing a mood, and though we understood the urgency of the situation, we needed some lighthearted moments to keep our sanity in check. I felt bad for him. The mayor wanted something for a press conference, and we had nothing, so Jimmy had to give him the standard *we have suspects, but we cannot provide details on an active investigation* speech to give reporters. The mayor was not pleased.

I checked my watch. We'd spent so much time talking to people, the last of our interviews with Ryan's activities class for home school program, I hadn't realized how late it was. "We couldn't locate the nanny, Flores. Went to her last known residence, but she'd moved out over a year ago. Bubba still hasn't found anything current on her."

"Any word on her pregnancy?" Jimmy asked.

"I've got someone looking into it," I said, referring to Joey. "As soon as I know something, I'll let you know, but she's illegal, so it's highly unlikely we have her real name and that she'd use her real name at a hospital or doctor's office. If she's even gone to one."

"If the girl is pregnant, I'm not confident it's Rockman's kid," Bishop said.

"Maynor was adamant about Rockman's devotion to his wife and kid." I paused. "But I've seen devoted men do things people never expected, so I can't say he didn't."

Michels bounced on his toes. "Chief, I've got three calls that we're looking into, and one is from a woman down the street from the crime scene. I'd like to go on the follow-up call with Detectives Ryder and Bishop, please."

"Didn't you hit everyone on the street?" Jimmy asked.

"Yes, sir, but this woman called because she remembered something."

"Go," he said.

"Jimmy," I said. "Can he take someone else? I'd like to—"

Michels opened the door. "I'll grab someone else," he said and left without another word.

Jimmy didn't question it. "Where are you two?"

"Behind a steel door," Bishop said.

Jimmy released a frustrated breath. "I'm not in the mood for jokes, Detective. We need this wrapped up quickly. Who's the best call for a homicide suspect? And what about the kid's abduction? Tell me we're going for a three-for here, not two separate unsubs." He headed toward the investigation room. We followed.

I took the lead on the update. "Right now, we have three persons of interest. No solid suspects, but one very strong motive and one very strong person of interest."

"Melodie," he said.

"Mary Hagerty," I said.

He blinked. "What?"

"It depends on which of us you're talking to," I said.

"I'm only in partial agreement," Bishop said. "If I was the one leading this conversation, I'd go with Melodie as the strong person of interest."

"Okay," I said. "I'll give you that. Let's talk through that route, then we'll go over Hagerty and see who Haus ties into best, because he's tied into this somehow, and it's important."

"Haus?"

"The jeweler without shoes."

"He wasn't wearing shoes?" Bishop asked.

"Detective 101, partner."

He snarled but in a playful way. "Melodie and Emily weren't typical identical twins. They weren't close, didn't hang in the same social circle, and their personalities were very different."

"Agree," I said. "And Emily, posing as her sister, had a relationship with Steve Rockman. Apparently he dumped her, but we can't get whether it was when he found out or later. The relationship was hidden from Melodie until they were engaged, and the mother knew but didn't tell."

"Damn, that's rough," Jimmy said. "And it points to Melodie as the doer."

"Just wait," I said. "It gets interesting."

"As I was saying, the twins are, or were, very different. For example, Melodie was structured, a planner," Bishop added. "Emily was more the fly-by-the-seat-of-your-pants twin. A free spirit, if you will."

"Who wanted her sister's life," I said.

"Was that the general consensus?" Jimmy asked.

"It was brought up a few times, and given their different lifestyles, I can see it." I grabbed the papers Bubba gave me earlier. "Emily's lifestyle wasn't in line with her sister's. Melodie had a career and a generous income. Emily worked various jobs, inconsistently, by the way. Was single, dated various married men, and struggled to maintain relationships."

I dialed Bubba's extension on the work phone.

"Yeah," he said when he picked up.

"Did you get the bank info I asked for?"

"Yup. You in the IR?"

"If that means investigation room, yes."

"Be right there."

Bishop furrowed his brow. "IR? Why don't these kids use full words?"

I looked at Jimmy and watched him try to fight the smile pushing its way across his face.

Bubba came into the room like a rocket ready to explode. "Emily Hagerty has a lot of debt, and none of it's been touched in almost four years. No payments, nothing. Most of it's already in collections, though some was written off before getting to that point."

"How much is a lot?" I asked, knowing he was fueling the fire under Bishop's suspect and dousing the flame under mine. I didn't care, as long as it helped find the kid.

"Over one hundred thousand bucks." He shook his head. "Just thinking about that kind of debt stresses me out."

"Wait until you have a kid in college," Bishop said.

"No way. I'm not having kids."

I identified with that feeling completely. "Four years? That's before the trip to Mexico. If that's the case, then we're probably not looking at a mutually agreed-upon life switch."

Bishop smiled. "Told you so. Emily gets in over her head financially and can't find a way out. So, she comes up with a plan to pose as her sister, then poof! Her debt, gone."

"And poof! Melodie's gone too. Probably dead."

"Or back for revenge."

Bubba added, "The last withdrawal on Emily's only checking account was in Tijuana." He handed us each copies of her bank statements. "The only changes in her balance are fees and minimal interest."

Jimmy groaned. "Fuck."

"I'm confused," Bubba said. "I thought that would be good news."

"It is for the real Emily, but not for anyone else," I said. "And it screws up Bishop's theory."

"How?" Bubba asked.

"Because if, and this is a big if, the two did switch lives, or if Melodie stayed in Mexico willingly, she'd need cash." I studied the statement. "And there's what, six thousand bucks just sitting in this account still? Why would Melodie withdraw some of what was there but not all of it?"

"Maybe she didn't have access to the account because her sister didn't give it to her."

"Okay, let's go back to the possible life switch. If they switched identities, Melodie would be posing as her sister and using her name. And it's possible, if she's in Mexico, that debt isn't an issue, and to keep it that way, she's staying off radar." I looked at Bubba. "Did you find any leases, bills, any debts owed, anything she acquired in Mexico or the States since that date?"

He shook his head. "She's gone dark. No other checking or savings accounts, and definitely none in Mexico, though that was a little harder to find."

I nodded.

Jimmy studied the notes on the whiteboards. "I would be pretty angry if my wife dated my brother and I didn't know about it until later. Plausible motive there."

"Years after they were married?" I shook my head. "I don't see it. She found out when Steve proposed to her. If she was upset, she would have called off the wedding, and the shit would have hit the fan then."

"Maybe something happened that brought up old feelings?" he asked.

"It's possible, but we haven't found anything yet," I said. "Bishop believes the revenge plot. I don't not believe it, but I believe Mary Hagerty is somehow wrapped up in this."

"Explain."

"For starters, am I the only one that thinks it's odd the woman gets a glimpse of her deceased kid on the floor and immediately says something's off but didn't once notice over the last three years?"

He looked to Bishop, who nodded. "I get it," Bishop said.

"She's inconsistent in her story. Plays a great mourning mother role but can't stay true to the character. One minute she's devastated, the next she's fine."

"It's called shock," Bishop said.

"She's not worried about her grandson. Today she barely mentioned him. If your daughter and son-in-law were murdered and your grandkid missing, wouldn't you be doing something? Bugging the cops, handing out flyers, looking for the kid yourself? I think she's got the kid, and she's keeping him from us."

"What's her motive?" Jimmy asked.

"Money. Maybe a life insurance policy, I don't know, but money's usually the reason. Or—and Bishop is on par with this too—maybe she's keeping the kid for Melodie."

"We need to find Melodie, then, don't we?" Jimmy asked.

"I've been going through the proper political channels, but I can't get anywhere."

"Let me see what I can do," he said.

Between interviews, I'd asked Bubba to run a check on Charlie Haus. I asked him for his information.

"The guy's a small-time con," he said, then smiled. "God, I love my job. I get to say all this movie stuff, and it's awesome."

"Go on," I said with a smile.

He rattled off a list of small arrests over the past thirty years, but of them all, only two convictions.

"Not enough to be a repeat offender in the system," Jimmy said. "Who is this guy, anyway?"

I filled him in.

"So, wait. Haus has been receiving money from both the Rockmans and Mary Hagerty and swears he didn't know it?" He glanced at Bishop. "And you don't find this suspect?"

"I do, but it's not enough to throw the grandmother under the bus."

"But her knowing where the kid is," Jimmy said.

"We can't confirm that she does," Bishop said.

"Then we need to get eyes on her now and find out."

He left the room, and I smiled brightly at my partner. "He's leaning my direction."

9

Lenny answered his phone on the first ring. "You okay, sweetheart?"

"If exhausted means I'm not okay, then no, I'm not okay."

"Perks of being an excellent detective."

"I wouldn't go that far."

Lenny and I go way back. So far back that he claims he changed my diapers, but he can't prove that. His daughter, Jenny, was my best friend until some drunk hit her on her way home from work. He'd also lost his wife, and since I wasn't all that close to my family, we'd become each other's family. He'd also been my boss, and he was close with Tommy, and when I needed an ear or a solid piece of advice, or just someone to bounce case thoughts off of, he was the man.

"Bad case?"

"Joey said it made the national news."

"Ah, the missing kid and double homicide. Sounds like a tough one."

"Aren't they all?"

"Absolutely. But I got to admit, the twins part sounds fun."

"I hope that was sarcasm because it's really a pain in the ass." I crouched down and watched Herman devour his gourmet pellet dinner. "Bishop thinks the twin who was the original wife has been hiding in

Mexico plotting revenge on the other twin that stole her family, and I think the grandmother's somehow involved."

"Do you think the twin came back for revenge?"

"We can't prove she didn't, but we can't prove she has either. We've made calls to the US Embassy in Mexico, but they're not exactly helpful. We have a DEA agent who I think we're going to have to ask for help with that. He's got contacts all over the world. He may be able to get information we can't."

I'd given Lenny bits and pieces of information about Kyle, but I wasn't ready to share the entire story just yet. It was his life's purpose to help me find love again, and I didn't want to lead him to believe Kyle and I had a future when I couldn't think on those terms myself.

When Tommy was murdered, Lenny explained what that loss would feel like in terms I was only beginning to understand. He said grief isn't something that ever goes away. It's something that becomes a part of our soul, that we live with every single day, in every single moment. When we begin to accept that, we can begin to move forward. Not on, but forward, because there is a difference. And I wasn't sure what I was ready for, so talking about it to someone so close to my heart and close to Tommy seemed wrong.

"What about you? Do you think the real one is still alive?"

"I'm not one hundred percent sure. I'm bordering on no, but I think we need to do our due diligence. Bishop's theory is like a Lifetime movie come true, and I can see how it would play out. Twin traps sister, steals her life, then sister miraculously returns, sees twin and her husband living the life, kills them both, then takes her kid and runs. In theory it sounds great."

"In reality it's a little hard to swallow."

"Exactly. Identical twins still have differences, so how could everyone in their lives not notice something was off with Melodie when she returned from Mexico?"

"Maybe they did, but they wrote it off. People don't pay as much attention as we think. They're too self-involved for that."

"I know, but the husband? The mother?" I shook my head as I spoke. "I don't get it."

"You don't have to get it for it to be true."

"Right, but if Emily, the twin that wasn't the wife originally, stole her sister's life and somehow left her in Mexico, why didn't she just kill her? Why would she take the risk in letting her sister live?"

"Maybe she thought she was dead."

"Or maybe the real wife planned it all and changed her mind?"

"You're right. It does sound like a Lifetime movie."

I laughed. After Tommy died, Lenny and I would spend my nights off watching TV movies and laugh about how so many of them were pure fiction. I was starting to believe that might not be true.

"Any leads on the kid?"

"Nothing," I said, glancing at my watch. I'd come home to shower and change, maybe sleep an hour or two, but it looked like that wasn't going to be part of the plan after all. "We've done everything by the book. There was a nanny, one rumored to be knocked up by the male vic, but we can't find her. I feel like she's part of this somehow, or she could help, but she's completely MIA."

"Illegal?"

"Her fingerprints have to be some of the ones our tech department ran, but nothing's come up, so it's likely. The problem is, we can't guarantee her prints are still around the house."

"This is a wealthy area, right?"

"Yes. Very."

"Have you had anyone talk to any of the other nannies? Away from their bosses, I mean. They might tell you something they wouldn't say in front of their employer."

I hadn't thought of that. "I'll get Michels on it. Thanks, Len, I appreciate your help with this."

"It's nice to feel involved, even if it is thirteen hours away."

"I gotta run. Talk soon?"

"You can count on it."

I closed my eyes for five minutes and woke up three hours later. I cursed myself for the missing hours, but I needed the shut-eye, and I hoped it would give me a fresh breath to find the missing child.

∾

Michels and Emmett headed out to the homeschool group meet-up locations to hit up the nannies. One of them had to know something.

"I matched the prints from Melodie's carry license application to Emily's last arrest record a few years ago," Nikki said. "They're a match."

I raised an eyebrow. "Identical twins don't share the same fingerprint. She had to manipulate the system so she wouldn't be caught."

Nikki shrugged. "My guess is she paid someone off."

"How long ago was the application submitted?" Bishop asked.

"Seven months ago."

He mumbled a cuss word under his breath and asked, "Why would she need a carry license?"

"Hamby is a dangerous place," I said with a hint of sarcasm. "So Emily, posing as her sister who had the perfect life, suddenly decides she needs a gun. Sounds like she felt threatened or scared."

"Because her sister returned and she knew it," Bishop said.

"Or someone local figured out her scam and threatened to tell, which would make sense since she's been depositing money into the jewelry account. What kind of gun, Nikki?"

"She purchased a SIG Sauer P365 the month before from a pawn shop in Cumming. And no, it wasn't the weapon used in the murders, but it's also nowhere to be found."

"Can you find out if the Rockmans have a safe-deposit box some-where?" Bishop asked.

"They don't." She blushed. "We already checked. We also determined she'd taken lessons at River Bend Gun Club in Dawsonville. Six lessons, basic gun handling and shooting." She dropped a paper onto the table. "Here's the contact info for the trainer."

"Nice work," I said, and I meant it.

She blushed again. "Thanks, ma'am."

Bishop laughed.

Nikki looked confused.

I sighed. "I know that's a form of respect, but it's kind of a pet peeve of mine to hear."

"Kind of a pet peeve?" Bishop said, still laughing.

"Shut it, partner."

Kyle had been back and forth for an assignment, helping us when he had the chance and helping save the world from a growing opioid crisis the rest of the time. I was so focused on my thoughts on the investigation, I didn't see him in the parking lot. He smiled and stood only an inch from me.

I took a few steps back. "Hey, what're you doing here?"

"Our bust just ended. Thought I'd come and check on the investigation."

"You look good," I said.

His smile stretched across his face. "Thank you."

My face reddened. "I don't mean good, I meant you don't look like you were in the thick of it."

"So, I don't actually look good?"

"Stop it," I said. "What did they have you do?"

"Work communications in the van."

"Ouch."

"It could be worse. I'm not supposed to be doing anything after such a big case anyway. But yeah, communications sucks." He turned and walked me toward my car. "Going home for the day?"

I laughed. "Right. I was already home. Slept for three hours and am still mad at myself for it. I just left something in my car."

"Still nothing on the boy, huh?"

"Not yet. Not even close. We've confirmed that Emily was posing as her sister, but no one, not one person we've talked to caught on, and none of them have any idea where Ryan might be."

"Confirmation is good for the investigation."

"A murderer and a found kid would be better."

He shrugged. "I've got people checking Mexico for the real Melodie, off the radar, of course. Any confirmation about why she stayed in Mexico?"

"Not yet, but Bishop's leaning toward Emily stealing her identity, not a mutual decision to switch. I can't quite decide. From what I've learned about Melodie, it's possible she suffered an emotional breakdown and set the plan in motion herself."

"What makes you think that?"

"Emily posed as her sister before and dated the man Melodie married under that guise. Melodie didn't find out until just after their engagement. It's hard for me to imagine her wanting to go on a trip with her sister to re-bond after that."

"Makes sense."

"Also, Emily had over a hundred thousand in debt, and she hasn't paid a dime of it since before they went to Mexico."

He rubbed his jaw. "That doesn't sound like a great switch option for Melodie, but even if this was her idea, it doesn't mean she actually took on Emily's identity. She could have stayed and created another identity altogether. Mexico excels at that kind of work."

"Right. It's always possible Melodie didn't know about the debt, but regardless, if she switched lives, she's gone off grid. No activity on Emily's bank account since one withdrawal right before Emily returned."

He leaned against my Jeep. "That's not good. That could be a murder-for-hire payment. How much was the withdrawal?"

"Six thousand bucks. There's still six thousand in there, though, which is strange. Why would she take half and leave the rest?"

"That doesn't make sense. Was the withdrawal in Tijuana?"

"How did you know?"

"Tijuana is a hub for human trafficking. Emily could have sold her sister into it, or Melodie was abducted into it there."

"So, what does that do to the murder-for-hire theory?"

"It's always possible."

I groaned. "Great. Just another confusing piece to the puzzle."

He bumped himself off the side of my Jeep and stood in front of me with his hands in his pockets. I caught myself admiring his long legs and trim waist, how the V-shape of his torso widened up to his shoulders. I inhaled and quickly looked away, embarrassed, but hopeful he was too deep in thought to notice.

"Did Melodie register her trip with the US Embassy?" he asked.

"Yes, but even though registered Americans that go missing are supposed to be immediately investigated, the embassy isn't doing anything."

"There's a process they have to follow. Melodie was just listed as missing and a person of interest in a murder investigation. She hadn't officially been missing before. They're working their system how they're supposed to, Rachel."

"Doesn't seem like it to me."

"I understand. The truth is, the odds of them finding anything are slim, and you need to be prepared for that. When an American goes missing in any country, the odds of locating them are small. International crime is a completely different ball game."

"I know, and Mexico isn't making it any easier for us."

We headed back into the building.

I made copies of important information on Emily and Melodie, including photos of each twin, and stuffed them into a file folder for Kyle. He had some things already, but he'd asked for more for a deeper dig. "I need you to sign a release for these."

He smiled. "Always the professional."

"The mayor is hot to make an arrest. When we do, I don't want some paperwork technicality being the reason the case is thrown out of court. Jimmy would take the hit on that, and he doesn't need that kind of pressure."

"Understood."

I grabbed a pre-printed release form from the filing cabinet in the room and slid it to him on the table. He signed it and slid it back. "I can do this in the open cubby here. If you need something else from me, you know where to find me."

I stood and bumped the file off the table, and the documents fell onto the floor. "Shit." I felt Kyle's eyes on me as I gathered the papers. "I...I've got to be back to work."

"I didn't know you'd stopped." He tipped his chin down and looked up at me with his eyebrows raised.

"I mean I have to focus on the investigation and not you." I blushed. "Oh hell."

He laughed as he walked over to me, took the file from my hands, set it on the table, and pulled me into an embrace. It was awkward, and I worried someone would walk in on us, but after a few seconds, I relaxed into him.

"This is just really different."

"I know. Baby steps."

Kyle was a good person. Patient, kind, and understanding. It was annoying how easy he made things seem. I still had a lot of baggage to unpack, and he was making it too easy to push that aside.

My cell phone rang. I checked the caller ID. Michels. "You find someone who knows where the nanny is?"

"No, but the search team found a shirt," Michels said. "It's the same one the boy had on in the photo we found in the doctor's home office, and there's blood all over it."

I glanced at Kyle. "Where'd you find it?"

Kyle headed to my cubby to make additional calls to his contacts in Mexico while I met everyone else in the interrogation room.

"We have no way of determining if the blood belongs to Ryan," I said.

"We have to assume it is," Bishop said.

"Just because the shirt looks like the one he had on in the photo doesn't mean it's his."

Ashley spoke. "I found a hair on it, and it matches the hair of the female victim, but the blanket came back with no matching DNA for the parents, or obviously the twin sister."

I sat in a chair. "This doesn't feel right to me. Anyone could take hair from a brush or a bathroom floor." I studied the shirt, holding it up for everyone to see. "And the blood, it doesn't make sense. It's not splattered, it doesn't appear to be soaked from the inside. In fact," I said as I turned the shirt inside out. "It's barely on the inside." I set down the shirt. "This is the same as the blanket. Someone's fucking with us. They're trying to distract us."

Bishop agreed.

"The shirt wasn't in the list of items in the boy's closet either," Nikki said. "But it could have been taken when he was."

"Do me a favor," I said to Michels. "Add where this was discovered to the map. I have a thought."

"Which is?" Bishop asked.

"Whoever planted these couldn't have gone far. They set us up to distract us, to put us off their path. Whoever put this stuff out isn't who's got the boy. They may be working together, but they're working two distinctly different jobs in this."

"Canvassing might not get us anywhere," he said. "It's always a needle in a haystack."

"I know, but right now, it's the only thing we've got," I said. "The clock is ticking. We don't have a lot of time to find this kid. I need someone at the homeschool program locations hitting up the nannies again. Go to the parks near them also. Have someone sit at these places if they have to. We need that nanny."

"Still no admissions to any hospitals, no contacts made to any urgent care facilities in a fifty-mile radius either," Michels said as he pushed pins into the map on the wall. "And we've checked every pharmacy and vet clinic for any requests for insulin twice now. Nothing."

"Thanks," I said. "Get back to me with anything as soon as you find it, please."

"Will do," he said.

I texted Joey. *Any news?*

He immediately called me. "Your case is still all over the news here. Even *Good Morning America* covered it."

I pursed my lips. "You watch *GMA*?"

"My mom has it on during breakfast."

"Wow. She makes you breakfast. Not at all entitled."

"Dude, I paid off her mortgage. It's my house too."

"Right."

"Anyway, you really have a way of getting the big shit, don't you?" he said, laughing. "No offense to the dead."

"None taken. I guess I'm just talented like that."

"Well, considering how much I know you appreciate me, I did a little digging for you."

"In other words, you hit a wall with the nanny?"

"If she's had any medical assistance with a pregnancy, it's not under her name anywhere. I've checked multiple times and in multiple ways. She could have a hundred different aliases, and without her real name, it's almost impossible to locate her."

"I figured that was the case. What did you find in that dig? And may I put you on speaker phone?"

"Are there cops with you?"

"It's kind of my thing, you know."

"Shit, okay. Just don't plan on me being a witness."

"I'd never expect that, and it wouldn't be possible anyway," I said and clicked the speaker button. "It's my contact in Chicago," I told the room.

"Youse guys got a good one in Detective Ryder. She deserves a raise," Joey said.

"What'd you find?" I asked.

"Emily Hagerty had an abortion a while back."

"We can't use this," Jimmy said. His face reddened. "We need something we can use. This guy is a hacker." He stood. "We can't work with a damn hacker!"

I held up my hand. "Just let him finish, Chief. Please."

"Look, I'm just trying to help. Had a little free time is all, thought I'd do some snoopin', but if you guys don't want my intel, then I'm out," Joey said.

"No. We want it," I replied.

"Can't use it," Jimmy mumbled.

I held up my hand again. "Please, let him finish."

"Go on," Jimmy said.

"Okay, so that abortion? It was paid on a credit card belonging to Steve Rockman." He gave us the date, which coincided with when the two were romantically involved.

"Damn," Bishop said.

The rest of the room, including Jimmy, stayed silent.

"Again, we can't use any of this without a subpoena," Jimmy said.

"If we need one, we'll get one," I said. "All this does is get us closer to some kind of motive, and we need that." I directed my voice toward the phone. "Anything else, Joey?"

"Not yet. Want me to keep looking, or are those Southern buttons too scared?"

I glanced at my fellow *buttons* knowing they probably weren't familiar with the term. Bishop confirmed that with a brow raise. "My buttons are fine, Joey. Keep me posted, and thanks for the intel," I said and disconnected the call.

"What the hell is a Southern button?" Jimmy asked.

"Button is a mafia term for police."

"That guy is mafia?"

I smirked. "No, he's an Italian millennial hacker living in his mother's basement. He's harmless but excellent at what he does." And very likely Vitamin D deficient, but I didn't mention that.

Jimmy stormed toward the door mumbling a string of curse words when the receptionist knocked and said, "The mayor for you, Chief. Line seven."

I stared at the investigation boards and the map searching for something, even a small clue, that could lead us to the kid. Kyle walked in and leaned against the table next to me. I jumped, having not heard him enter. "Jesus, you scared the shit out of me."

"Deep in thought?"

"I can't figure this out. It just seems impossible that Melodie could go off radar like that for so long, then find her way back to Georgia to kill her sister and husband. But other than her, the only semi-viable person of interest is Mary Hagerty, but I have no real evidence to support that theory either."

"What do you have?"

"Strange deposits into a jewelry bank account the owner swears he doesn't use."

"Deposits?"

I nodded. "From the Rockmans' account and Mary Hagerty. And the guy is slimy, but we can't find anything on him other than a few assault arrests that never amounted to anything."

"Shows a pattern."

"I know, but nothing connects him to the women or to Steve Rockman other than the deposits." I shook my head. "I have shit.

Absolute shit. We need to find that kid, and we need him alive, Kyle."

"Find the killer, and you'll find the kid."

"That's what I've been saying, but it's not getting us anywhere. We need boots on the ground in Mexico, but I don't have the resources for that, and the mayor would never approve the cost."

"I can do it."

I turned toward him. "You can do what?"

"Go to Mexico and look for Melodie. My contacts will—"

I cut him off with a headshake. "No. You can't do that. It's not in the budget, and like I said, the mayor wouldn't approve it, anyway."

"Actually, that's what I was coming to tell you. He already did. My contacts can get me intel, Rachel, but it comes with a price. Our embassy is willing to negotiate intel for three separate missing women, but Mexico will only give it in exchange for six mules caught at the border six months ago. They've been part of an ongoing investigation, but the embassy is willing to take the hit in exchange for intel on the three women."

I couldn't believe my ears. "I—six mules? Mexico will execute them the minute they arrive in Mexico."

He nodded once. "It's likely."

"Let's call that what it is, Kyle. Murder."

"It's how the system works, but if I can get info on Melodie Rockman and two other women, the States can potentially solve three investigations. That's three Americans, Rachel. Two of the women have been missing for over five years."

"And the embassy thinks they're still alive?"

"They have reasons for wanting to know."

"What are those reasons?"

"Nothing they want to share with us low-on-the-totem-pole law enforcement."

I dragged my incisor tooth over my bottom lip, fighting myself to stay emotionally detached from the situation. "And Jimmy's okay with this?"

"I told him I was available to assist in the investigation in this capacity, and you're right. Initially he said it wasn't an option, but I made a call to the DEA's legal counsel, who made a call to the embassy, and the wheels turned. It's not coming out of the department's budget. It's coming from the embassy. I came back to Jimmy, and he's on board. I'm leaving for the airport in a few minutes." He moved toward me. "If I can get anything on Melodie Rockman, wouldn't you want that?"

A burst of emotions soared through me. I couldn't distinguish what ticked me off the most, Kyle going over my head to my chief, or, and I could barely admit this to myself, the fear simmering inside me about what could happen to him on my time, in my investigation. "This is crap, Olsen." I used his last name with the tone a mother used when calling her child by its full name. "You can't just...just walk into my investigation and act like you own it."

He stepped back and stared at me. "You invited me into your investigation."

I flung my arm up, waving my hand in frustration. "I asked for assistance, not for you to be the hero and put your life at risk." I closed my eyes and leaned back against the conference table, focusing on my breathing while counting to ten. I made it to four. "I'm sorry. I'm out of line." My heart raced as memories of Tommy's murder flashed through my mind. I breathed in deeply and let out the air slowly.

He stepped back toward me and put his hands on my waist. As if he'd read my mind, he said, "This isn't the same, Rachel."

I didn't like talking to Kyle, a man I'd begun to care for in a way I couldn't even understand, about Tommy. I wanted to keep them separate, different, but his words made it impossible. He nailed my emotions perfectly and pissed me off even more. "It sure the hell isn't. You're not Tommy."

His hands fell from my waist, and he put a few feet of room between us. "Okay, then, on that note, I'm heading out. I should only be a few days. I'll call when I can." He walked out of the investigation room without another word.

From either of us.

I sat there for a moment, processing what had just happened. I wasn't wrong. He was putting himself in danger for me, and if something happened to him, I'd never forgive myself. I leaned against the table again and heard Tommy's voice in my head. *You're full of shit, Ryder, and you know it.*

My mind traveled back to a particularly intense investigation at the Chicago PD. I'd been assigned a homicide, and when it came out that Tommy had worked with the victim and suspect on another drug bust, he offered to help. I accused him of trying to steal my thunder and set me back career-wise. As if that was something my husband would have ever done. Really, I was just afraid for him. I didn't want him involved in my dangerous investigation because if something happened to him, I wouldn't have forgiven myself. He said the same thing to me then. *You're full of shit, Ryder, and you know it.*

And when his voice whispered those words in my brain again, I knew he was right about Kyle too. He was trying to help, and that was his choice. I grabbed my phone and sent him a text, not ready to have the discussion about my actions yet.

I'm sorry.

My heart raced until the little blue dots appeared.

Baby steps, Ryder. I'll be in touch soon.

My body tensed, preparing for the explosion I felt building as Jimmy marched down the hall toward the room, cursing like a truck driver.

"Son of a bitch! I can't have this shit on my time!" The door swung open, and Jimmy stormed in. "Where the hell is everyone?"

I blinked. "Uh, working an investigation, I think."

He slammed his hands onto the table. "The mayor is riding my ass hard, Ryder. He wants the kid, and he wants him now. I'm moving you and Bishop to just focusing on the kid. Michels can handle the murders."

My back stiffened. "No, you can't do that."

"My job is on the line here. I need you on that kid."

"We are on that kid, but the key to finding him is in figuring out who killed the Rockmans, and Bishop and I have been busting our asses trying to do that."

"Michels and his team haven't found anything. We need someone with more experience on lead."

"I am on lead. Everything is coming through me, and everything Michels and the team are doing comes from me and Bishop. Jimmy, I've been down this road before. We'll find the kid. Michels is doing everything right. The teams are out searching, we've got the tip lines covered and worked aggressively, and we're interviewing and re-interviewing everyone associated with the kid right now. We'll get something. Just don't take me off the murders. Please."

"You're no closer to finding the killers than the night they were murdered."

Jimmy was completely on edge. I wasn't sure the mayor was the real reason, but regardless, I felt the need to walk on eggshells with him. "We are working on both the grandmother and the biological mother. They're our best bets. One of them is good for this, I can feel it."

He relaxed a bit.

"Listen, I'll be honest, I think Melodie Rockman is more than likely dead, but if anyone can find that out, it's Kyle. What he finds out will be key in the investigation. In the meantime, we have to continue moving forward with both persons of interest and see where that takes us. And the only people who can effectively do that are me and Bishop."

"You've got nothing on Mary Hagerty."

"Just circumstantial stuff, but we're digging, Jimmy. It's there. I know it's there. Let us do what we do best."

"Guts don't get convictions."

"Pick what you want, Jimmy. We can focus on finding the kid without anything to go on, or we can focus on the murders, which should lead us to the kid. And in doing that, we have to hit every single person of interest. I'm not a magician. I can't make things happen as fast as you'd like. We've got questions for Hagerty, but I'm not ready to ask them. I don't want her knowing what we know yet. We need to set this up like a game of dominos, and that's what we're working toward."

"She's the grandmother. She's going to pressure us for information."

"That's the thing, she really hasn't. And if she ever does, we give her a bone, but she can't know where we are with this."

"We aren't anywhere with this, that's the problem."

He was so tense, so angry. I'd never seen him that way before. I tried to calm him with a softer tone and more information. "And I've got another call into the twins' father. The divorce was nasty, and we need to do a little digging into Mary's life. Once we get more intel, we'll talk to her. Question her. Can you just give us more time before you make any changes?"

He tipped his head back and then, out of nowhere, kicked a chair. It smacked into the table. "A fucking grandmother? What the hell is happening in this world?"

"Jimmy, what's really going on here?"

He looked at me with some unidentifiable emotion trapped in his eyes. It set me back. I'd never seen Jimmy out of control or angry. The look worried me.

He dragged his hand down his chin and sighed. "Savannah's pregnant."

My eyes widened, and my jaw dropped. "Oh my God, Jimmy!" I covered my mouth and whispered, "That's amazing!"

A slight smile nudged at his mouth. "It's really early. She's going to the doctor this week. We aren't telling anyone, and you can't tell her I told you. She wants to keep it under wraps for the first trimester."

I knew my best friend, and there was no way that woman could hold that kind of news from me for three months. I finally understood Jimmy's frustrations. "It's Ryan Rockman, isn't it?"

He nodded. "In part. I can't understand how someone could take a child like that in the first place, but murder his parents and take a child that's got a disease? What's wrong with people?"

"A lot, Jimmy. A lot is wrong with people. Listen," I said, remaining as calm and steady as possible because that's what my friend, not my boss, needed. "There are a lot of bad people in the world, but your kid, it will be so loved and protected by so many. And those people are the ones who are going to find Ryan Rockman safe. We've got this. Don't let the mayor or your emotions push you to move this case any faster than it has to go. We've got this, I promise."

He nodded. "Aren't I the one who's supposed to be giving you the pep talk?"

"Are you saying I'm not good at it?"

He smiled. "Actually, I'm a little surprised that you are."

I whacked his arm. "Watch it. I can blackmail you now, you know. I know your secret." My cell phone rang before he could respond. I hit the button and answered. "What's up?"

"You should be paying me the big bucks for this shit, Ryder," Joey said.

I checked my watch as I put him on speaker. "I'll ask the taxpayers. Did you find out something on the nanny?"

"Still nothing, but I did learn that your Emily had a little tryst with someone while in rehab."

"Rehab?"

"Oh, you didn't know?"

He gave me the dates and the location. I recognized it as the same place we'd gone to for a recent investigation, a place Bishop knew well.

"Dude was shot in the head two weeks before your girls left for Mexico." He paused for a moment, then said, "Shit, man. I'm sorry. I shouldn't be so cold."

"It's okay," I said. Joey was close to Tommy. He didn't take his murder well, and I appreciated that he was sensitive to my feelings.

I grabbed a pen and paper. "Go on."

"Jeremy Jackson. Found unconscious with a bullet in his head in Smyrna. Was on life support for a few days until his aunt unplugged him."

"They get his killer?"

"Yeah, drug dealer."

"So, no connection to Emily Hagerty?"

"Nah, just some good shit."

Jimmy rolled his eyes.

"Thanks, I guess. Hey, did you check on the other thing?"

"I've only checked three months, but in each, the wife, or the imposter wife, I guess, made deposits at that bank in person into two separate accounts—the jeweler, and from my excellent hacker skills, one belonging to M. Hagerty. And the one to M. Hagerty was cash, not a check." He spelled out the last name.

I slammed my hand onto the table. "Bingo!"

Jimmy stared at me.

"Thanks, Joey. You rock!"

"It gets better. Cameras show the older woman coming in with scarves around her head and engaging with the reps at the same time withdrawals from the account were taken."

"That's perfect, Joey. Thank you."

"You owe me for this one, Detective."

"I sure do," I responded and then disconnected the call. I smiled at Jimmy. "Looks like Emily's been paying her mother to keep quiet for a few years now."

10

Bishop dragged his hand down the sides of his face. "Shit."

Ashley grimaced. "A grandmother? That woman is going to hell in a handbasket right quick."

I smiled. She was so unbelievably Southern sometimes. It was endearing.

"Let's not jump to any conclusions, but we definitely need to move on this," Jimmy said.

"We don't know what the money is for," Bishop said. "It could be payment for helping with the boy or even financial support. Mary Hagerty's divorced, and she doesn't work. She might be struggling financially."

I laughed loudly. "You're joking, right? First, it's going into a separate account entirely under M. Hagerty. Explain that. Second, she divorced one of the highest-paid lawyers in the Southeast. Money isn't a problem for her."

"Unless she doesn't know how to manage it," he replied.

He had a point, but I didn't see the woman struggling. Mary Hagerty played tennis and golf and spent a lot of cash on clothing and social events. She lived the country club lifestyle. She wasn't doing that on a few thousand bucks a month. That could lead to mismanaging her cash flow, but based on what we'd already learned about her finances, she'd have to spend a hell of a lot of cash to be struggling. Possible, but not likely.

I paced a circle around the large conference table. "We've got to get moving on this. The mayor's on Jimmy's ass." I glanced at the chief. "No disrespect intended."

"None taken."

"When we hear from Agent Olsen about the biological mother, that may give us a suspect," Bishop said. "But I still think she's the one to focus on here."

"She's been off grid for three years. That doesn't look good for a white woman stranded in Mexico."

Ashley cringed. "I hate to think what could have happened to her."

"Any number of things," I said. "Tijuana is one of the largest human trafficking locations. It's possible the sister could have sold her into it or she'd been abducted into it."

"Wow," Ashley said.

"Here's where we are." I grabbed a dry erase marker and stood in front of the board with the list of persons of interest. I added Ana Flores to the list since she'd gone entirely MIA after supposedly claiming Steve Rockman got her pregnant. Under Ana was revenge for being fired, the possible pregnancy, and money. I also added Heather Maynor to the suspect list, with secret crush not returned as a possible motive. Listed under Melodie were two things: revenge and Ryan. Mary Hagerty's possible motives included money and passion killing for discovering the switch. I added blackmail in parentheses. I also added Charles Haus. "I think he's connected to the mother, whether it's to manipulate her for cash, or something else. I'm not sure yet."

"You're assuming Hagerty knows what happened to her daughter," Bishop said.

I whipped around and glared at him. "Yes, I am."

"But we don't know that she does."

"Bishop, stop defending the woman. Anyone can commit murder. The drive-through girl at Dunkin', the pastor at your church. This is detective 101. Stop letting your emotions get in the way of this."

"It's not emotions. Give me some solid evidence to prove she's involved."

The receptionist spoke into the speaker in the room. "Chief Abernathy, they've found another shirt, and this time, they think the blood is real."

The wooded area in Roswell was the last place we expected to find anything belonging to Ryan Rockman, but it was quickly identified as his by photos Michels had received from one of the homeschool programs, and though we couldn't get a match on the blood, the K9s reacted immediately. The blood wasn't splattered, and it wasn't planted. Where the shirt was ripped matched the stains, and it was clear something happened to Ryan Rockman.

"Shit!" Bishop paced a path around the small wooded area off the creek.

One of the K9 handlers yelled, "Found something!"

We froze.

"It's a shoe," he hollered.

Ashley whimpered. "This poor child." She rushed toward the creek and retrieved the shoe. By the time she got back to us, it was tagged and bagged. "I'll bring it in, but it's definitely a shoe he had on in the photo, so I'm guessing it's his."

Our earlier plans changed. Michels and his team went on a canvassing spree in the area. For me and Bishop, it was time to talk to Grandma.

Mary Hagerty lived in a large home off Providence and Freemanville Roads in Hamby. The area was one of the priciest in town, with homes so big they could fit at least five regular-sized homes in them. Mary lived next to a well-known businessman who'd built a life-sized replica of the old main street from historical Tombstone, Arizona, onto his home. It made all the papers when he built it, and since then he's used it for political fundraising events, movies, charity events, and antique collection shows. I'd had the chance to walk the ten-thousand-square-foot addition a few months ago and was amazed at the attention to detail. Had I been around back in the days of

Tombstone and that dry, dusty road through the small town, I wouldn't have known the difference.

"She's got some serious cash to be living next to this guy," I said. "Cancels out your theory that she's struggling."

"She got the house in the divorce. It was paid in full."

"But it's got to be expensive to maintain. Look at the size of it."

Mary's home wasn't fifteen thousand square feet like many of the others in the area, but it was close. I'd been in town long enough to get used to the home sizes and the extravagant landscaping, not to mention the pricy interior design, but I still found myself surprised sometimes. Mary Hagerty's home was one of those times.

Her maid answered the door. Her accent was so thick, I barely understood her. "Ms. Hagerty isn't available. You leave message?"

I moved my light jacket to reveal my badge. "What's your name?"

"Juanita Lopez."

"Ms. Lopez, where can we find Ms. Hagerty?"

The maid blinked and stumbled over her words. "She's, uh, she's...are you *policía*?" Her English suddenly disappeared.

"Yes, ma'am," Bishop said.

"*Ella está* the club."

"And which club is that?" I asked.

"*Puedo pregunta por qué busca a la Sra. Hagerty?*"

I glanced at Bishop, who looked completely lost. I answered her question about why we were looking for her boss. "We need to see Ms. Hagerty to discuss the investigation into her daughter's homicide and her missing grandchild. Now, which club?"

The housekeeper gasped. "*Ryan está desaparecido?*"

"Yes, he's missing. Please, where is Ms. Hagerty?" I caught Bishop's eye, then glanced back at the woman. "We aren't here regarding your immigration status. We just need to know where Ms. Hagerty is."

Her English improved immensely, though her accent was still thick. "She's at the, uh, Atlanta Golf Club. I do not know where it is located."

"Thank you. We can find out," I said. "When was the last time you saw the boy?"

"The other day. Mrs. Rockman dropped him off at about ten. She stayed awhile, then said she had to go to meet someone. Ms. Hagerty was to watch the boy."

"And did she? Watch the boy?" Bishop asked.

"Well, yes, but she had a date with her gentleman friend, so of course, I was watching him when she leave."

Bishop and I shared another look.

"Ma'am," he said. "Did Mrs. Rockman seem distressed when you saw her last?"

"Mrs. Rockman is, how you say, strung high."

"You mean high-strung, like tense?" I asked.

She nodded. "*Sí.* Always on high alert because of the diabetes. She was very protective of the child."

"Yet she left him with you?" I asked.

The muscles in her neck bulged. "I've worked for Ms. Hagerty for *quince*, fifteen years. I understand his needs."

"I'm sure you do," I said. "Are you aware of how his insulin pump works?"

She nodded. "*Sí.*"

"Do you know of anyone who might want to take the boy?" Bishop asked.

She gasped and reverted back to Spanish again, but she spoke a mile a minute. "*No! La familia Hagerty muy conocida y se rodea de gente de confianza. Nadie que conozcan querría lastimar a ese dulce niño!*"

"I'm sorry," I said. "I didn't get half of that."

"The family is good. They wouldn't let anyone hurt the boy."

"We have spoken to Ms. Hagerty several times, and this case has been all over the news," I said. "And yet not once has she mentioned you or having you watch the boy. Why do you think that is?"

"I don't know."

"Can you explain why she's at the golf club now, then?"

She crossed her arms over her chest. "Ms. Hagerty has obligations. She volunteers."

"Did she tell you her daughter was deceased?"

She shook her head.

"Why do you think she didn't mention her daughter's murder to you?"

"I don't know."

"Obviously," I said. "Have people come to the house asking to see her? News reporters, maybe?"

She shook her head.

"Ma'am," Bishop said. He took out a photo of Charles Haus. "Have you seen this man before?"

"*Sí.*" She nodded. "That is Charlie. Ms. Hagerty's special person."

"And this person?" He showed her a photo of Heather Maynor.

She shook her head. "I don't see her before."

"Thank you," Bishop said.

"What was the club's name again?" I asked.

"Atlanta Golf."

"Thank you," I said and took two steps back toward the stairs to the large front entrance.

We stood there after she closed the door and waited, watching to see if she'd peek out a window or do anything. After a few seconds of nothing, we headed to the car.

"Atlanta Golf Club?" Bishop asked. "Then back to the jewelry shop?"

I shook my head. "The housekeeper is going to tell her we were there. Let's sit on it and see what she does. If her grandson matters to her, she'll be in touch the minute she knows we came to her house."

"She's at a golf club."

"Says a lot about how worried she is, doesn't it?"

He sighed. "I think you're right."

I smiled. "I'm pretty sure I know what you're going to say, but can you just say it anyway?"

"You're a pain in my ass."

I laughed. "But you think she's involved now too, don't you?"

He nodded. "She's not at all worried about the kid, is she?"

"Nope, because she knows where he is, and she knows he's safe."

Bishop drove. Bishop always drove. He turned right onto Highway 9 instead of left, which would have taken us back to the department. "Keep this way," I said.

"Where we going?" he asked.

"Randy Rockman's house."

"Michels has already been. Even cleared him of any suspicion."

"I know, but we haven't talked to him. We need to do our due diligence."

He stopped at the light in the most congested part of downtown Alpharetta and studied the people walking across the street. "Still got that gun in your boot?"

I raised my brow. "Yes. Why?"

"Then nothing."

I whacked his arm and laughed. "I'm not going to shoot you. Just say it."

"I thought maybe you could try and soften your approach when we talk to Rockman. Southern men are different than the men in Chicago."

"You have no idea, but what's your point, partner?" I emphasized *partner*.

"You're a little rough around the edges. That doesn't always work here."

I scowled. "I don't treat family members of the victims bad."

He smirked. "You've told family you'd drag their butts into jail on an impeding an investigation charge for not telling you what you wanted to know."

"I only did that a few times, and they deserved it."

"The guy I'm talking about believed he was a person of interest."

"Everyone's a person of interest in a murder investigation." I kept my nose close to the window.

Bishop laughed. "All I'm saying is maybe work on your communication a little. A little extra sugar sweetens the pie."

I turned toward him and narrowed my eyes. "That's the stupidest Southern expression you've ever said. And by the way, I can be sweet, but I'm dealing with a double homicide and a missing sick kid. I don't have time for sweet."

"I'm just making a suggestion."

I sunk in my seat. "If you have an issue with me, submit a ticket to HR. In the meantime," I pointed to the light, "that thing ain't getting any greener."

≈

Randy Rockman lived near the dividing line between Johns Creek and Alpharetta in a reasonably large home with a white picket fence. It was in a congested area filled with other reasonably large homes with white picket fences.

"The fences," I said. "So obvious."

Bishop pulled into the driveway. "What do you mean?"

"I mean it's obviously a statement to the whole American dream about a house with a white picket fence thing, and it's just pathetic."

"Who pissed in your coffee this morning?"

I sighed. "I'm tired. I know we're doing what we're supposed to be doing, but I want that kid found."

"You *are* focused on finding the kid. We are. Find the killer, find the boy. You said it yourself."

My partner had a way of using my words against me, and it annoyed me sometimes. "I know. I'm just frustrated." I pushed the door open and climbed out of the car.

Bishop sighed.

I knocked on the door. Bishop eyed me. "Let me start at least, okay? I don't want the guy getting jittery because of...tension."

"Read him his rights."

He stared at me. "He's already been cleared." He shook his head. "I don't know what's going on with you, Ryder, but get your shit together."

I couldn't reply because the door was opened by a man who looked a lot like Steve Rockman.

"Detectives, come on in." He held the door open.

I kept my mouth shut and my eyes focused on his body language as Bishop took the lead.

"Mr. Rockman, the Hamby Police Department offers their condolences for your loss."

"Thank you."

"We'd like to ask you some questions about your brother and his relationship with his wife."

We sat in a formal living room with ornately designed furniture. The couch was horribly uncomfortable and worsened my mood.

"Which wife?" he asked. "The real one or the imposter?"

"Let's start with Emily," Bishop said. "Are you aware the two dated prior to his relationship with Melodie?"

He nodded. "What a mind-fuck that was. He thinks he's meeting Melodie, who he'd talked to me about a few times after seeing her somewhere, but it was Emily. She posed as her sister. Who does that?"

"More people than you know," I said.

He shrugged. "I can't even imagine that."

"When he found out he was actually dating Emily, what did he do?" Bishop asked.

"At first, nothing. He continued to date her, but something happened, and he ended it."

"What happened?"

"I don't know. Unfortunately, he never said."

"And then he met the real Melodie?"

"A while later, yes."

"And that relationship progressed quickly?"

He nodded again. "I wasn't sure it was the right thing. He continued to talk about Emily sometimes, and many times he'd referred to Melodie as Emily. I think he had feelings for Emily still, but because of what she did, he couldn't be with her."

"So, let me get this straight. He dates Emily, thinking she's Melodie, then learns she isn't, but stays with her until something happens, and then dates Melodie but still talks about Emily?"

"Yeah. I always thought he was in love with Emily, and Melodie was his second choice."

"Did you know he paid for Emily to terminate a pregnancy?" Bishop asked.

He blinked. "What? No." He shook his head. "No way. Steve wanted kids. He wouldn't let her abort one."

Let her was an interesting choice of words.

"We have no way of confirming if the child belonged to your brother or someone else," Bishop said.

"Why do you think he married Melodie?" I asked.

"On paper, Melodie was the perfect wife. Career oriented, well known, and liked in the community. Melodie had a great reputation. Emily, on the other hand, she was the rebel sister, and everyone thought that. Whatever happened between them, it was too much for my brother. I can't say if he'd had enough of the lie or what, but I suspect that was it. He had a reputation. He's an excellent doctor, and I can't imagine he'd want people to know he stayed with a woman who impersonated her twin, even if he loved her. Melodie, though, she hit all the markers on his list."

"So, you're saying Steve married Melodie because she fit an image?"

"I'm saying that's my impression, yes, but Steve never said that exactly."

"What did he say?" Bishop asked.

"Nothing. It was Melodie that said something."

"Go on," Bishop said.

"She approached me on their wedding day. She'd found out about Emily and Steve after they got engaged, and she struggled with it, which everyone understood. But she got through it, or so I thought. A few hours before the wedding, she called me. I went to the church and talked with her. She wanted to know if she was making the right decision. If her fiancé still loved her sister."

Bishop took notes. "What did you say?"

"I told her I didn't know." He exhaled. "And that was the truth. I might have thought he was, but I didn't know for sure."

Bishop nodded.

"Mr. Rockman," I said with as much politeness as I could muster. "We've estimated that Emily began posing as Melodie approximately three years ago. Did your brother say anything in that time that makes you think he knew?"

"No, I don't think he knew, not until recently, that is."

We waited for him to continue.

"I see things a little clearer in retrospect, and I've had time to think about it now, so I'm not sure if that stains my thoughts, but I recall things changing when Melodie, or Emily, I guess, returned from Mexico. Steve was happier, less stressed, but I don't think he made the connection at the time."

"Why is that?"

"I can't say exactly, but my brother's moral foundation was strong. He couldn't pretend. He wouldn't do that to his son. But yes, he seemed happier, and when I asked him about it, he said Melodie returned from Mexico different. Less Type A, more relaxed. She claimed it was the renewed relationship with her sister, and how Emily's carefree lifestyle made her drop some of her control issues."

"Your brother's office manager said Melodie changed too, but that she became more paranoid, more intense," I said.

"Definitely when it came to Ryan, yes. Looking back, I know that Emily lived on the edge, but she wanted kids and told me she would protect them with her life."

"When did she tell you this?" Bishop asked.

"When she was dating my brother. We had them over for dinner, and she said she couldn't wait to have kids. Wanted a house full of them, and if anyone messed with them, they wouldn't know what hit them."

"Interesting," I said. "It's our understanding they weren't out and about a lot."

"No, they weren't. Initially, Steve said she liked to spend her time with just him, but I suspect it was because her secret would get out sooner."

"So, you were close to your brother?" I asked.

"For a long time, yes. But things changed about two years ago."

"What happened?"

"My wife and I were at their house, and Melodie—Emily, I guess in retrospect, slipped up. She referred to a small, private event we'd gone to when Steve was dating Emily. She gave some details Melodie wouldn't have known because she wasn't there. It stood out to my wife because it was the only event we went to with them, again, because Steve said she liked to keep things between them. My wife was pretty upset about it. I told her it was probably a simple mistake on my wife's part, but she insisted, and a few weeks later, she said something to Melodie about it."

"What did she say?" Bishop asked.

"That it was strange Melodie would know the details of an event we attended with Emily."

"And what happened?" I asked.

"Melodie became defensive. They argued. Steve showed up here that night and told my wife to stay out of his marriage. He basically threatened me too. I didn't think much of it at the time, but now..." He shook his head. "I think he knew then."

Bishop and I shared a look.

"So," I asked. "That changed your relationship with your brother?"

He nodded. "We didn't see them much after that, until a few weeks ago."

"What happened then?" Bishop asked.

"Steve came to my office after hours. He wanted to talk about what happened, but I told him I'd done what he asked, and I wanted the same from him. I wanted him to stay out of my life." He sighed. "Knowing what's happened, I think he was trying to make amends. I think maybe something was happening, and he needed me, but I wasn't there."

"Where can we find your wife?" I asked.

"She's in China. We're trying to adopt a child, and she's got to stay there for another month at least."

"Can we contact her there?"

"Yes, I'll give you her contact information."

"Do you know of anyone who might have wanted your brother and his wife dead?" Bishop asked.

"Absolutely. Melodie. Wouldn't you want revenge if your sister stole your life?"

"You don't think Melodie willingly walked away from her family?"

"Not for a second, no. She loved that kid. Sure, she might have wanted to leave my brother, but not her son. She was devoted to that kid."

"Anyone else?" Bishop asked.

"What about Mary Hagerty? Do you know anything about the relationship she had with her daughters?" I asked.

"Other than what I read in the papers about her divorce, I don't know much. I never really interacted with her."

"And you don't know of any problems your brother had with clients or former employees?" I asked.

"No. Steve was well liked. He wasn't a saint, but people liked him. If Melodie didn't do it, I don't know who did."

"Do you think Melodie is capable of killing two people?" Bishop asked.

"If what I think happened, happened, then I think anyone would be capable of killing two people."

"What exactly do you think happened?" I asked.

"Like I basically said before, I think Melodie went to Mexico in good faith, and somehow her sister stole her life." He paused and asked, "Have you looked for Melodie in Mexico?"

"We're working on that," Bishop said.

"Let's take Melodie out of the picture," I said. "Do you know of anyone else who might have done this? Someone who maybe wanted Ryan?"

He shook his head and sighed. "I wish I did, but like I said, I wasn't involved in Steve's life recently."

"Thank you," Bishop said. He stood.

"I'd appreciate it if you'd let me know what's going on. I'm worried about my nephew."

"Mr. Rockman," I said. "We haven't found a will for your brother or his wife. The only known relatives are you, Mr. Hagerty, and Mary Hagerty. Do you have any idea who your brother wanted to raise his son in the event something happened?"

"It never came up in conversation. I don't think it's something a parent wants to think about. But my wife and I will gladly raise Ryan if we're asked."

"Thank you," I said.

"We'll be in touch," Bishop said. He handed him a card. "In the meantime, if you think of anything else, give us a call."

"Will do."

Bishop thanked me in the car. "I appreciate you handling him the way you did."

"Gee, thanks."

"I'm serious. You did good work in there."

"I don't need you to head my fan club, Bishop."

He glanced over at me. "What the hell's wrong with you? And don't tell me it's the investigation because I've worked with you long enough to know you don't get like this from an investigation."

I raised my eyebrows. "Like what?"

"Pissy." He flinched when he said it.

"You seriously just called me pissy?"

"I call it like I see it."

I tipped my head back and groaned. "Jesus."

"Listen, I'm not trying to be an asshole. But is this about Kyle?"

"What? No. Kyle means practically nothing."

He rolled his eyes. "Right."

"Fine. If you want to know the truth, I don't think he should be the one to go to Mexico for our investigation."

"Why not? He's got contacts that can help, and we really need to be here."

"He could have connected me with his contacts, and I could have gone."

He laughed. "You're saying you think you, a white female cop from Georgia, have a better chance of getting information on a missing and assumed dead woman than a world-traveled DEA agent with serious connections?"

"He's working with the embassy. Anyone can do that."

He shook his head. "That's not what this is about." He pulled into a Starbucks drive-through and faced me while we waited in line. "I'm calling bullshit."

"Call whatever you want. I'm just saying we could have done it."

"You're worried something's going to happen to him."

I sunk lower in the seat. "Okay, fine. I'm worried. It's our case, and if something happens to him, it's on us, okay? Don't you worry about that at all?"

"He's a professional. He knows what he's doing, and he made the decision himself. You can't shelter him from harm just because of what happened to Tommy."

I narrowed my eyes at him. "I know that."

"Then act like it."

~

I called Savannah from my office. "Hey, I have thirty seconds. Just wanted to let you know I spoke to the twin mom and say thanks again."

Savannah exhaled into my ear. "How's the investigation going?"

"Not well. We still don't have a rock-solid suspect, and your husband is stressed, which makes the rest of us stressed. We need to find the kid, and the clock's ticking."

"You will. Hopefully, Kyle gets resolution to the Melodie part of this. At least that would be one less suspect."

"You know Kyle's in Mexico?" I asked.

"I have a mole in the department."

"Nice."

"How you holding up with that?"

"Why does everyone keep bugging me about that? I'm fine."

"I'm sure everyone knows that's not true."

"Jimmy said I was upset, didn't he?"

"A little birdie might have said something, yes. But it wasn't Jimmy."

"Bishop?"

"Honey, you need to put your personal feelings aside and close the case. He didn't tell me because he's upset with you. He told me because he thought I could talk some sense into you. Kyle's a big boy. If he puts his life in danger, which he does as a DEA agent every day, that's on him. Not you."

Jimmy walked into the investigation room.

"Gotta run, boss is here," I said and disconnected the call.

"Thought I sent you home an hour ago," he said.

"Pretty sure it wasn't an order, and besides, there are so many tentacles to this thing, I need to sort through them and see if I can find a real connection."

He pulled out a chair and sat, then pointed to the whiteboard. "Let's discuss it."

"Shouldn't you go home?"

"Not until we close the case."

I nodded. "Rockman's brother thinks Rockman knew Emily was impersonating her sister at some point before they were murdered."

"And that makes you think Emily set Melodie up in Mexico?"

"I'm back to the same questions on that theory, and I can't come up with an answer." I walked over to the easel and flipped to a fresh page, then jotted down what I'd learned about Emily. "Emily and Melodie were very different people and led very different lives, but they wanted the same thing. Steve Rockman." I added more to the page. "First Emily's got him. Life is good. She's happy, but she's got a dirty little secret too. Steve thinks she's Melodie. She tells him the truth and they stay together, which, yeah, is a shock, but love is blind."

"So Savannah says."

I smiled. Savannah would say something like that. "But things get tense. Steve decides the dishonesty was too much, maybe? Or maybe he realized he wasn't into her because she had a drug problem. That part, I don't know, but something happened, and they broke up. Soon after, Steve's with Melodie. The real Melodie, and then bam! Emily winds up pregnant. Steve pays for the abortion, but we can't confirm it's his. You know why?"

"Because she was in rehab when she found out."

I nodded. "So, she tells Steve she's knocked up."

"I'm assuming you don't think the guy in rehab knocked her up."

"Timing doesn't fit."

"Impregnation isn't that specific."

"But ultrasounds are." I went to the room's laptop and typed into the search bar. "See, ultrasounds can predict due dates with a one-point-two week margin of error."

"Let me guess, your guy in Chicago got you Emily's medical records for the abortion?"

I nodded.

"Jesus. You know we can't use that."

"We can get a subpoena, if necessary, but I don't think we'll need it."

"When was the procedure?"

"At nine weeks."

"How long had she been in rehab?"

"Six weeks."

"Damn."

I nodded. "Steve knew it was his child. He paid for it."

"You think Melodie found out?"

"I don't know." I bent my neck from side to side. It made loud cracking noises. "I think this case is a damn soap opera. Toss in some world domination and a mafioso, and we're set for daytime TV. But I don't think any of that matters. We've been chasing these false motives and getting caught in the drama, while the motive has been right in front of us the whole time."

"What's that?"

"Money." I continued after gathering my thoughts. "I think Emily loved Steve. I think she'd planned to reconnect with her sister and took her to Mexico with the purpose of killing her and stealing her life again because she thought Melodie stole hers."

"But she didn't succeed, and Melodie came back for revenge."

"That's what I'm saying about false motives. That's an entirely separate situation, and like I've said, I don't know if Melodie's alive, but I think someone else found out and blackmailed Emily, then, when her pockets ran dry, they killed her."

"Mary Hagerty."

I nodded. "With a little help from her boyfriend."

11

Jimmy's eyes widened. "The jewelry dealer."

I nodded.

"You got eyes on Hagerty, right?"

I cringed. "Not exactly."

"What? I told you to get someone on her."

"I know, and we've got people watching her house."

"Then what's the problem?"

"The problem is we're a small department with a smaller budget and a shit ton of small crimes. The officer watching her had to take a call."

"So, she's what? Gone?"

"Not really. To the best of his knowledge, she hadn't left. When we went there to talk to her, she was gone."

"Did you find her?"

"We confirmed she was at a golf club. Our guy played eighteen holes behind her and has been in the tavern watching her for hours already. According to him, Hagerty's only distraught when someone asks, but she has slipped away a few times to make a private call."

"On her cell?"

"Nothing shows up in the call list."

"Burner phone."

I made the shape of a gun with my finger and said, "Bang!"

"She's got someone watching the kid."

"I think you're right. She told us the nanny was pregnant with Steve's kid, but not to throw her under the bus. She wanted us to think the nanny disappeared."

Jimmy pressed his lips together. "We need to find that nanny."

"I know, and I have a plan." My cell phone rang. I glanced down at it and saw Kyle's contact information. "It's Kyle." I hit the button to take the call and put it on speaker. "Jimmy's here."

"I'm getting on a flight now, and I'll be there in a few hours. Melodie Rockman is all but confirmed dead."

Someone knocked on the door and opened it slowly. "Detective Ryder," the officer said. "There is a woman here to see you."

I walked Mary Hagerty's maid into an interview room. She twisted her hands into a knot and bounced in her seat.

"Can I get you some water?" She didn't need any caffeine, that much I knew.

"No, thank you."

"Ms. Lopez, why are you here?"

"My name isn't Lopez. It's Flores."

My eyes widened. "Are you Ana Flores?"

She shook her head. "I am her cousin, Juanita."

"Do you have a photo of Ana?"

"On my phone."

"May I see it?"

She handed me her phone. I texted the photo to myself, then handed the phone back to her. "Do you know where Ana is?"

She shook her head again. "She...she is disappeared. I cannot find her, and I'm worried. I hear Ms. Hagerty talk, and I think she knows, but she don't tell me." She cried. "*Mi prima no es una asesina. Ella mantiene a su familia. Ella es una buena persona.*"

I handed her a tissue. "I'm sure she is a good person. Why are you saying she is not a murderer?"

"Ms. Hagerty, I hear her talk to her Charlie. She knows something. She uses my cousin. I do not understand what's going on."

"When did you hear her talk about this?"

"Before you came. I didn't know. I'm...I'm not...I don't want to go back to Mexico. My family...I..."

"Ms. Flores, I'm not worried about your immigration status. I'm worried about the child. Do you know if Ana was pregnant?"

"No, no. She was a good girl. She didn't do that."

"Could she have gotten pregnant and not told you?"

She cried again. "No. Not Ana."

Three hours later, after countless questions reiterated until my gums were swollen from excessive talking, I had a photo of Ana Flores, but that was about it. I made sure her photo was put into the system and set up a BOLO, *be on the lookout*, for her.

Ashley yelled from outside the investigation room. "I can't open the door!"

Bishop jumped up, opened it, then grabbed a bag Ashley stuck out in front of her.

"Food," she said. "Guess who bought it?"

"The mayor?" I asked jokingly.

"Haus Jewelry."

Bishop laughed. "No shit?"

"That depends on your definition of shit," Ashley said.

I laughed. "How do you know?"

She tossed a note across the table.

I read it out loud. "Sorry for any misunderstanding. I have closed the account and donated the money to charity."

"My ass," Bishop said.

"I'm on it," Bubba said.

"Sit and eat," I said.

"Please," Bishop added. "There's a lot of food in these bags."

We all ate and discussed a plan of action. I stared at the photo of Ana Flores that Juanita Flores had brought in earlier. "She's so young."

"And if she's supporting her family, she might have to do work she didn't want to do," Bishop said.

I nodded. "Like work with a killer." I wrapped up the leftover half of my sandwich and pushed it aside. "If Ana was fired, which her cousin says is true, and she hadn't found another job, Mary could have approached her and paid her off to work with her."

"And her cousin has no idea where she is?" Bishop asked. "No suggestions?"

"Nothing, but she's going to keep her ears close to Hagerty, and that's where my plan comes in."

"We don't have time for plans," Bishop said. "We have a kid who's going to need medicine."

"Not if he's with his nanny. And not if Mary Hagerty gave her the supplies she needs to keep him well. She already knows what to do and how to do it. Hagerty doesn't want the kid dead."

"We don't know that. The DNA on the shirt and the shoe are matches to the parents. They belong to Ryan Rockman," Bishop said. "And it looks like he's been hurt."

"No, I don't think so. Barron studied those stains. Based on the doctor's medical records from the child's last exam, the boy has never had any injuries. No scars, nothing. The stains could correspond with scratches he might have received from walking in the woods. And how many times do shoes come off kids' feet? Ashley and Nikki didn't find anything to say the kid was dragged through the area. They can't find anything to show any type of injury happened there other than blood on a few shrubs. He walked into them as kids do. I truly believe he's somewhere safe."

Bishop couldn't get on board with that. Since learning that Melodie Rockman was likely dead, he determined the killer could be Haus. He proposed Haus got money from them, then killed them, only to discover the kid was home and watching, so he had to enlist help from the grandmother, who then employed the help of the nanny. The resolution, he said, once the case exposure died down, would be the kid dropped off somewhere safe.

I disagreed. My theory was that Mary was the lead and Charlie Haus did the grunt work. Only neither of them planned on the kid being there, and everything after that wasn't part of the plan.

"You need to get over your *grandmothers aren't capable of murder* issue," I said. "I'm not saying she's Marybeth Tinning, but mothers kill their children all the time. Just because her daughter had a child doesn't mean she wouldn't kill her."

"Who's Marybeth Tinning?" Bubba asked.

"A woman with nine children that all died under suspicious circumstances."

"Holy balls," he said. "Did she do it?"

"She was indicted for three of them but only prosecuted for one, but the consensus is she murdered them all. They just can't prove it."

"Damn," he said.

"I think Ryder's right," Jimmy said. "Mary's the lead on this. Hagerty duped Haus into helping with the promise of more cash. But when he killed the parents, the kid walked downstairs, and he panicked. He called Hagerty, who thought the boy was with someone else."

"Right," I said. "Which goes with the idea that Emily would no longer let her mother blackmail her into keeping the secret. She wouldn't leave the kid with her mother because it was too much of a risk."

"So," Ashley said, "Mary Hagerty gets the kid and what, goes to her maid who sets her back up with Ana?"

"No," I said. "Juanita Flores isn't involved."

"She withheld information," Bishop added.

"And if necessary, we'll charge her, but it would be better to use her as a witness. The point is," I said after taking a breath. "Hagerty intentionally told us she deleted Ana's phone number from her phone. She didn't want us finding the nanny because she was worried the woman would give us the kid. What she didn't tell us was that she's got a burner phone, and that's what she's used to communicate with Ana, which is why we don't see her worried about the kid at all."

"Why hasn't Ana reported the boy as safe?" Bubba asked.

"Fear. Money. It could be either of those. She's illegal. Mary could have threatened to report her and her cousin. We won't know until we find Ana."

"What we need," Jimmy said, "is what Ryder's proposing, you two on Haus and Hagerty."

"Seems like a waste of time for us to be staking out possible suspects when we could be doing the real work." Bishop groaned.

Jimmy narrowed his eyes at him.

"Fine," Bishop said. "I'll take Haus."

"Works for me," I said.

"Michels and Emmett will take the golf course and the jewelry store," Jimmy added. "Give the officer on the course a break. Let's get this one on the books ASAP." He tossed his food trash into the garbage and walked out.

"Well, here we go," Bishop said.

Stakeouts are important elements of investigations and, contrary to what happens on TV, usually don't end up balls to the wall or with someone dead. They're more like an extended stay in the hospital with lukewarm coffee and no cable TV. They take forever, and if you're lucky, you figure out what's going on.

I answered Kyle's call on the first ring. "You're back?

"I am. You at the department? I'm about ten minutes out."

"I'm on a stakeout."

He laughed. "I love how you call it that."

"That's what it is."

"It's surveillance."

"Same thing."

"Surveillance sounds better."

"Word snob."

He laughed. "I'll meet you. Send me your location."

I shared my location over text message, and he arrived shortly after. Instead of pulling behind my rental, he walked up and tapped lightly on the back of the SUV. I unlocked the doors, and he climbed into the passenger seat.

He smiled at me. I blushed.

"Miss me?"

"She's dead? Are you sure?"

"So much for a little romance."

"I'm kind of on a clock here, Agent Olsen."

"Her remains were located two years ago. Not much left but the teeth."

"And you could confirm from the teeth without a dentist?"

"Barron compared the photos to her dental records. It's not a perfect match, but it's close enough for comfort. Of course, it's always possible those records were manipulated. It's easy to do, and if someone has the right amount of cash to make it happen, they will."

"Wait." My tone changed. "You talked to Barron while you were there?"

"Yes."

"Why didn't you go through me? I'm the lead on this investigation."

"Because I thought it would be quicker to go to Barron and then report the facts as best I could to you and the rest of the team."

"I don't appreciate that."

"Rachel, can we just get past the territorial stuff?"

I folded my hands on my lap. "I'm not being territorial."

He raised his brows. "Then why the pissy mood?"

"What the hell is it with you men and that word? Is a male cop working a double homicide with a missing child considered pissy? I'm stressed, and frustrated, and bored off my ass sitting here waiting for a probable murdering grandmother to mess up. That doesn't mean I'm pissy. It means I'm doing my damn job."

"Okay, then."

We were quiet for a moment. Kyle had some mints and popped one into his mouth.

"Do they know how she died?" I asked, pretending I hadn't just acted exactly how I said I wasn't acting.

He shook his head. "But she was used in sex trafficking. We'll probably never know how she got there or what happened."

"I know," I said. "Her sister."

We were quiet again, then he said, "So you still think the grandmother's involved, huh?"

The tension in the vehicle was palpable, but we pretended it wasn't there and discussed the investigation to hide whatever was brewing between us. I couldn't decide if it was something sexual and intimate or the beginning of the end, even though there wasn't much of a beginning in the first place. When the garage door opened and a vehicle backed out, I started the rental but kept it in park. "That's not hers."

"I'll take it, then." Kyle climbed out of the car, turned around and smiled back to me, then said, "I'm only here to help, Rach, because I have feelings for you. Just roll with it, okay?"

He closed the door before I could say anything.

"CVS called," Bishop said. I put him on speaker. "They had a call about the prescription. A woman with a Hispanic accent asked if it was time to fill."

"Is she coming to pick it up?"

"They told her it will be ready at six o'clock."

"The nanny. I'm on it."

"I'll meet you there."

"Kyle followed a vehicle out of Hagerty's garage. It wasn't Hagerty, but no word on who it is yet."

"Our buddy Chuck's been at the jewelry shop all day."

"Mary's not left the house either. Not that I can tell, anyway." I turned onto Mayfield Road and headed toward CVS.

I sent a text to the patrol down the street and told him to keep eyes on the home. I didn't care if we were obvious. If Hagerty questioned it, we'd figure it out.

"Something's off," Bishop said.

"I'm with you on that. We've been sitting here watching these two, and they're doing nothing. It's a complete waste of time."

"Maybe not," he said. "I see you. I'll come to your vehicle."

He opened the door and groaned as he sat. "I'm going to end up with butt sores from this."

"Ew. Please."

"What're partners for?"

"Definitely not that." I smiled. "So, why is this not a complete waste of time?"

"The jewelry store is closed now. I got eyes on Haus's vehicle, and I made sure eyes were on—" He stared at the entrance to the store. "Is that the nanny?"

I studied the woman carefully. "She's got her fucking head covered and it's hotter than hell out still."

We both got out of the car and went inside. I kept my distance, hanging near the entrance in case the woman tried to bolt while Bishop followed her toward the back of the store to the pharmacy section.

The next thing I knew, Bishop was screaming a string of curse words worthy of a long-haul truck driver on Interstate 80. "Son of a bitch!"

The woman knocked down a display of cheap jewelry as she ran toward the exit. I moved to the side of the door and stuck my foot out when she reached it. She fell to the ground with a thump.

When she rolled over and saw my weapon pointed at her, she waved her hands. "No, no. Don't shoot!"

"On your back with your hands behind you, now!" I kept my weapon aimed steadily on her. The scarf had fallen from her hair and face, and I caught enough of a view to see she wasn't Ana Flores.

Bishop finally made it over to us, though he was panting like crazy. "She just ran. I...I don't know what the—" He dropped to the ground with his cuffs, secured them around her wrists, then lifted her up. "Come on, we're going in."

"It's not her," I said. I placed my gun back in its strap and swore under my breath.

Bishop handled the woman while I went to my vehicle and contacted dispatch and requested the interrogation room.

Bishop leaned toward the suspect with his palms on the table. "You have no ID, and your prints aren't in the system. You know what that tells us, right?"

My eyes widened. Bishop's tone and composure were genuinely bad cop, which was rare, and I was proud of my fatherly partner. The young woman cried. I glanced at Bishop, and he nodded once for me to share the scene. That's what interrogating a suspect often was, a scene. We played very defined roles to extract information from suspects and witnesses. They always knew more than they wanted us to believe.

I pulled out the chair beside the woman and spoke softly. "Listen," I said as I leaned in toward her. "I know you're afraid, but I'd like to help you. I just need you to help me. If you do that, I'll do my best to make sure my partner here doesn't send you back to Mexico. Okay?"

She nodded.

I started with the basics. "What's your name?"

"Maria Peréz."

"Where do you live?"

"I...no live. I visit."

"Okay, where are you staying while you're here?"

"*Familia*."

Bishop asked in a loud voice with strong enunciation, "Where does the family you're staying with live?"

She glanced at me.

"She's not deaf, Detective," I said as I rolled my eyes at him. It was all acting.

"Maria, do you have an address for your family's home?"

She shook her head. "I know it's in the Cummings. I have *direcciones en mi bolso*."

I asked Bishop to get her things from the locker. "She's got directions in it," I said.

When he left, I smiled at the woman. "Maria, you were driving a vehicle with no license plates, no registration, and no sales information connected at all to the VIN number since it was sold to a used car lot two months ago. Do you understand that?"

"No."

"There is no record of the car being owned by a person. It's owned by the car dealership, which means either they're letting you borrow—uh, *prestámo*, maybe, or you took it without permission—*robó*."

Her eyes widened. "No, no! *Yo no lo robé. Mi primo trabaja allí. Me dejó usarlo. Le pagué la mitad de los quinientos dólares que me pagó la mujer.*"

She rattled that off so quickly all I got was the woman paid her five hundred dollars.

"Maria, I need you to either repeat that slowly, or speak English, please." I knew she understood the language because she didn't appear to struggle to understand me. And she'd blurted out "don't shoot" at CVS, among other things.

Bishop returned with the purse and put the directions on the table. He watched her carefully.

"My cousin, he work there. He borrow the car to me, and I pay him from the monies the lady gave to me."

"A lady paid you to pick up the medicine?" I asked.

She nodded vigorously.

"I've got someone going to where she's staying," Bishop said. He pulled a photo of Mary Hagerty from a file folder and slid it over to her. "Is this the woman?"

She examined the photo, looked at me, then the photo again, and shook her head. "*No quiero ir a la,* how you say, *policía cárcel?*"

"English, please, Maria. You're talking very fast, and I can't keep up." I was fluent in Spanish, and not only from the years of schooling. In fact, most of my Spanish came from my work with Hispanics, mostly gangs, on the streets of Chicago. Fluent, however, didn't mean I could catch it all when it was spit out faster than bullets from an automatic weapon. "Don't worry. If you tell us about the woman and what she paid you to do, we'll do our best to keep you out of jail."

"She just pay me to, uh, you know...pick up the thing."

I pointed to the photo of Mary Hagerty. "This woman."

She nodded. "*Sí.*"

"And that thing is a prescription for what kind of medicine? Do you know?"

She shook her head.

"Did she tell you why she needed you to pick it up?"

"She say she need help. She pay me lot of money and tell me it will be good."

"Did she say why she couldn't get it herself?"

"No."

"Did she tell you who it's for?"

She glanced at Bishop. "I gave the woman at the *farmacia* a note."

Bishop glanced at me. "Didn't get a note from the pharmacy." He stepped out to contact them.

"Okay, where were you supposed to bring the package? Were you supposed to meet her somewhere?"

"No, she give me address." She pointed to her purse.

I grabbed the purse and searched through it until I found the paper with Mary Hagerty's home address on it. I set it on the table. "Here?"

She nodded.

"When were you supposed to drop it off?"

"Right after I pick up."

I loosened the bun of brown hair at the back of my neck. I was getting a headache from lack of sleep, lack of regular meals, and the investigation.

Kyle stepped into the room. "A minute?"

I smiled at the woman. "I'll be right back."

"The vehicle belonged to Mary Hagerty, but she sure as hell wasn't driving it."

"That's what we thought. Who was?"

"A Hispanic woman. Claims a woman hired her to leave the house and drive around for a few hours. She's in the other interrogation room now, but she's not saying much, and she's not in the system."

"Son of a bitch!" I exhaled deeply and blew it out. "She's playing us. She knows we're onto her and she's trying to distract us. How the hell is she getting these people in and out of her place without us knowing?" I charged toward the pit, the heart of the department. "Where's Chief Abernathy?" I asked an officer.

"In his office, I think."

"Thanks."

Jimmy stood at the door as I approached. "I could hear you a mile away. You find the boy?"

"No, but I'm pretty sure that POS grandmother's got him. We need a warrant for her house. Right away."

"What do you have?"

"Two women. One sent to pick up Ryan Rockman's insulin. The other used as a dummy to ditch us."

He walked behind my desk. "Let me make a call."

"Jimmy, they're not in the system."

"Shit. I have to go to a judge with two illegal accessories?"

I cringed. "I told one we didn't care about her immigration status, and—"

"You told her we'd help her, didn't you?"

My cringe intensified. "She was scared, and I needed her to tell the truth."

"Son of a b—motherfu—fine. I'll see what I can do."

I smiled, and before I walked out of his office, I whispered, "You're going to have to cut back on the swearing, Chief."

He yelled, "Screw off, Ryder," as I walked out.

12

Bishop and I executed the warrant at Mary Hagerty's home with a team of patrol officers and crime scene tech at our side. Kyle came along for the ride and, of course, to assist.

Juanita Flores answered the door. "Is my cousin found?"

"No, ma'am. We're here to search the home. Is Ms. Hagerty here?"

"Search? No, no. She's not here. I cannot allow—"

Bishop showed her the warrant. "Ma'am, it's not up to you."

"I do not understand."

"Perhaps you can tell us about the woman who left the house a few hours ago in Ms. Hagerty's vehicle?" I asked.

"I do not understand."

"Candela Martinez," Kyle said.

"Is she a cousin too?" I asked.

The team moved into the home.

Bishop gave them directions. "We're here for anything related to the boy, her twin daughters, properties she might own, bank accounts, financial records of any sort, medical information, rental paperwork. You find anything that might lead us to Hagerty or the boy, you let me or Detective Ryder know immediately."

"Ma'am," I said and silently cursed myself for falling victim to the

Southern courtesy I swore I'd never use. "Are you saying you know nothing about the woman that left the home in your boss's vehicle a few hours ago?"

She nodded. "I...I leave early today. Came back when Ms. Hagerty call. She tell me to stay the night. She go away. She said it was important."

"Why didn't you call us to tell us?"

"I...I'm just doing my job."

"Did you tell Ms. Hagerty we were here, that we talked to you, or that you came to the police department?"

She shook her head. "No. I tell her nothing. I want to help my cousin. That is all."

I nodded. "How many vehicles does Ms. Hagerty own?"

"Two, maybe three. I don't count."

"And did she tell you where she was going?"

She shook her head.

"Did she say who she was going with?"

Another headshake.

I removed the photo of Charles Haus from my file and showed it to her. "Was he with her?"

She shook her head. "I haven't seen him, no."

"Juanita, Ryan Rockman needs his insulin soon. We believe whoever took him had enough insulin for a few days, but I'm beginning to think otherwise. Whoever has the boy sent someone to CVS to pick up his prescription. Do you understand?"

"Ms. Hagerty sent the woman?"

I nodded. "She was identified by the woman we caught picking it up, and another woman was paid to drive one of Ms. Hagerty's vehicles around town. We believe your employer has her grandson. Do you know of any other properties she owns? Some place she would go to vacation or something?"

"I...I...she didn't tell me anything."

"Okay. Tell me about Charles Haus. Do you see him often?"

"He comes by, yes. They are romantic."

"Do you know what kind of vehicle he drives?"

"I don't know cars."

Charles Haus had been at the store, and to the best of our knowledge, still was, but I had a feeling that was a load of BS also. I got on my phone and contacted the two officers who replaced Bishop. We hadn't heard from them in a few hours.

"He's still inside," one said.

"Every strip mall shop has a back entrance. Did you keep tabs on that?"

"His vehicle is still in the parking lot."

"Doesn't mean he is. I need one of you to go in and check. Now, please."

"Got it," he said.

I asked a patrol officer to sit with the maid while we did the search. I didn't believe she knew anything, but I wasn't about to send her off before we finished the search.

I scanned the large living space looking for something, anything, to catch my eye. The place was straight out of the pages of a decorating magazine, yet void of personal connection, just like the Rockman home. The only photo of a person from Hagerty's family was one of Ryan and Mary at a park. I picked up the photo and studied it carefully. I yelled for Bishop the minute I recognized the wood and metal chimes in the playground.

"That's the park near where we found the first planted evidence," he said. "Is she playing us?"

"I think she thinks she's too smart to be caught."

My cell phone rang. It was the officer at the jewelry store. "He's gone. There's another employee here. Said he left a few hours ago. Best guess is it was between when Detective Bishop left and we arrived."

"Did the employee say where he went?"

"Just that he was expected back tomorrow."

I said thanks and told him to bring the employee in for questioning.

"He's not under arrest," he said.

"You did pass the police academy final exam, right? We don't need to arrest him to bring him in. Just tell him we have more questions. Do not tell him it's about the missing kid. Leave him in a room, and we'll take over when we get back."

"Yes, ma'am."

I hung up the phone. "Dammit. She picked him up," I said.

"In what vehicle?" Bishop asked.

I headed toward the garage. There were two spots clearly used for vehicles. The one closest to the home's entrance was relatively clean. The other one looked like someone had been off-roading or mudding recently. Dried mud flecks were splattered on the cabinets next to the spot, there were remnants of Georgia clay.

Bishop stared at the dirt. "Shit."

"Looks like Mary's an adventurer," I said. "Or someone she knows is."

He picked up a piece of the clay. "And the kid is somewhere close."

Bishop stayed at Hagerty's home to finish out the search. We had three women and one man in separate rooms at the station awaiting additional questioning. Bubba dug through both Charles Haus's and Mary Hagerty's recent financial transactions one more time to see if he could pinpoint a location where they might be hiding out, while Ashley and Nikki returned from the search with evidence to process.

"Michels and Emmett are interviewing our guests," Jimmy said. "But none of them seem to have any information about where Hagerty might be."

I stared at the whiteboard, every bit of information and each photo formed into one big, blurred mass. I chewed on my fingernail, then removed my bun and let my hair fall over my back. It had grown so much since I moved to Hamby. Bishop once called me Rapunzel, but it was the perfect length to toss into a bun and forget about, except when that bun gave me a bigger headache than I already had. "She's been playing us all along."

Jimmy stood beside me. "It seems so. What I don't get is why she needed the extra insulin. If she had enough in the fridge at the Rockmans' house, why would she need more? Are they planning to run, or did whoever she's got watching the kid screw it up?"

"To run. Here's how I see it happening. Charles Haus is the doer. He pulled the trigger, but the kid was home, and he came downstairs when he heard the shots. Haus freaked because Ryan wasn't supposed to be there. He calls Hagerty, who rushes over, grabs what she can, and leaves with the kid. The murders happened sometime after noon and probably before five thirty, which gave Hagerty time to make arrangements for Ryan. She plans to hide the kid until the pressure's off, and then she'll have whoever's got him drop him somewhere."

"Because she wants custody of the kid?" he asked.

"I can't see that. Not with her current lifestyle, but if something happens to the kid, then the estate left to him from his parents' deaths would go to whom?"

"When you get the answer, let me know. This just makes me realize I've got to start planning for my own kid's future."

I smiled. He would be a great dad. "I'm really excited for you two."

"I know, and once this case is over, and Sav's ready to share the news, we're going to get drunk, or, I'm going to get drunk, but we'll celebrate."

I laughed. "Sounds like a plan."

He went back to investigation talk. "I'm assuming you've had people on Hagerty's neighbors to check if they've seen anything?"

"Do you know where Hagerty lives?"

"Just in town."

"She's next to the Tombstone house. Those people can't see their neighbors over their privacy fences."

"Figures. What stumps me is why Mary would think the kid wasn't home? She even said her daughter was overprotective."

"I'd say that was BS, but Heather Maynor confirmed it." I jotted a few things down on the side of the whiteboard. "I think maybe Emily did have a plan for the kid, but it either fell through, or she wasn't honest with her mother. Maybe Mary wanted to take the kid, and she didn't want her to, so she lied." I thought about that for a minute. "And given that Emily's been depositing cash into an account for M. Hagerty, I'm guessing she didn't trust Hagerty and didn't want her near the kid, so she lied." I tapped my pencil on the table. "The why, Jimmy. It's got to be something bigger than money. Why would Mary Hagerty kill her daughter for a couple thousand bucks a month?"

"Why did Jeffrey Dahmer chop people up and eat them?"

"Because he was a fucking psycho."

"Aren't all killers?"

I shook my head. "Some are desperate. Some manipulated. Some angry."

"Then maybe that's Mary Hagerty."

"Which one?"

"All of them." He took a dry erase marker and drew a circle around Charles Haus's photo. "What if he's the mastermind of this? What if he manipulated Hagerty into the murders?"

"Don't tell me you share Bishop's *grannies don't commit murders* theory."

"I'm just looking at this from every angle."

"Understood. So, what, you think she could have pulled the trigger because Haus manipulated her into doing it?"

"I think we have to consider it."

"Emily's been paying Haus for a few years, but he's never touched the money. She's been paying Hagerty too, and she's taken it."

Jimmy nodded. "And she's also giving Haus cash. It could be the cash her daughter was giving her."

"Right. The money in her regular account from Emily is being spent on rich-people crap along with the twenty-two thousand bucks a month her ex gives her. The cash deposited into the account goes in as cash and then comes right out in cash. We don't know where it goes from there, but I think it's safe to assume it's going to Charles Haus, which is probably part of the reason he's not touched that other account."

"Saving for a rainy day or vacation money?" His tone was lighthearted and frustrated at the same time. "Or biding his time until the bigger payoff?"

"He said he closed the bank account, so maybe he thinks the bigger payoff is coming, and he wanted to make sure he got that other cash before we caught on? I can't say why he was holding onto that money, but it's out of the account now, and we couldn't do a thing about it."

"You think the big payoff is the money from the Rockmans' estate."

I nodded. "Whether the kid is alive or not, Mary's probably one of the people that'll get some of the cash. Maybe she wanted it, and this was the plan all along. I don't know, but it's the money, it has to be."

"Then I think we're right. The kid wasn't supposed to be there. Now she's covering her ass."

"But she's taunting us, Jimmy. She had to know we had eyes on her."

He shook his head. "You're overthinking her intelligence level. She's desperate. She's covering her ass because she's worried we're getting close, not because she thinks we're already onto her."

"I guess that's the way we play it, then."

"Go home, Detective. It's past midnight, and you're running on empty."

"I will, but I want to make sure I'm right about what happens to the money."

I desperately wanted to talk to an attorney, but it was close to three a.m., and while normally they don't request fees from police for legal information for investigations, at this hour, it would probably be double. I did talk with the DA, but wills and estates weren't her specialty, and she didn't want to commit to anything.

After several deep dives into the web, I did find something about estate laws in Georgia, which took me down a rabbit hole of legal jargon similar to a foreign language, but the best I could guess was anything left to or in the name of Ryan Rockman, who, to the best of my knowledge, though I'd asked Bubba to check, did not have a will, would go to the next person in the family line. Probate court would make the decision who that person was, and if it was more than one person, there would be an agreement made if possible, or the judge would decide where the cash went.

I played it out in my head. Mary Hagerty discovers one twin impersonating the other. She confronts her, learns Melodie is dead. She begins blackmailing her daughter to keep her secret. She tells her boyfriend, who decides to join the party, manipulating them both financially. But Emily's had enough and tells her mother she's not paying anymore. Desperate for the cash, she and Haus work a plan and kill the father and Emily so Hagerty gets the kid and the cash to raise him. It would be a big life change, but nannies and maids would probably be the ones raising the boy. But when the kid winds up home at the time of the murders, they panic and take him. Their choices are to hide the kid and let the police find him, have him mysteriously appear, or kill him.

But a dead kid's money would be split between family members, and that included Randy Rockman and Hagerty's ex-husband. Less for her, which I suspected Haus didn't think was cool.

But I wasn't sure they'd take the risk with the kid living too. It's possible Rockman's brother could have won a custody battle against Mary. He's got a wife and the means to raise the kid. Mary's past her prime, single, and not living a life a kid could easily fit into. But did she think killing the kid would get her a chunk of cash? Probate court could decline a case at the request of the family if they agreed upon a settlement between them, but I couldn't see Hagerty taking the risk to find that out before killing the kid.

If this was about money, either Mary Hagerty was ill-informed about estate law, or she'd been manipulated by someone else.

I picked manipulated by someone else, and the pieces of the puzzle finally began to fit together.

I took a shower in the department's fitness center and felt refreshed. It wasn't a night of sleep, but it was the best I'd get until we had the boy back in our hands. I headed to the room we'd put the man in, checking my watch along the way. He'd been there for hours and would be pissed off that no one had come in to talk to him after telling him why we were keeping him, but that wasn't my problem, and given his record, he was probably used to it. We had the legal right to hold him for up to forty-eight hours without charging him with anything, and we hadn't passed that mark yet.

"He's not going to be happy," I said out loud. "But hopefully he—" I yelped when someone tapped on the back of my shoulder. I turned around with my fist drawn back.

"Whoa." Kyle put his hands out in front of him. "Hold on there, Detective. I'm unarmed."

"What the hell are you doing sneaking up on a cop?"

"I've been looking for you for over an hour."

I blushed. "Oh, sorry. I was in the shower. What's up?"

"We sent Marshall home."

"Marshall?"

He flicked his head toward the door. "The guy you were just talking to yourself about."

"*You* sent him home? Why?"

"Technically, Jimmy sent him home, but I recommended it."

"Did anyone credible question him?"

"Do you consider me and Bishop credible?"

"I didn't mean it like that. So, he doesn't know anything?"

"I didn't say that."

I checked my watch again. "Can we move this along, please? I'm trying to find a kid." I immediately regretted the harshness in my tone.

"Frederick Marshall, or Freddie, as he prefers to be called, has six arrests and two convictions for assault and battery, and theft by taking. He did time in Alabama."

"I know that. He got out of prison a year ago."

"Where he shared a cell with Richard Haus."

My eyes widened. "Holy shit. Is he—"

He smiled. "Chuck's brother. We made the executive decision to send Freddie on his way, knowing he'll lead us to good ol' Chuck. We've got his cell tapped and eyes on him. We'll find the boy, Rachel. Soon."

My stomach growled, and my cheeks reddened again.

"When was the last time you ate?"

"When good old Chuck had food delivered. Still angry with myself for eating it, but I was starving."

"How about we make a quick run to Waffle House? It's not gourmet food, but I don't think your stomach cares. We can't do anything now, anyway. God's not even awake yet, and Bishop went home to catch some shut-eye."

"Fine," I said, though I was going under duress. I wanted to stare at the whiteboards until something made sense because nothing in this investigation made sense.

Kyle drove to the Waffle House on Main Street in Alpharetta. I ordered the all-star special with a side of hash browns and laughed when the server read off the order to the cooks.

"That really is a unique ordering system," Kyle said.

"I read a blog about it shortly after moving here. It's pretty intense."

"I can admit to being a fan of the food."

"Drunk or sober?"

"Yes."

I laughed. "In Chicago the drunk food of choice is White Castle or Taco Bell. I tried the White Castle equivalent here but wasn't impressed." I realized then I had no idea about Kyle's past. Where he grew up, if he'd been married before, what made him become DEA.

"Krystal's takes a special kind of person to stomach."

"So does White Castle, trust me." I sipped my coffee. It wasn't great, but as long as it had caffeine, I was happy. "So, we never talk about you. Where are you from?"

He smiled. "Ah, I see we're into the getting-to-know-each-other stage. Progress."

I shrugged. "Baby steps, remember?"

"My father was Air Force, so I've lived all over the world, but I was born in Sacramento. We moved to the booming metropolis of Altus, Oklahoma, when I was in seventh grade. I went to college in Oklahoma, then dropped out and headed south. I lived the beach life in Panama City for a few years, then went back to college, got my degree, and applied to the DEA."

"Why did you choose the DEA?"

"Panama City is a party town. Always has been. While there, I got involved in the scene and wound up in the back seat of a DEA agent's vehicle for being involved in a situation I shouldn't have been involved in. He let me go, and it changed my life. Scared me straight, I guess. And I decided to try and do the same for other idiots like me."

"Wow. That's not at all the story I expected."

"Most DEA agents have some history with drugs. It's usually a family member with an addiction, but in my case, I was the one heading that direction."

"Did you go to rehab?"

He shook his head. "I wasn't an addict. Yet."

I nodded. "You ever see the guy who let you go?"

A smile stretched across his face. "I reported to him for three years."

I laughed. "That's awesome."

"It was. He's a great man. Retired a few years ago, but we keep in touch."

They brought our food, and I changed the subject while I devoured the greasy plate of heaven.

"We need to find the kid. Today. We put BOLOs out on both Haus and

Hagerty, and they're now officially suspects, but it's not enough. We need that kid alive, Kyle. Today."

An hour later, Kyle knew every detail of the investigation. His input wasn't any different than mine, so at least we were on the same page.

Bishop arrived back at the department shortly after us. He'd gone home to sleep but couldn't. Instead, he showered and returned with a change of heart. He'd finally turned ahead in the book and landed on the same page as me too, though I knew it disappointed him to realize a grandmother could be so evil.

"I have seen five-year-olds show no remorse for killing a dog," I said. "Some people are just innately evil." My cell phone rang. I didn't recognize the number. "Detective Ryder."

"This is Juanita Flores. I left the house this morning, and someone was here while I was gone. The front door was open. I think the lock is broken, and the house, it is a mess."

"Are you in the home now?"

"*Sí.*"

"Okay, I need you to get out of there immediately. Get in your car and drive to the end of the street and wait for us. I'll call you as soon as I'm there and it's clear. Do you understand?"

"*Sí.*"

I disconnected the call. Bishop and Kyle stared at me. "Someone's been to Hagerty's place." I contacted dispatch to send patrol there as we rushed to our vehicles.

13

Bishop stared at the ransacked living area. "She said the place was a mess? That's an understatement."

"Someone was looking for something," Kyle said.

"The question is, did they find it?" Bishop asked.

"And what was it?" I asked.

Ashley and Nikki worked in tandem photographing the scene and scanning for prints. They worked well together. Ashley stood and studied something on her phone, then she walked over and handed it to me. "Look at this."

It was a split-image photo with a fingerprint on each side. "Those look the same."

She nodded. "I freaking love technology. I'll have to run it for verification, but it looks like our jewelry guy was here and..." She took the phone back and then swiped to another split-image photo. "So was your buddy from last night."

I examined the photos. "Shit. We have eyes on this guy. How'd he get away?"

I immediately contacted the officer watching Freddie Marshall.

"He's not left since I got here, Detective."

"Who was there before you?"

"Uh, Jenks, but his shift is over."

"Okay. Make yourself invisible, please."

"Yes, ma'am."

"Who's Jenks?" I asked Bishop. "I thought I knew everyone now."

"He's one of the new guys."

"We put a new guy on a homicide investigation? Son of a bitch!" I called dispatch and had them give me Jenks's cell number. It went to voicemail after five rings. I disconnected and tried again.

Five tries in and he answered. "What the hell? I'm sleeping!"

"This is Detective Ryder with Hamby PD. Did you sleep on your watch last night?"

"What? Who...oh, shit. I mean, yeah, I might have dozed off once or twice, but the guy was home sleeping. He wasn't going anywhere."

"You dumbass, he was watching you a hell of a lot better than you were watching him!"

"Shit, did he leave?"

I held the phone to Bishop. "I can't with this idiot."

Bishop ripped him apart, but in that soft Southern way he had. I just wanted to kick his ass.

Kyle remained calm while I tried to chill.

"I need a fucking cigarette."

"This is good, Ryder. It's all good."

I raised my upper lip. "Are you serious? We lost a suspect. How's that good?"

"Look," he said. He stood behind me and made me stare at the rifled-through room. "You know what this means?"

I took a breath, and when it hit me, I turned around and my nose hit his shoulder. "Hagerty's not with Haus!" I stepped back and chewed my fingernail. "Well, I'll be damned. Maybe Bishop's right. Maybe grandma has a heart after all."

If Haus tossed Hagerty's house, it was either because he was looking for something or because he was pissed. I figured it was both, which meant she changed the game on him. We could solve this thing a hell of a lot faster with the two main suspects at odds. We just had to do it before one killed the other.

Richard Haus worked at a small car repair shop in Roswell.

He didn't greet us with open arms. "I don't have to talk to you."

I smirked. "Nope, but I'm sure your parole officer would love to hear what we have to say."

He threw the greasy blue cloth in his hands onto the car hood and spit out the toothpick he'd been chewing. "What's this about? I ain't done nothing wrong."

"Murder one sounds like something," Bishop said.

"What the fuck? I ain't involved in no murder. You got the wrong guy." He picked the toothpick up off the grimy floor, swiped it on his also grimy pants, and stuck it back in his mouth.

He pled the fifth to every question we asked. It would have been funny if he wasn't such an asshole.

"Okay, that's enough," I said as I removed my cuffs from my belt. "Let's take this to the station and see if you change your mind."

Panic filled his eyes. "I gotta work. I can't go to the station."

"Then you'd better start talking."

"I told you, I ain't involved in no murder."

Bishop crossed his arms over his chest. "You and your brother close?"

"Not close enough for this shit."

"He owns a jewelry store. Seems a lot classier than you."

"He ain't classy. He solders shit together, that's all. Only reason he owns the place is because the owner sold it to him for a buck when he was dying. Said he didn't want his kids to make any money off him. Guy was a shitty-ass father just like mine, treating his kids like that."

Interesting but beside the point. "Do you know anything about your brother's relationship with Mary Hagerty?"

"Is that the woman from the country club? With the big hair and lots of paint on her face?"

That was an on-point description of her. "Yes."

Bishop removed a photo from the file and shared it with him. Richard Haus nodded. "Yeah, that's her. What about her?"

"Can you tell us about their relationship?"

"I wouldn't call it that," he said, laughing. "I'd say it's a mutually beneficial opportunity."

"How so?"

"She's got cash and needs, and Charlie can fulfill those needs."

I cringed.

Bishop cleared his throat. "Are you referring to sex?"

"If that's what you wanna call it with an old lady."

I pressed my lips together. The old lady was about Bishop's age. He wouldn't take kindly to that. "Where can we find your brother?"

He checked his watch. "At work."

"Nope. Guess again," I said.

"I don't know, then. Told you we ain't close."

"He's not at work, and he's not at home. Is there anyplace else he could have gone? Maybe a family property or something?"

"We don't got none of that, but he's got a small cabin in Ellijay. You check that?"

I furrowed my brow. We hadn't found anything on record for him in Ellijay, but a cabin in a small town made sense. "He owns it?"

"The store owner gave it to him too."

"When did the owner die?"

He shrugged. "'Bout five years ago, I reckon."

"You know his name?" Bishop asked.

He shook his head.

"You know where the cabin is?"

"Said Ellijay."

"Where in Ellijay?" Bishop asked.

"Don't know. Don't care."

We asked a few more questions that got us nowhere, but he did answer about Freddie Marshall.

"That POS ain't right in the head. If my brother's hanging with him, he's doing something bad. I'm tough, but even I don't mess with Marshall."

"Mr. Marshall was recently released from custody, and we'd like to ask him more questions. Do you know where we can locate him?"

He shook his head. "I'm clean and following the law. My year in with him was more than enough to scare me straight."

I handed him my card. "You hear from either of them, you let us know, okay?"

He gave me a once-over, his eyes trailing over my body so slowly I wanted to throw up. "Oh, I'll be callin' you, babe."

Bishop stepped in front of me with his hand on the grip of his gun. "Back off." His face was blood red as we walked to the car. "Did you see the way he looked at you? Asshole."

I smiled. "Thanks for sticking up for me, Dad."

He rambled on about respect and manners until we were back at the station. I spent the time half listening and wondering how we would find Charlie Haus and where Mary Hagerty and Ryan Rockman were hiding out. We couldn't just drive to Ellijay and start knocking on doors. We needed an address or something close to one.

I'd been going through Mary Hagerty's ever-increasing file trying to figure out where she could be and if she had the kid. If it was Haus that ransacked her place, why? What happened between them? Did she change plans? Did she hide something from him? Where was Mary?

Bishop and I spent the better part of the day circling back over everything we'd done and what we knew. Bubba searched real estate records for Ellijay, but he hadn't found anything in Haus's name. He'd discovered the name of the jewelry store's previous owner, but he hadn't yet found anything about a home in Ellijay. The home could have belonged to someone else, a family member, perhaps, and never transferred into the next owner's name. It was common practice for small towns and cabins in the woods, which didn't make our situation any easier. But Bubba was good, and he'd find something. It would just take time.

He rushed into the investigation room. "I found him!"

I glanced up at the clock. It was past seven. I had no idea the time had gone by so fast. The clock was ticking. She'd have to get medicine for him soon if either of them was still alive. "Who?"

"Charles Haus. I got an alert for his credit card. He's at Old Timers in Ball Ground."

I grabbed my things. "Text me the address," I said, and rushed out the door, saying, "You rock, Bubba!"

Bishop knew the bar and the back roads to get to it. It was a dump. As a female, I wasn't comfortable, but as a cop, I knew I could handle the crowd. I examined the bar as we walked in. Large tables set up like a family-style restaurant sat in three rows in front of the long bar. There were at least twenty-five seats at the bar itself, and in total, probably forty people in the place. There were just as many outside. They weren't my crowd, and I had a feeling they wouldn't like me and Bishop either, whether they knew we were cops or not.

We had to handle this delicately. The crowd was big enough to cause a problem, which was why Bishop called for backup, but I requested they stay outside while we handled things inside. Bringing in too many uniforms into a dive bar filled with people never ended well. We were better off two on one—if, of course, the rest of the crowd wasn't interested enough to jump in. I had a feeling that was the case. Charlie Haus didn't appear to be all that popular, sitting alone at the bar with a bottle of whiskey and a shot glass in front of him. He wasn't dressed in his fancy suit, and he hadn't brushed his hair probably since we met. He was stressed, and the worry and frustration on his face solidified that for me.

I walked over to the man and flipped my jacket to show my badge. He knew I was a cop. He'd already seen the badge before, but sometimes it's just fun to piss off an asshole, and I wanted to make a statement to the rest of the patrons. "Charlie Haus. I'd like you to come to the station for a little chitchat."

He swiveled around to me, then back to face the bartender. "For what?"

"We'll talk about that when we get there."

"I'm busy."

"We don't much care, sir," I said.

"Let me finish my bottle," he said.

I assumed he meant that for me, but since he wasn't facing me, I couldn't be sure. "You talking to me? Seems a fine gentleman like you would talk face-to-face when talking to a woman."

He swallowed back another shot of whiskey. "A woman? I don't see no woman. All I see are pigs."

At least he was finally showing us his true self. I shrugged when the bartender made eye contact. "Well, then." I took a few steps closer and whipped his chair around. "Let's finish with the politeness, then."

Bishop stepped toward us. I motioned for him to stay back. He wasn't far, but far enough that Haus knew he was dealing with me and not with my partner. I needed to make a statement. If Bishop handled it, the room full of men would be on him, but they were less interested in taking on a woman. I couldn't guarantee that, but I played my card that way, and I won the round.

Haus removed his feet from the lower bar of the stool and stood. Big men didn't intimidate me. I had a gun. Two, actually. One on my side and one in my boot. Unfortunately, I didn't know if he had any. I did a quick visual body scan, but there were no substantial lumps anywhere. And I mean anywhere.

He stood on the heels of his boots, which I estimated gave him about nine inches on me. I guessed his weight at about two-fifty, which was double my size.

This could escalate quick. I knew it, but I didn't care. I wanted him to come at me. I prayed for it. Sometimes the sweet release of someone pushing back was the best part of an investigation. Unless, of course, he had a weapon.

Thankfully, I had Bishop as backup.

"I want a lawyer," he griped.

"For what?"

"For whatever you're framing me for."

"Relax, you're not under arrest. Yet. My partner here is looking for a one-of-a-kind ring for his girlfriend, that's all."

He snarled at me. "Uh-huh."

"Fine, you're right, Chuckie. My partner isn't into trashy jewelry. We've got some questions, and we're pretty sure you know the answers. No harm, no foul. Just conversation."

His voice was hoarse, barely over a whisper. "What did you call me?"

"Your name."

"Fuck you, bitch."

Apparently, he wasn't a fan of the nickname I'd chosen for him. "I'll take your bad mood and raise you fifty."

He snarled again.

"Listen, I don't have all day, okay, so let's get a move on."

Haus casually poured himself another shot and pounded it back. He probably thought he was tough when he slammed the shot glass on the wood bar. "I don't give a shit what you want. You hear?"

Bishop stepped forward. I held up my hand and shook my head. "I can handle this kid."

"You fucking calling me a kid?"

"You called me a pig." I smiled. "I figured I owed you." I paused for effect. "You know what's funny? When we first met, you acted all civilized, but I saw right through that. I knew you were a piece of shit the moment I laid eyes on you. And look at you here, proving me right."

He stepped toward me.

I stood my ground and decided to play with him. Bishop would drag me over the coals afterward, but meh, such is life. "I know what you did."

"I didn't do nothing, and you couldn't prove it if I did."

I laughed. "Try me."

"Get off my case, bitch. You got something on me, then you deal with my attorney."

"Can you afford one, or should I contact the public defender's office?"

His chest was now an inch from my face. Bishop coughed.

"You don't want to do this in here," I said. I needed him outside. It would be easier to handle him in a less confined space. The fewer things for him to throw at me and the smaller the crowd to interfere, the better.

"I'll do what I want, where I want."

"Good, me too. So, let me be clear here, Chuckie. I'm taking you in whether you like it or not. We can do this the hard way, or we can do it the easy way. Easy way is you come outside, and we go happily on our way. Hard way is you come outside and do something stupid. Either way, I'll meet you out there." I walked toward the door and flipped around casually. "You coming?"

I turned and walked outside with Bishop lecturing me in my ear. "This guy is dangerous, Ryder. Knock it off."

"It'll be fine. We have backup if needed." Though I was pretty sure it wasn't needed. Chuckie was big, but he wasn't bright, and that was all I needed if he came at me, which I was confident he would. And I looked forward to it. It was always fun to take down a dumbass in front of his peers.

The parking lot was full of cars and motorcycles, and a small group of people had gathered near a red Ford F-150. When they heard Haus dropping multiple f-bombs in my direction, they stopped and stared.

Two cop cars were parked near the side of the lot. Both officers had stayed in their vehicles as requested, so the crowd wasn't too interested in them.

Haus smiled at the group, gave them a fist pump, and yelled, "I fucking hate pigs."

The group cheered him on. Cop haters were always the best part of my job.

I stepped close to Bishop's vehicle. He got on his radio and spoke to the two squads there. They stepped out of their vehicles and stood beside their doors.

Best I could tell, Haus won fights because of his intimidation skills, not because he knew what he was doing. He was strong, but strength didn't always equate to good fighting, and my hunch was Haus was more bravado than skill.

He glanced around at the onlookers and laughed. "Y'all want to see me kick these pigs' asses? I'm starting with the bitch."

Wow. He was a real sweetheart. Big difference from the reasonably polite guy he portrayed at the jewelry shop.

This would go fast. He popped his neck from side to side and came at me swinging. I leaned toward the right and stepped to the side when he tossed a left jab. "Missed. If you can get one in before I lose my patience, maybe I'll push for a lighter offense."

"Fuck you." He raised his leg and tried to kick me in the vagina.

I rotated and moved further away. "You do know that doesn't have the same effect on women as it does on guys, right?" I glanced at his package. "Probably can't feel a thing when it happens to you, though."

He kicked at me again and missed...again.

Bishop put his hand on his weapon. "Ryder. Enough."

"I haven't touched the guy." I moved around him in a circle. Years of kickboxing and specialized training gave me an edge. Haus's stupidity was just an added benefit.

"I'm going to beat you in front of all these people, and then, when you're home alone, I'm going to have my way with you and shoot you in the head."

Bishop dropped his own f-bomb. Everything about that could trigger me, and he knew it.

I maintained my senses, though my first instinct was to beat his ass. Out of nowhere, Haus punched me in the face. My cheek screamed in pain and went numb seconds later.

Bishop drew his weapon. "On the ground, asshole! Now!"

Haus ignored him, following up his punch with a left hook, but I stepped back and avoided it. "One punch is all you get." I smiled, though I really wanted to rub my cheek back to life.

He was in the zone. Bishop screamed at him to back off and drop to the ground, but he didn't hear him. He was too focused on me. His face was burnt red, and sweat poured down his cheeks like a summer thunderstorm on a hot day.

It was time to make a decision. Should I continue to play with his head, push him so he ended up with serious charges, and hopefully get him to confess to the murders and tell us where the kid is, or should I back off, keep it as professional as possible and walk away? Either way, he knew we were onto him, and that's what mattered.

Being a cop and doing the right thing when faced with someone like Haus was a challenge. I voted for the latter knowing he only had a few good punches in him and taking him down would be the highlight of the investigation.

I glanced at Bishop. "I've got this," I said.

He kept the gun aimed at the moron. The backups had their guns out too. The crowd just watched in silence. A few had their cell phones up, recording. Jimmy would have me for dinner if this got out.

When he drew his right arm back for the third shot, I stepped forward, hooked my right arm up under his, pushed him off-balance, and knocked him with my hip. He went down quick. I dropped into a squat and rolled him onto his stomach, balanced the weight of my knee on the middle of his back, then grabbed my cuffs and whipped them onto him in less than a minute flat. "You're under arrest for impeding an investigation and assaulting an officer. You have the right to remain silent. Anything you say can and will be used against you in a court of law. You have the right to an attorney. If you cannot afford an attorney, one will be provided for you. Do you understand these rights as I've just read them to you?"

Chuckie told me what I could do to myself.

I smiled up at Bishop. "All done."

He shook his head. "Jesus Christ, Ryder."

"What? Can't a cop have a little fun?"

The two officers stuffed Charles Haus into a squad car and took off for greener pastures while Bishop read me the riot act. "What the hell was that? You could have gotten us all killed." We walked to his vehicle as he continued. Once inside, he really let it out. He scrubbed his facial hair and dropped a few f-bombs. "You've done some dumbass things, but this one, this one takes the cake, Ryder. You put three officers and a parking lot full of people at risk. And we don't even have anything on this guy!"

My patience hit the wall. "Like hell we don't! We've got thousands of dollars deposited into his account by a dead woman and her mother. We've got a known relationship with the mother, who is also a suspect. We get him to talk, we've got the boy, Bishop. And forgive me, I might have gone a little off track, but that asshole wasn't going to go easily no matter what you did. Better I take the hit than you. If you would have had to fight back, the entire crowd of men would have been on our asses. You know that as well as I do."

"This wasn't the way to handle it. They got it on video. If that shows up online, we're screwed. The mayor will have Jimmy's ass, and shit trickles down, Ryder. You know that."

"I didn't do anything wrong. Let them post it."

"You don't have to do anything wrong. The country is anti-cop. You can breathe on video, and we lose our jobs. If you've got some sort of career death wish, that's fine, but don't drag me along for the ride."

I took a deep breath and exhaled. "You're right. I'm sorry. It was selfish and unprofessional. But he's involved, Bishop, and there was no way he'd come in without a fight. I thought I was doing right by you."

He smiled. "How's your face?"

"He's got a nice swing, but it'll be fine."

He glanced at my cheek. "It's going to bruise."

Dispatch interrupted me before I could respond. "All available units—"

Both of our cell phones rang. We looked at the phones and answered at the same time.

"We've located Mary Hagerty," Jimmy said. He repeated the address dispatch had just provided.

"She's dead?" Bishop asked.

"Affirmative," Jimmy replied.

"We'll be there ASAP," Bishop said.

We disconnected. I said, "We need to find that kid. Now."

14

There's always a countdown to finding a missing person. Every show on TV says it's three days or they won't be found, but that's only partially true. Most of the time it takes weeks, even months to find someone, deceased or alive. Often, missing people are never found, and that's the worst way to drop a case. Homicide is horrible, but it's worse when a family doesn't have closure and doesn't know what happened to their loved one. I couldn't let that be the case with Ryan Rockman. We had to find him. We had to bring him home safely, even if that home wasn't the one he'd had before, and even if he'd lost all of his family members. It was heartbreaking, but it was a much better option than the kid being dead.

Mary Hagerty's body lay on top of a dirt path just a few hundred feet from the Ellijay cabin belonging to the great-grandfather of the original jewelry store owner. When the body was discovered, Bubba was able to search the location by address and learned who owned it. It was still in the great-grandfather's name, which didn't make sense, but sometimes that was how things went.

We didn't have an exact time of death but knew it was within the past twenty-four hours. The heat sped up the stages of decomposition, and she'd already progressed quickly.

Bishop stared down at her, gagging into his handkerchief. The smell was awful, and the minimal amount of food I'd eaten threatened to make a return.

"How can you stand there and smell her like that?"

"I can't stand it," I said. "But as I've told you every time you ask me, I'm used to it."

"I'm never getting used to this."

Jimmy walked over. "Jesus, Mary, and Joseph. That's awful."

"Death usually is," I said.

Once the heart stops beating, the body stops working and its cells can no longer maintain homeostasis. But instead of just hanging out and waiting for embalmment or cremation, things happen, things inside the body erupt, and the consequence of that are disgusting. Doctors respectfully label it skin slippage, but it's more than that. It becomes an open environment for bacteria to feast, and Mary Hagerty's remains were a smorgasbord for bacteria.

Michels walked over and cussed. "Holy shit, that's—" He choked and then turned around and threw up.

I smirked even though I felt bad for the guy. It wasn't the first time he'd done that, and it wouldn't be the last.

Since Hagerty was part of our investigation, the Gilmer County Sheriff's Department and coroner gave us the case and body, but the sheriff's deputies stuck around to assist just in case. I figured they wanted to make sure we didn't screw anything up.

Barron walked over dressed in a pair of jeans and a fishing vest. "Looks like we got ourselves a winner," he said.

"Sorry to take you away on your day off," Jimmy said.

"I left the lake hours ago, just haven't had the desire to switch out of my fishin' clothes." He glanced at the remains. "Looks like a feeding frenzy going on here. Let me do my exam and get her in the cooler."

"Please," Jimmy said. His cell phone rang. He ignored it. It rang two more times, but he didn't even bother looking at it.

My cell phone rang then too. I glanced at it. "It's Savannah." I answered it. "Hey, we're at a scene."

"I need Jimmy, please. Is he there?"

Her voice worried me. "I, uh, yeah. Hold on."

He grabbed the phone from my hand and spoke without a greeting. "Babe, we're at a crime scene."

Jimmy's mouth dropped. I heard Savannah on the line, but her words were mumbled, and she was crying. "North Fulton? I'm on my way." He handed me the phone. "I gotta—"

"Oh my God! The baby!"

"I need you two to handle this," he said before racing away.

Bishop and Michels stared at me. I dropped my head into my hands. Tears immediately pooled in my eyes. I shook it off and swallowed back the massive lump forming in my throat.

"What's going—baby? What baby?" Bishop asked.

I realized my mistake. "They...Savannah's pregnant, but they haven't told anyone yet. She's not very far along. I hope she's okay."

He wrapped his arm around my shoulder. "I'm sure she'll be fine."

I toughened up, straightened my shoulders, and wiped the tears from my eyes as I stared at Mary Hagerty's remains. "We need to get this done, Bishop."

"Then let's do it."

Processing the scene took nine hours. I didn't know what day it was, what time it was, or what state we were in. I was exhausted, emotional, and distraught, all from the investigation and the fear of what was happening to Savannah and her baby. I hadn't had a call from Jimmy, but I knew he wouldn't call either until he knew something or at least had the chance to check in. And it was likely he didn't want to disrupt the investigation with bad news. Which meant it was probably bad news.

Poor Sav.

Poor Jimmy.

The poor baby.

I left the scene and headed straight to North Fulton Hospital. Charles

Haus was still sitting and sweating in a jail cell, but I didn't care. He could sit his butt there for another day and a half for all I cared.

The volunteer at the front desk sent me to Savannah's room. Jimmy stood at the edge of the bed while she slept. I snuck in quietly, stood beside him, and whispered, "How's she doing?"

"She's okay."

"And the baby?"

"He's okay now."

"What happened?" It hit me then. "Wait. He?"

He smiled. "He."

"Oh my God, Jimmy," I whispered. "Is she farther along than you thought?"

"Appears so."

Savannah spoke, and her voice was groggy and tired. "He promised me a girl first."

"I tried," Jimmy said.

"I knew he told you," she said. She still hadn't opened her eyes.

"I had to tell someone, so I figured your best friend was the least dangerous option."

"Unfortunately, I blurted it out at the scene." I shrugged as I glanced at Jimmy. "I'm so sorry."

"It's okay," he said.

I walked over to Savannah and cautiously grabbed her hand. "Are you okay?"

"I feel like garbage, and I could really use some caffeine, but that's a big no."

"Everything's a big no," Jimmy said. "Bed rest for the rest of the pregnancy, so basically five months."

I blinked. "You're that far along?"

"That's what they tell me."

"Wow. You're going to start showing any day now."

"Shut your mouth," she said softly.

I laughed. "What happened?

"I'm not really sure. One minute I was fine, and the next I was standing in a puddle of blood. I thought I was miscarrying." Tears filled her eyes, and the machine next to her beeped faster. It was her heart rate.

"No, don't tell me. Just relax, okay?"

She nodded and closed her eyes again. "Get out of here, Ryder. You have a kid to find."

"I'm on it." I grabbed her hand and squeezed. "I'm so glad you and the baby are all right." I meant that more than I could ever express with words. I hoped she knew it too.

Jimmy walked me out of the room. "What's the status?"

"She was killed there. The cabin's got enough stuff for someone to live there for a month at least. The garbage is filled with food and clothing we think belonged to Melodie Rockman."

"Do you think she has the kid?"

"If she did, he's gone now, and Chuckie doesn't have him."

"Then we're missing something."

"I know. We'll figure it out. You stay here."

"No, I'll be back. Savannah needs rest. She's been telling me to leave. I'm going to grab a shower and head back to the department."

"What exactly happened?"

"I'll fill you in later. It's a lot of technical terms, but at least she and the baby are going to be okay."

"Can I do anything?"

"Find the boy."

∼

I leaned against the table in the investigation room as Bishop and I traded ideas again.

Michels and every available officer with an assist from the Gilmer County Sheriff's Department were still on scene searching for Ryan Rockman. There was no sign of him anywhere at last update.

"Where the hell is the kid?" Bishop slammed his hands down on the table. "He's dead, Ryder. Someone's cleaning up after himself, and he's sitting in a cell next door." He was referring to Charles Haus. "He and Mary had a fight. Maybe she wanted to turn herself in for the boy's sake, so he killed her and did something to the boy."

I sighed. It was time. We'd batted softball theories for the last hour and couldn't come up with any hardballs. We were stuck. The case wasn't like any other. The only rule was there were no rules, and these people played the game well. "Let's go talk to Haus."

Nikki walked into the investigation room before we got up to leave. She held onto a single piece of paper. Her hand shook so much the paper blurred from the movement. "Detective, we have a problem." She handed me the paper. "It wasn't him."

"What do you mean?"

"It wasn't Haus. His fingerprints aren't anywhere." She handed me the paper. "Look at this."

"But it's his cabin. Could it have been wiped clean?"

"Sure, if he's talented enough to wipe just his prints. I don't think he's ever gone to the cabin. I couldn't find one print belonging to him anywhere. Neither could Ashley, but"—she smiled—"we found this."

I studied the image and notes, and my eyes widened. "Are you serious?"

She nodded.

"How did you get Melodie Rockman's hair?"

"From her wedding veil. It was in storage at the Rockmans' house."

"That's brilliant!"

"I was in a wedding a few weeks ago, and the bride got her hair extensions caught in the clips on the veil. I saw the dress in the box, and figured I'd give it a shot."

I handed the paper to Bishop. "You were right. How the hell could this happen?"

Bishop studied the paper. "But Kyle and Barron confirmed her death."

"No, Kyle confirmed a body was found, and Barron confirmed it was likely a match based on the dental records, but they weren't a one hundred percent match, and they were only photographs. Kyle even said they could have been manipulated, or Melodie could have paid off someone in Mexico to fake it all." I tipped my head back. "We were set up to believe Melodie died in Mexico."

He stared at the paper in disbelief. "I was right. I can't believe it."

I was proud of him and mad at myself for not following his gut. "That's why we didn't find any of Haus's prints at the Rockman house."

Bishop was energized. "She's killed three people and kidnapped her own son. Talk about wanting revenge."

"Let's just hope she hasn't killed her child."

Bishop was hot under the collar. He couldn't sit any longer, instead choosing to pace a circle around the table. "She did this for the child, Ryder. He's alive. He's got to be."

"She's been in Mexico for God knows how long, and we have no idea what happened to her there. We can't predict anything about her. We don't know who she is now."

Locating a missing child is hard enough, but locating a missing child and a previously presumed dead mother who's ghosted her life for three years is virtually impossible.

"We're starting over," Bishop said. "We need all hands on deck." He'd put together a list of people to interview again and divided them between me, himself, Michels, Emmett, and Kyle. "Best we can assume is Rockman returned from Mexico somehow and recently. She's killed three people, and if she's got her son, she's not going to be able to keep him long. He'll need medicine. He'll need food. She can't hide for long.

"I want her picture all over the news. I want it in every store, on every wanted list. I don't care what we have to do, but people need to see her so they can recognize her."

Michels said he'd make sure of it.

"Bubba," Bishop continued. "You check airlines, buses, anything coming in and out of Mexico, and any accounts directly or indirectly related to her with alternate middle names, first names, switched names, whatever you can think of. She's got to have money, and depending on how long she's been back, she could be running out of it. Find the money.

"Emmett, go to the school programs, the doctor's office again. Talk to everyone. Ask if they noticed anything different recently. Don't tell them why. Michels, I want you on that nanny. She's somewhere, and we need to find her. Talk to Juanita Flores. She's got to know something. Give her Hagerty's death notice. Oh, and contact Mr. Hagerty and let him know too. Maybe one of them knows something. Get to Juanita, and I don't care if she sits in a cell all day. Make her talk."

The fire in Bishop's eyes proved he'd had enough. I'd never seen that kind of anger from him, and I was glad to. It was my perfect motivation. It was time to find Melodie and let her pay for her crimes.

"I'll handle Haus," I said.

"With me," Bishop said. "He's in this, and we're going to find out how."

"I'm here to help," Kyle said.

"We need you on your Mexico contacts. We need to know what really happened to Melodie Rockman," Bishop said.

"Got it," Kyle said.

"Updates to me and Ryder every hour. You get something solid, any of you, you tell us stat. Everyone understand?"

We all understood.

I grabbed a cup of coffee and added a straight-up shot from an espresso pod to it. I needed the jolt of energy to handle Haus. Bishop's face was still red, and the scowl hadn't disappeared. We walked into the jail hallway, and I grabbed his arm before we reached the doors to the cells. "Maybe it's best I take him to interrogation."

"Why?"

"Partner, you look like you're about to stroke out. Go splash some water on your face or something. He'll be fine with me. I promise."

He took a deep breath and exhaled slowly. "I'll come in in a little bit. I need to calm down. Don't mess with him too much."

"Oh, I'm going to mess with him all right, but I'll wait for you to join the party for the good stuff."

He turned and jogged off with an impressive determination in his step.

I sauntered over to Haus's cage and gave him a big, toothy smile. "Hey, Chuckie, how's it hanging?"

He told me where I could stick it, if, of course, I had the tool for sticking.

"I understand men who constantly refer to the penis do so because they feel inadequate, so let me be clear. I'm not the least bit interested in your small penis."

He mumbled something about what he'd do to me when he was released.

I laughed. "Chuckie, you ain't going nowhere anytime soon." I guided him to the interrogation room, smiled up at the camera, and told him to smile too. "You look like less of an asshole when you smile."

Bishop walked in. I thought he'd at least give me a few minutes alone with the guy, but apparently not. He looked and acted refreshed. Splashing water on his face must have been magic.

He sat across from Haus. "Mr. Haus, how are you enjoying your accommodations?"

"Attorney."

I stood. "All right, then. We're happy to oblige, but I'll tell you right now, any potential deal we might have come to is off the table once the attorney arrives. You want to negotiate murder one charges, then I suggest we have a little chat first. You decide to take the risk, that's cool too. But let me explain what's going on so you can make an educated decision." I sat at the corner of the table. "Let's talk about how your prints are all over Mary Hagerty's house, and let's talk about homicide."

"Attorney."

"I'm not asking you to answer any questions, Haus. I'm educating you on your charges. Homicide is tricky. We have you for murder one, which, as I'm sure you know, in Georgia, is the only murder charge there is, and it comes with a pretty tough sentence."

He was stoic.

"Murder one encompasses three levels, and based on what we've learned, I can promise you one of these applies to you. First, a person acted with intent to kill another. Second, a person acted with depraved disregard for human life, and third, a person killed someone while committing a felony. That one, by the way, doesn't need to be intentional. It just needs to happen. You can also be a participant in a crime that resulted in murder and still go down for murder one, even if you didn't pull the trigger." I leaned back in my chair. "So, the way I see it, you talk, or we go with murder one." I laughed. "Who am I kidding? We're going with murder one anyway, but maybe we can stop you from getting the needle."

Bishop smirked. "Why don't you give it some thought?" He checked the clock on the wall. "You get one minute."

"I didn't kill nobody."

"We've got three bodies and a missing kid," I said. "At this point, we've got to assume the kid is dead too, and I'll be honest here, Chuckie. Child killers don't last long in prison."

"Think Dahmer," Bishop said.

He stayed quiet.

Bishop stood so aggressively his chair fell backward. "Okay, you want that attorney? Let's do it. We're going for the needle, and we'll get it. I'm tired of this bullshit!" His face reddened again. "You're going down for it, asshole, whether you pulled the trigger or not."

I sighed loud enough to switch Haus's eyes from Bishop to me. "Bishop, chill." I smiled at Haus. "My partner's got a kid. He's a little sensitive."

Sweat poured down his face. His hands shook so much he hid them on his lap. He licked his lips.

I tried a softer approach. "Listen, I know we kind of got off on the wrong foot, you calling me a pig and all, but the truth is, we can help you. But for us to do so, you need to help us. Just give us something we can move with."

He took a deep breath. "The kid ain't dead. At least not as far as I know. I swear."

"Where is he?"

"I don't know! Mary gave him to the nanny and was supposed to get him back, but she's ghosted me. I haven't heard from her for at least a day."

"Mary Hagerty's dead," Bishop said. "And we think you killed her."

"I didn't kill no one."

"But yet you're involved in three murders now. Maybe you should explain how that happened," I said.

"I'm a jewelry designer that owns his own store."

"Guess again," I said. "Business owners don't use shadow bank accounts to hold cash. The Rockmans and Mary Hagerty were paying you. We already know that." I looked at Bishop. "We tagged him from the start."

"I'm a jewelry designer that owns his own store," he repeated.

"And somehow, that makes you an accessory to murder," Bishop said.

Chuckie's cockiness disappeared. "You told me you'd work on the charges if I talked. I told you the kid ain't dead. Now, what're you gonna do for me?"

I smiled. I'd been the bad cop, the middle-of-the-road cop, and the good cop, and unfortunately, that one seemed to work best. I preferred bad cop, but I did what I had to do. The trick was making it seem real when I knew the guy was a dirtbag. I leaned forward, took a deep breath, and smiled even bigger. "Look, we want to help you, but we can't go to the DA without something that brings in Melodie Rockman. And when I say something, I mean damning evidence. Worst-case scenario. Best case would be her in cuffs." I leaned back. "You've got to know more than you're saying. Let us help you help yourself."

"I don't know where she is."

I nodded. "Let's try this, then. How did you meet Mary Hagerty?"

"She's a client. She likes diamonds. I made her a ring once. We got along, and we've spent some time together. Nothing serious."

"How did you meet Melodie? Where and when?"

He scrubbed his chin with his thumb. "About two weeks ago. She came into the store with Mary."

"How do you know it was her?" Bishop asked.

"Mary introduced us."

"Was this the first time you'd met her?"

He nodded.

He was lying, and I knew it.

"And Mary never said anything about her daughter to you before?"

He shook his head.

"But yet you know her grandchild isn't dead."

"Attorney."

"Fine," I said as I stood. "We'll get you that attorney."

I walked to the door, and Bishop followed. He held it open for me and then closed it behind him.

"He's lying his ass off," I said.

"Yup," Bishop said. "He's been in on it all along."

"Definitely. Now we let him sit there and sweat a little more. The longer he's stuck in that room, the more trapped he'll feel, and the more desperate he'll be. That's what we need. We'll get him an attorney, and he'll talk."

"We need more than that. We need Melodie Rockman and the kid alive."

I made arrangements with an officer to handle Haus's request for an attorney while Bishop and I headed to the investigation room to determine our questioning strategy, but Michels walked in before we even got started. "Pickens County Sheriff just found Ryan Rockman."

15

Bishop kicked his driving into high gear, leading the convoy of Hamby PD through the back roads of Fulton, Cherokee, and finally Pickens County toward the boy's location.

The curved, hilly roads of Pickens County didn't allow for NASCAR speeds, but at least the drivers had the courtesy to move to the sides of the two-lane roads to let us pass.

I checked the GPS. "We're still twenty-five minutes out. Where the hell is this place?"

"Bumble fuck."

I laughed. I'd used that term a time or two when I first moved to Hamby. "You're catching on."

Bishop turned right onto a narrow dirt road. It was less than a block long, ending at a T-intersection with a large white church on the top of a hill. It was one of those old Southern Baptist churches with the steeple in the front and large windows resembling eyes beside it and a long group of windows below.

I wondered if the windows would glow red like in the horror movie I saw years ago. "Dear God, that's an *Amityville Horror* house."

He laughed.

"You're in the Appalachian Mountains. There's a lot of sacred grounds in the area, but I'd say this is more along the lines of *Deliverance* than *Amityville Horror*." He shuddered. "Every man's worst nightmare."

I laughed as I leaned my head against the window. "I don't hear banjos."

"Thank God for that." His tone turned serious. "I hope the kid is really okay."

I tapped my foot on the floorboard, trying to release my anxiety about that very thing. "He is. You heard the deputy. Paramedics said his vitals are good, his blood sugar levels are normal, and his pump is working fine. Looks like whoever had him took care of him."

"And dumped him. The kid's lost everyone."

"He's still got his uncle. That's more than what a lot of kids have." I knew that better than most. The streets of Chicago are filled with broken families, missing fathers, addicted mothers. The children rely on grandparents or gangs to form connections and find a sense of belonging, and most of the time, the gangs win.

We arrived at the small gas station off Old Burnt Mountain Road. Bishop parked to the side of the ambulance. We couldn't see the boy, but given the crowd of officers around the ambulance, we knew right where to go.

A deputy approached us. "Detectives Ryder and Bishop? Deputy Rubens, Pickens County Sheriff."

Bishop nodded. "I'm Bishop, and this is my partner, Detective Ryder. How's the boy?"

"A little tired. Confused, but overall, he's good."

"It would be great if we could see that for ourselves," I said. "Though we are eternally grateful for your work."

"Of course."

We only took a moment to study the child and then retreated to a less populated area of the parking lot.

"The attendant said a woman brought him into the store and wandered around with him for a bit. He thought the boy looked familiar but was distracted by another customer. Next thing he knew, the woman disappeared, and the boy was left in the candy aisle. He checked online, saw it was the missing kid, and called it in."

"Does he have cameras?"

Deputy Rubens pointed to the camera in the front corner of the store. "Just a live feed."

The best advice I could give any business in any place in the entire country—the world, even—is to pay the extra monthly fee to record the live feed. Why more companies didn't was a mystery to me. "Where's the attendant?"

"We've got him inside still."

"I've got it," I said.

Bishop nodded and spoke to the deputy as I walked toward the building.

The older man stood behind the counter and fiddled with the small boxes of mints and gum near the front of the register. He smiled when he saw me. "Good evening, ma'am."

I showed him my badge. "Detective Ryder with the Hamby PD. I understand you're the one who called in the boy?"

He nodded. "Sure did. Thought he looked familiar, but I got a customer who couldn't get the pump to work right, so I went out to help, and the next thing I knew, the woman was gone and left the kid. Found him munchin' on a bag of Oreos in the back of the store. Boy didn't seem to notice he was alone."

He didn't know the half of it. "Did you speak with the woman at all?"

"No, ma'am. She come in, took the boy to the pot, and kept her back to me the entire time. I didn't even see her leave. Just heard the car and turned to watch it head left out of the parking lot."

"What kind of vehicle was she driving?"

"Not sure, ma'am, I didn't much pay attention to the car. Just wasn't thinking about it at the time."

"That's okay," I said. I could tell by his frown he was upset with himself. "I'm sure she left him with you because she knew you'd do the right thing."

He smiled. "I got me six grandkids and three greats. Can't imagine someone leaving her kid like that."

"I'm with you on that. Can you tell me what the woman looked like? What was she wearing? What color her hair was?"

"I gave the deputy a description, but I'm happy to tell you. She was

Hispanic. She had on a pair of them yoga pants. My daughter wears them. Black, and a big red sweatshirt."

"Tell me about her hair. Was it short? Long?"

"Hung down past her waist. My grannie used to have long hair like that. Always wore it in a braid until the day she died. Don't think she ever cut it once."

It had to be the nanny. "Did she hunch her shoulders or walk tall?"

He shrugged. "Can't say. Just saw the boy and the hair, then I got busy with my other customer."

"How did the boy seem? Did he ask for anyone?"

"Not a once. Just said he was thirsty, so I gave him some water. I asked his name, and he told me it was Ryan. That's when I knew for sure he was the boy in the pictures."

I smiled. "Thank you. Someone may be here to ask you more questions. In the meantime, if you think of anything else," I handed him my card, "please let me know."

"Will do." He bent down under his counter. I quickly placed my hand on my weapon. When he popped back up, he had a pack of mints in his hand. "For you. I know your job ain't easy."

I took the mints. "Thank you, you're a kind man."

"Do my best."

I headed over to the ambulance, pushing my way through the crowd of deputies and medical staff to at least introduce myself to the boy and see if I could get any questions answered.

I recognized the look of the woman sitting in the ambulance with him and knew I'd be out of luck. Her entire persona reeked of DFACS, Division of Family and Children Services. The scowl present on her face unless she was looking at the boy. Her protective posturing, shielding him from the growing crowd, and the biggest tell, her hand in my face when I stepped up into the bed of the vehicle.

She tossed out a firm and confident, "No, ma'am. He's mine until he's safe from harm, but first, we're getting him to the hospital to make sure he's physically okay." She smiled at Ryan. "And I'm sure you are fine, little guy. We just want to make sure you've got a warm bed and a lot of things to eat and drink, okay, sweetie?"

The woman was large and intimidating. Her dark curly extensions hanging just below her shoulders softened her militaristic attitude, but not enough to make me comfortable. She was the perfect representation of DFACS, and I suspected she did her job better than most. From what I could tell, Ryan was happy and healthy, but we'd need to talk to him soon. Sooner than later, if we had our way.

"What hospital?" I asked.

"What do you think?"

An officer standing next to me smiled when he saw my eyes bulge as I responded. "I'm not familiar with the area."

"The only hospital we take our precious children, Children's Healthcare of Atlanta. You're a cop and you don't know that? You might want to go back to the academy and learn your job."

I bit my lip to give her the respect she deserved, though I thought she could use a good smack of the realities of my job. It wasn't easy to keep my mouth shut, but walking away helped.

"She's a tyrant," Bishop said.

Deputy Rubens laughed. "She scares every deputy in Pickens."

I laughed. "I can see how that's possible."

Pickens County had a similarly sized crime scene tech department, which was ridiculously small but appropriate for the less populated cities. Ashley and Nikki assisted in processing the scene because it could take hours given the amount of traffic coming through the store daily. They needed to find something, anything, that would help our investigation and add the extra needed nail into the case. Something to verify who left the boy.

News traveled fast. Every major station in the greater Atlanta area planted themselves on the sides of the streets surrounding the gas station. People gathered, bringing toys, food, and gifts for Ryan Rockman. Most of it would end up in shelters, but it would be put to good use, and that's all that mattered.

Randy Rockman arrived at the scene about three hours after us. He rushed over to me. "Where's Ryan? Is he okay?"

"Your nephew is fine. They brought him to Children's in Atlanta, but his sugar numbers were good, and he was in a good emotional place. He's being handled by DFACS, but if you can get there to verify your relation-ship and fill out the thousands of pages' worth of forms, I'm sure you'll be granted temporary custody once we locate his biological mother and he's safe from harm."

"Who left him here? Did he say?"

"He said the lady, that's all."

"Then it couldn't be Melodie, right? He'd know his mother."

"That's not necessarily true, Mr. Rockman." It was interesting that he assumed it could be Melodie, that she was back, and that she'd come for her son.

"I...I don't think it was her. It couldn't be. She'd never leave her child."

"People do things we can't imagine."

"Do you think she killed Steve and Emily?"

"We're working hard to find out, Randy, and I promise you, we'll get to the truth." He didn't need to know the facts yet. Telling him could possibly put him in danger.

"I need to get to the hospital, but I want to get some of Ryan's things from Steve's house so he's got them with him. Can someone help me with that?"

"I'll make sure someone goes with you in the morning. Can you meet them there at eight?"

"Sure thing." He hugged me.

"Oh, this is..." Awkward.

"Thank you for finding my nephew, Detective."

If only I had.

"Mr. Rockman, even though it's likely you won't get to take your nephew home anytime soon, I suggest you get with an attorney about the process. It might not be as simple as it sounds."

"Thanks, Detective Ryder. I appreciate it."

Nikki rushed over to Bishop and me as we stood next to his vehicle. "There's thousands of possible pieces of evidence in that place." She waved her cell phone in my face. I grabbed her wrist to keep it steady. She blushed. "Sorry, this is just so freaking cool. I love technology."

I studied the photos. "How did you find this?"

Bishop looked at them. "Think those are the nanny's prints?"

Nikki nodded. "They were in the boy's room at the Rockmans' house. If it's not the nanny, whoever it is had that kid in this gas station."

"It could be Melodie Rockman," I said.

"I don't think so," Nikki said. "When Ashley found the wedding dress and veil, I found the wedding album stuffed in a box in the storage room. I ran prints from it. I can't say they're Melodie's, but there were only two sets of prints on the thing, and neither match the ones we found here."

"Where did you find the prints here?"

"On the bag of Oreos the kid had. Other than that, she didn't touch a thing. There weren't any of her prints on the bathroom door, so I'm assuming she used her shirt to open it. Probably did the same with the store entrance too."

I carried around a thing of sanitizer to kill the billions of germs attached to the stuff I touched, but even so, I usually tried not to touch anything in a bathroom with my bare hands. "Good job, Nikki. You're awesome."

She smiled, and as she walked away, I heard Ashley tell her, "I told you she'd like you!"

I eyed Bishop. He shook his head and laughed.

"Shut up."

He laughed, then his tone turned serious. "We can't guarantee the prints belong to the nanny."

"No, but we can go off the assumption they do."

"Assumptions don't get convictions."

"Then we need to find proof that our assumptions are right."

"Why did she leave the kid at a gas station?" Bishop asked.

"Maybe she was supposed to meet someone with the kid, and when that person doesn't show up, she gets scared and drops the kid off."

"Melodie Rockman?" he asked.

"Or Mary Hagerty."

"I think we need to turn up the heat on Haus," he said.

"Ditto."

~

Bubba manipulated photos of Melodie Rockman to match possible disguises and distributed them across the state. Michels had already sent the photo of the nanny out before, but he updated it with the most recent description we believed was her at the gas station. Emotions ran high throughout the department as we searched for a triple-murdering, child-abandoning dead woman and a nanny.

Jimmy called just before two o'clock. I'd been in the investigation room trying to connect the dots of everything we'd learned. I hadn't checked my watch in forever, and the early number immediately made me tired. My adrenaline cooled to lukewarm. I yawned when I answered, then immediately apologized and asked how Savannah and the baby were doing.

"They're holding their own. Update me."

I did.

"What're the odds of the woman at the gas station being Melodie Rockman and not the nanny?"

"Slim. Outside of the fingerprint, the description doesn't match."

"If Rockman's alive, she's coming for that kid. We need to find her."

"I know, and we're trying. She's been the invisible woman since her return. She planned this out well, Jimmy."

"Ryder," Bishop said as he walked into the room. "Put him on speaker."

"You're on speaker, boss. Bishop's here."

Bishop spoke. "Just got word from Bubba. There were three large withdrawals from Hagerty's account. Fifteen thousand."

"Three? So, not a check?" Jimmy asked.

"Cash at three separate ATMs," Bishop replied.

"Who's got cash withdrawal approval for fifteen thousand bucks?" Jimmy asked.

"A woman who gets twenty-two thousand a month in alimony," I said.

"Melodie's got her card," Bishop said.

"Hold on," I said. I put Jimmy on hold and called Ashley. "Was Hagerty's debit card in her wallet?"

"Nope."

"Thanks," I said and went back to Jimmy. "Ashley's confirmed Mary Hagerty's bank card wasn't on her when they found her."

"Get the bank's cameras. We need to see what she looks like."

"On it," I said and disconnected the call.

Bubba was crashed in the tech room. I hated waking him, but we needed him to get on the phone with the banks as soon as they opened. We needed to confirm it was Melodie taking the money from the ATMs.

I searched through my case notes. "Bubba said Mary was getting cash for a while and then it stopped. Could Melodie have been using Mary to bribe her twin for cash?"

"Doesn't sound right to me," Bishop said. "Why would Melodie take the risk of Emily finding out she was back?"

"Maybe she didn't care? Maybe she didn't come back with a plan. Maybe she and Mary made some kind of agreement? I don't know." I yawned. I was exhausted.

"Do me a favor, go home. Get a shower and a clean change of clothes. Maybe even catch a power nap. I'm going too. We need to be at one hundred percent to ride this out."

"We can't go home," I said. "We're so close."

"We can't afford to mess this up, either, and we're both exhausted."

Kyle waited in my driveway. An instant flash of relief washed over me, followed quickly by an uncomfortable wave of guilt. Lenny's words echoed through my head.

Tommy would want you to move on. He'd want you to find love again.

Lenny said that to me at least a hundred times, but I chose not to believe it because I wasn't ready. But in that moment, the guilt felt less damning, less intense, and I wondered if that was a sign from my dead husband. Maybe Lenny was right? Maybe Tommy did want me to love again, and maybe I deserved to be loved too.

I stepped out of my Jeep as he walked into my garage. "Hey, shouldn't you be sleeping?" I asked.

"Sleep's overrated."

I smiled. "That's what I tell Bishop."

"I know."

"I just came to grab a quick shower and head back to the station."

"I know, but I thought I'd check on you, and I wanted to apologize for getting it wrong about Melodie Rockman."

"You didn't get it wrong. The information wasn't right, and that was on purpose, but not by anyone you know."

"Still, I'm going to figure out what happened."

I sighed. "We'll get there. You haven't gone home yet, have you?" Kyle lived in the city, far enough to be a pain to drive to in the middle of the night.

"Nope. Didn't think it was worth the drive just to turn around and come back."

"You need to get some rest."

"So do you."

I couldn't argue that. "You can stay in my guest room if you'd like."

"How about a shower instead?" He quickly added, "In the guest bathroom."

"Sounds like a plan," I said.

I visited with Herman for a few minutes, feeling bad that he'd been neglected so much since our move to Hamby. Not that he noticed or cared. Fish don't engage with people, probably because of that whole threat-of-being-a-meal thing, but Herman and I did have an understanding. I provided a safe home and regular meals, and he provided an ear without any unsolicited advice.

It worked for us.

"I'll keep him company while you shower," Kyle said. "And if you'd like, I can make you something to eat. I'll shower after you so we don't ruin each other's water pressure."

"Okay, but you don't have to make me something to eat. My fridge is empty."

He held up his bag. "I brought provisions."

"Wow. You're like a God or something."

He smirked. "That's the way my mom made me."

I laughed as I walked back to my bedroom. As I showered, I tried to relax, breathing in and out slowly, stretching my shoulders, flexing and unflexing my muscles. My thoughts split between the investigation and Kyle, or really, my relationship with Kyle and how it impacted my relationship with my dead husband. It felt strange to think on those terms, but everyone with a deceased spouse will tell you it's possible to still have a relationship with a dead person. Granted, it's one-sided, but it's still real. I shook that off, forcing myself to focus on the here and now. The guilt surrounding my life with and memories of Tommy wasn't going anywhere.

Kyle made a salad with plenty of veggies, as well as tomatoes, cold chicken breast, and some dressing I couldn't identify. It was fantastic, and I didn't realize I was as hungry as I was until I smelled the dressing. "Wow. You've definitely defined your position as the chef in this baby-stepping relationship."

"Is that a compliment?"

"Best you're going to get."

I finished my meal and checked the clock on the wall. It was already five o'clock, and we'd had no word on Melodie Rockman or Ana Flores. I needed to be back in the office. "I'd love to chat, but I need to get back."

"I'll clean up," he said.

"No, don't." I set my things in the sink. "I'll get it later. Follow me back to the department?"

"Be happy to," he said.

I glanced at the photo of Tommy and me on the small table by the garage door as we walked out.

16

Kyle and I talked when we arrived back at the department.

"I've got some calls to make," he said.

"Kyle, it's okay. You don't have to—"

"No, I do, and I have an idea, so let me just run with it, okay?"

"You're not going to Mexico again, are you?"

"Not if I can help it."

"Good."

While Kyle worked his idea, I followed up with the DFACS woman, who hadn't softened at all, to check on Ryan Rockman. She said Ryan was doing well so far, but that he wasn't going to be part of any investigation on her watch. I told her I'd never put a kid in jeopardy.

But if the illusion of the appearance of the kid brought out a killer, I'd make that happen.

Bishop and I grabbed an extra standing whiteboard from storage and hiked it up to the investigation room, then filled it with the new details of the case. We couldn't wipe off the other boards, not until the case was complete. We'd have to take pictures of them for the DA, because if we left out anything in our reports, the photos might help us figure out what we missed.

Ashley went into the evidence removed from the house and grabbed a planner of Melodie's from the year she left for Mexico.

"Thanks," I said. "I thought I'd seen this."

"We weren't going to take it, but Nikki thought it might be important."

"She's almost as smart as you," I said.

"She's totally smarter."

Bishop and I reviewed it, put together a detailed map of the year leading up to the twins' trip, and we realized she had been struggling long before leaving.

She'd gone to a therapist, a behavioral specialist, and a psychiatrist. She'd lunched with Leah less and less as the year progressed, and even noted three separate times she saw Emily. She'd barely worked out, her business had decreased drastically to barely part-time, and there was very little social interaction outside of the home that included her husband.

"They were having problems," Bishop said.

"It looks like it."

∼

The receptionist knocked on the investigation room's door hours later. "The Haus public defender is back to talk to you."

"Back?" I smiled at Bishop. "Guess Haus had something to tell her, huh?"

The receptionist smiled. "I checked the sign-in log. She was here for about three hours last night."

Bishop smiled. "Here we go."

We met a young blond-haired woman dressed in black pants and a white-and-black striped blouse in one of the interrogation rooms.

"I've talked to my client," she said. Her voice squeaked like she was nervous. She looked like she was barely out of law school. "And he said you're willing to work with him. I'd like to know what you propose."

"We don't propose anything," I said. "We offered to help him, but he chose to invoke his right to you instead, so any possible deal is off the table."

"He won't talk without a deal."

"Then perhaps you should talk to him again." I stood. "Now, we have a triple-murder investigation to complete, so if you'll excuse us."

Bishop opened the door, and we left.

"Jimmy needs to change the way things are done around here," I said.

Bishop paid attention to traffic. "That's an understatement."

"No, I'm serious. We had eyes on Mary Hagerty, but she slipped through the cracks, and now she's dead."

"This isn't Chicago, Ryder. We don't have the staff or budget for that kind of work. We stick patrol on them, and if they get a call, they gotta take it. Shit happens. It's no one's fault."

"And that's why things need to change."

"I'm sure Jimmy's working on it." He pulled into the Dunkin' drive-through and ordered us coffees.

With still nothing on Melodie Rockman's or Ana Flores's whereabouts, Bishop and I decided to take a drive to Haus Jewelry to have a little one-on-one with Freddie Marshall and take him in for a minor parole violation. It was the best we could get on him, but we figured he knew something, and if we played our cards right, we'd have him spilling the beans about it. It was a long shot, but if nothing else, we'd parade Marshall by Haus's cell and let him think we knew more than we did.

Marshall wore a black blazer, blue slacks, a light blue shirt with a full cutaway collar, a solid black tie with a diamond clip, diamond cuff links, and black shoes. He'd shaved his head and face, going from ratty and redneck to bald and scary. The fancy clothes and diamond jewelry didn't cover his criminal soul, they'd just made him even creepier.

He glanced up at us as we walked into the store. Bishop flashed his badge, and Marshall quickly looked away. He knew we had his buddy. If he listened to the radio or watched TV, he had to know Ryan Rockman was found, and he knew why we were there.

"Mr. Marshall," Bishop said. "Surprised you're here today."

He smiled. "Got a job to do."

"Tell me this," I said. "Does a scumbag like you wearing the diamonds you're pushing actually make people want to buy them?"

"Eat shit, pig."

I nudged Bishop with my elbow. "Oh, look at that. He knows us."

"Well, I did show him my badge. I wouldn't say he's smart," Bishop said. "Classy dude, though, huh?"

"Very." I set my handcuffs on the glass counter. "Looks like you're closing for an undetermined amount of time, Freddie. You're in violation of your parole, and it's time for a meeting with your parole officer."

He blinked. "I didn't violate nothing."

"As you know," Bishop said. "We had people on you. Sure, you eluded them for a bit, but you're not as bright as you dress, and we clocked you arriving home two hours past your assigned curfew. That right there is a parole violation."

At least this round of eyes on someone worked.

A woman walked into the store with a parade of kids behind her.

"Store's closed," I said.

She tilted her head. "The sign says—"

I moved my jacket, and she stared at my waist.

"But I have something to pick up."

One of the kids tugged on her dress. "Mommy, that lady is mean."

"Honey, shush," she said. "I'm talking to the lady. I...I have something to pick up, and it's important I get it today."

"Sorry, but I'm pretty sure the store will be closed indefinitely."

"That's unacceptable," she preached and stomped her high-heeled foot. "I have six thousand dollars of diamonds, and I demand you let me have them!"

One of her little minions dressed in a white sundress and cowboy boots stomped her foot too. "Mommy! You said we could get minis from *Chick A Flay*."

Bishop turned and faced the woman. "Ma'am, we are in the middle of a criminal investigation. Best you walk out that door, get your kids Chick-fil-A, then go home and call your credit card company to cancel your transaction. We're closing this location for possible fraudulent activity."

"Fraud?" She stared at her obnoxiously large solitaire diamond wedding ring. "Are you saying my diamonds are fakes?"

Freddie Marshall didn't say a word. He just stared at the handcuffs on the counter as his sweat dropped little dots around them.

"I'm calling the police!" the woman exclaimed.

"We are the police." I rolled my eyes and walked toward her. "I'll tell you what. Wait outside," I said as I opened the door and let her minions run onto the sidewalk. "I'll get someone here to file a report, but you need to stay outside and away from the door. Am I clear?"

She huffed. "You don't have to be rude."

God, I hated women sometimes.

Bishop and I waited for the officer to arrive, allowed Freddie to lock up the store and switch the answering machine message to "on vacation," and headed back to the department with him riding silently in the back seat. We didn't bother making small talk. Letting him sit and sweat was a better option.

We walked him right past Haus's cell, slowing down so they could get a good look at each other. As Freddie began to speak, I squeezed his fleshy tricep to quiet him.

Bishop gave Chuckie a toothy grin. "How you doin', there, big guy? We brought your friend in for a visit."

We placed Freddie Marshall in a more secure cell with real walls instead of bars and a metal door. The men couldn't speak, which was exactly what we wanted. The plan was to let them sweat it out a bit, walk Freddie out to meet with his parole officer, bring him back a while later, then pull Chuckie out and tell him his buddy dropped the bomb of all guilty bombs right on his boss's chest. We'd eventually tell Freddie the same thing, blaming Chuckie for giving him up to us.

It was the easiest way to get someone to talk.

Jimmy met us in the investigation room with an update from Pickens County. He looked exhausted, but there was a small light in his eyes that gave me a ray of hope. I gave him a concerned, questioning look, and he shot me a thumbs-up. At least that was something.

"We'd had multiple sightings of a woman matching Rockman's general description. Right now, we've got people searching a private community. It's over a thousand homes and thirty-seven hundred acres. I'm sending Michels and Emmett out to take lead."

I eyed Bishop, but before I could say anything, he shook his head. He knew I wanted to be there when Rockman was caught, but he was right. We had people here to deal with, and they were just as important to this investigation. If they caught her, we'd get a call and get there ASAP.

"Anything on the nanny?" I asked.

"Not yet."

"When we finish with Haus and Marshall, we'll help," I said.

"We need you here," Jimmy said. "We need to know what happened."

"Yes, sir," I said.

Jimmy walked out.

"You ready?" Bishop asked.

I tapped my foot on the floor. "More than ready."

He stood. "Let's do this, partner."

We chose the weaker of the two links as our first victim. When working a suspect, it's always best to pick the loose cannon, the weaker of the bunch. Let them talk, share a few key details important to the investigation, then use those with some added creative verbal gut punches to make the big suspect spill the tea. That manipulation of suspects, stressing them out and getting them to throw their partners under the bus was the best part of the job, and I took great joy from it. I wasn't sorry for that, either.

Bishop knew my strengths, and every cop knew a bitch with a badge had more impact on an investigation with men involved than any male detective could have.

Why?

Because in general, men are intimidated by women, and female cops know how to use that to our advantage. It was a game, and it wasn't always easy, but it was worth the effort.

"Wait," Kyle said. He ran up from behind us. "That idea I had panned out, and it's perfectly timed, I might add."

"Really? What'd you find?"

"I got Marshall."

"Oh? How?" I asked.

"He set up a bank account for Melodie Rockman."

"What?" Bishop asked.

We followed Kyle back to Bubba's office.

"I contacted the bank, and the representative who helped him open the account still works there," Bubba said.

"Wait." I looked at Kyle. "I thought you were going to contact people in Mexico?"

"I did," Kyle said. "I told them we'd learned Melodie was still alive, and they did a little research. Turns out a truck carrying women turned over and caught on fire. Most of the women escaped, and I got in touch with someone who's part of the sex trafficking recovery group that's working to rehab the women. She connected with one of the women in the truck, showed her the photo of Melodie, and the woman confirmed it was Melodie."

"Shit," Bishop said. "That's great news, but how's it connect to Marshall?"

"Through Haus, who was in Mexico at the time of the truck accident."

"Haus? How? Why?" I asked.

"He was working as a mule for the cartel. He used an alias, but I had a hunch and was able to get his picture out to our team there. One of them recognized him."

"He came to me to run a check on Haus's bank accounts," Bubba said. "Because he thought Haus might be laundering money for the cartel or something, and that's when I discovered something funky with that account he just closed. I did a little digging, and we found the connection to Marshall."

"So, Haus was in Mexico when Melodie was?" Bishop asked. "Un-fuck-ing-believable."

Bishop and I were in shock. It took over an hour, but Kyle and Bubba provided a detailed evidence map that confirmed murder one charges for Haus and Rockman. And if we could find Melodie, she would go down with them too.

We'd stuck Marshall in a cold, impersonal interrogation room, one of three the department called "the dungeon" even though it was on the main floor of the building. It got its name from the gray-painted cement walls, matching cement floor, and sterile steel table with hard, extremely uncomfortable metal chairs, and a solid metal door. It was designed that way intentionally, and it was the favorite spot for intimidation.

I walked in with Bishop following behind. I played good cop with a heavy dose of intimidation to drive my point home. "Mr. Marshall, thank you for waiting. We've had a busy several hours, but I'm happy to report things are moving in the right direction. Of course, that direction is only right for us, and I do apologize for that, but when a guy like you plays in the big leagues, the pitches are harder to hit." I smiled. "Sorry, Cubs fan here. I like to reference sports in my regular conversations," I lied. I pulled the seat out across from him, set the stuffed file folder on the table, and sat. "You like baseball, Freddie?"

"I'm not here for sports. I'm here about my parole violation, and I'd like to see my parole officer, please."

"That's not exactly how it works."

He shrugged. "Then make it work that way."

I held up my finger. "Let me get back to baseball first. I'm not a big Braves fan, but the department is hoping they'll take it all the way this year. I don't know enough about the players to take that bet. Besides, once a Cubs fan, always a Cubs fan. Even if it takes another hundred years to win again." I crossed one leg over the other. Bishop leaned against the wall next to the door, his arms folded across his chest. I knew because I could see him in the round mirror in the corner of the wall to Marshall's right.

"What the hell does this got to do with my parole violation?" he asked.

"It's called an analogy. If you'd have let me finish, I would have told you that your jump to the big leagues working with Charles Haus got you a prime spot on the field. The field being prison, that is."

"I sell jewelry for Haus. That's it."

"Really? Let's talk about that relationship." I opened the folder and removed a clipped section with a white piece of paper on top. On it typed in a large, bold font was Freddie's name. I flipped through the pages and pulled out his prison ID. "You met him through your cellmate, correct?"

"I want an attorney."

"For parole violation? I mean, sure, but that's kind of a waste of time, don't you think?"

"Then let me talk to my parole officer."

"We've contacted him, and he's expected sometime today. You know how busy those people are. Lots of convicts like you to babysit. While we wait, I thought we could chat about your involvement with Haus and his money laundering and murder charges."

"I don't know anything about those."

"You sure about that?" Bishop asked. "Murder one is a big charge, but we'll consider dropping it down to something..." He pushed himself off the wall. "Less intense." He smiled. "If, of course, you tell us what we want to know."

"Murder one? What the fuck are you talking about?" He blinked rapidly and twisted his hands on his lap. Tiny beads of sweat appeared on his temples. "I...I didn't kill nobody."

"Murder one's tricky," I said. "Georgia law doesn't hold just the person who performs the kill action accountable, but like I told Haus, it does hold everyone involved to the same level of judicial justice. Let me give you an example. Let's say a woman is somehow trapped in another country, though no one in her family has any idea she's there or they're not telling if they do. She's able to make a connection to a mule, one who, fortunately for us, has a brother in prison who has a cellmate with his own special connections." I pressed my lips together as I revealed the big intel Kyle provided. "These things have a trickle-down effect, if you know what I mean." I waited for him to respond. When he didn't, I pressed the issue. "You do know what I mean, right, Freddie?"

He shifted in his seat. "I want my attorney."

I glanced at Bishop. He nodded and left the room.

"He's going to get you set up, but until then, let me tell you what I know. If you feel like talking, then great. If not, at least you'll know what we've got on you and how we're getting you at least life in prison."

When he didn't respond, I leaned toward the table, pressed my forearms flat against its top, and rubbed my hands together. "Let me continue, then. You assisted Charles Haus after Melodie Rockman returned to the States, set her up with a bank account in a fake name, then carefully funneled money from a dummy account under Haus Jewelry. It took our people a while to figure out how you did that, but we did." I smiled again. "I'll admit, your work is impressive, as are your connections." I shrugged. "Who knew a simple con artist like you would have relationships with bank personnel?" I didn't expect him to respond, and he didn't.

"Here's what I think. You might be a crook, but I know murderers, and I don't peg you for that." I eyed him up and down. "You're a little weak looking, and I don't mean only physically. In my experience, people capable of committing the act of murder have a very specific look," I lied. "It's in the eyes mostly, but it does include their entire aura, if you get my point.

"The problem is that even if you didn't physically pull the trigger, like I said, your actions resulted in the deaths of three people as well as the abduction of a child with a potentially deadly medical condition. The law sees you as equally responsible whether you pulled the trigger or not."

He eyed the door. "You can't make me talk. I know my rights."

"I'm not asking you to talk. I'm asking you to listen."

He shut up.

"We have your phone records, Marshall. We know you've been in contact with everyone involved with the case. And we know you've tried to contact Haus since he's been staying with us. Let's just say that during our time with him, he's shared a plethora of information about your involvement."

"I didn't do nothing."

I smirked. "Now come on, we all know that's not the case. Let's just put our cards on the table, okay? That way, you'll know what you're dealing with, and you can decide how this all plays out. It'll be your turn to deal. How's that?"

He crossed his arms over his chest and grunted.

I took that as *go ahead.* "First, I'll read you your rights because you're officially under arrest for the murders of Emily and Mary Hagerty and Steve Rockman." I read him his rights and kept going. "I think you should know what Haus has told us, and if, perhaps, you have something you can give us, we may be able to make a better deal with you than we have with him."

He stared at me through slitted eyes.

I tilted my head to the left. "So, anyway," I said casually. "Haus mentioned that this was all your idea, funding her return through a dummy account in his company's name, working your trick to manipulate Mary Hagerty into thinking she was saving her daughter from a life of sex trafficking in Mexico." That wasn't how it went down, but if I convinced him his buddy said it, I could get him to tell me what we wanted.

"I didn't set up nothing on my own. Haus came to me. I made a few calls, and that's it. He did the rest."

Bishop returned then. He walked around the table and stood behind Marshall. He bent his head to Marshall's ear and whispered softly.

"Where's my attorney?" Marshall asked.

Bishop stood up straight and pulled the chair out next to him. He sat on it backwards, with the back of the chair against his chest. It was a typical cop move meant to appear casual but always intimidated the suspect. "Your public defender is on his way, but know this, any offer the DA might have put on the table now is out. It's straight-up murder one, three counts, child kidnapping, one count, theft by fraud, one count, and the list goes on. Just one count of murder one gets you life behind bars, my friend. The rest is just gravy, but we can always toss in the possibility of parole. If you talk now, that is."

Marshall leaned back in his chair and ran his hand over his head. I watched him carefully. He was smarter than he looked but played dumb to benefit his cause. The problem with that was me. I was smarter than I looked too, and I knew how to play him a hell of a lot better than he knew how to play me.

"You're barking up the wrong tree, Bishop. This guy's done. He's not going to talk. He knows we've got him. Let's just let the judge decide what to do with him." I smiled at Marshall.

Marshall's upper lip stiffened.

I eyed the camera in the corner, then rubbed the side of my nose. Bubba had been watching—and recording—the entire interrogation and knew my sign for sending someone in to create a little more intensity. That someone knocked on the door. I stood and opened it.

Ashley stepped in with urgency. "Detectives, they've found Melodie

Rockman. She's in holding room three, and she's waived her right to an attorney."

Bishop stood, patted Marshall on the shoulder, and said, "Ain't looking good for ya, pal."

He closed the door behind him, said, "Thanks, Ashley," and we headed to Haus's room.

"Nice one," I said. "He's going to shit himself now."

"Probably already has," Bishop added.

"Actually, I do have something," Ashley said. She handed me a small, clear evidence bag. "Charles Haus's hair."

I looked into her eyes. "From?"

"The Rockman home, two feet away from where the victims were killed."

My heart raced. "How'd you find this?"

"I found it that night, but it didn't match anything in our system. When y'all brought Haus in, I decided to give him a new hairbrush, and we got a match."

"This is fantastic. It puts him at the scene, which is exactly what we need," I said. "The DA is going to love you."

"Thanks," she said. "Sorry I couldn't get a print, though. This is good, but a print would be much better."

"No, this is perfect."

"Thanks," Bishop said.

"Anytime," Ashley said and walked away.

"We got him," I said.

"Damn straight," Bishop said.

Chuckie was less pleased to see us than I'd expected.

"Anything that asshole said is bullshit."

I set down the file I'd brought into the other room. "Really? Are you saying you didn't know he'd set up that account in Haus Jewelry's name to funnel money from Mary Hagerty and Emily Hagerty?"

He blinked. "I didn't do that."

His public defender placed her hand on his. "Mr. Haus, please say nothing."

I smiled at her. "I'm sorry, I don't think we introduced ourselves before. I'm Detective Rachel Ryder, and this is Detective Rob Bishop." I pointed to her notepad. "You might want to write that down."

She straightened her shoulders. "I'm Cassie Brighton, and I know who you are." Her meekness seemed to instantly disappear. If she weren't working for the defense, I'd have applauded her for the confidence switch.

"Okay, then," I said. "I'll continue." I looked at Charles. "According to your buddy, here's how things went down." I laid out everything Kyle had told us previously as if Marshall was the one throwing Charles under the bus. "You're paying off debt to the cartel, only at the time, you're doing it under an alias." I glanced at the paperwork Kyle provided earlier. "Johnny Walker." I chuckled. "Not at all original, but whatever." I twirled the paper toward him. Ms. Brighton read it and then pushed it away.

"I guess mule identities are like stripper names. The play on words is key, right? So, there you are in Mexico, traveling back and forth between the two countries, working as a mule to pay off your debt to the cartel, and someone approaches you about a woman who's looking for a way back to Georgia. She's got some cash, but she needs more. She knows how to get it once she's back in the States, and she's willing to pay you big for your troubles. All you need to do is get her out of Mexico and back to Georgia where she can get a hold of her cash. And she tells you she'll give you whatever's left once the job is done, plus I'm assuming money from a life insurance policy for her dead husband. The one you helped murder."

Brighton whispered something to Haus. When he nodded, she said, "Go on."

"You knew who your brother was in prison with, so you make arrangements for his help. And when you came back to the States the last time, the jewelry store owner you swindled into leaving everything to you dies, so you've got the perfect solution to your cartel problem as well as a way to work another scam against the woman and her family."

"These are separate incidents, Detective," the attorney said. "Are you planning additional charges?"

"We know you're moving drugs and cash through the jewelry store for the cartel, Haus." I smiled at Brighton. "The DEA is finalizing the charges now." I looked back at Haus. "Oh, and by the way, we've contacted the deceased owner's children. They're on their way here to talk with us now. Apparently, they've got information to share."

"I am a jewelry designer," he said.

"Mr. Haus, please let me speak for you."

"I'm not arguing that," I said. "The scam was to stash Melodie somewhere she couldn't be found, then connect with Mary Hagerty on a more personal level. Once that was achieved, you'd bring Melodie into the picture, and the two of you would convince Mary that Emily betrayed them both. She kept them apart, put Mary in a bad position, or whatever it was you claimed. It was just gravy when you discovered Mary believed Emily was posing as her sister already." That part was a guess, but from the look on Haus's face, it was a good one.

"You convince her there's only one solution. Emily's got to go," Bishop said. We didn't know how the murders went down, but it was important to let him think we knew he was responsible.

Haus breathed through his nose. "I didn't kill no one."

"Mr. Haus," Brighton said.

"No," he said. "They got it wrong. Marshall's full of shit, and I can prove it."

"I don't recommend you say anything, Mr. Haus," she said.

"I don't care. They're not gonna pin this one on me."

"I'd like to know what kind of proof you have, because I think your buddy in the other room said you bragged about pulling the trigger," I said. "And we have you at the scene. So, let's just cut the BS." Saying Marshall flat-out pegged him for the killing could mess up the trial, but saying I thought he said it was different.

"I said I didn't kill anyone. Mel—"

Ms. Brighton cut him off with an authoritative voice and hand in the air. "Mr. Haus, shut. Up." She looked at me. "Felony murder."

I leaned back in my chair and smiled. "We want his proof before we take it to the DA."

"May I have a few minutes with my client, please?" she asked.

Bishop and I left the room.

"He's going to talk," Bishop said.

"I want Melodie. He needs to give us Melodie."

"He will," Bishop said.

17

"My client has informed me he's willing to move forward with the possibility of a reduction in charges," Ms. Brighton said.

"Great," I said. "Let's get a move on, then." I sat back down and smiled at Haus. "Go ahead."

"Melodie Rockman killed them."

"I'm going to need a little more than that, Mr. Haus."

He glanced at the attorney. She nodded.

"She killed the husband and the sister. I was there. I didn't know she was going to do it. That wasn't the plan."

"Then what was the plan?"

"She wanted the kid. She'd spent months working on an exit plan, and when she was ready, she went for the kid, only the kid wasn't there."

"And what happened?"

"She shot them."

I took a pad of paper I'd brought in the room with me and slid it across the table to Haus as Bishop removed a pen from his pocket and handed it to him. "Write it all down," I said. "From the minute you learned about Rockman till we picked you up. Every single detail."

I smiled at the attorney, said, "Pleasure doing business with you," and left the room.

Haus was a slow writer, and by the time he'd finished the thirty pages of his handwritten confession and account of the situation, he was cranky, his attorney was cranky, and Bishop and I were too. We processed him, then stuffed him in another cell until his get-together with the judge. When we finished, we went ahead with charges against Marshall. His attorney talked with him privately, but given Marshall's history, he knew the odds of winning his case were slim. Once Marshall was processed, we had him transported to Fulton County, where all parolees under arrest were stuck until their court dates.

Bubba picked up food at a local Mexican restaurant and brought it to the investigation room. We updated the team on what we'd learned.

"But Haus isn't saying where Melodie is?" Jimmy asked.

I nodded. "According to him, she went off the radar completely. He thinks she and Mary Hagerty had a fight and that Melodie killed her too."

"They fought about the kid," Jimmy said.

"That's our assumption," Bishop said. "She'd been staying at the cabin where Hagerty was found."

"Melodie Rockman's DNA was all over that cabin."

"Haus said he wasn't there when it happened, which is why he's just assuming it's true. Claims he never went to the cabin," I said.

Kyle stepped into the room. He got a round of applause and took a comical bow. "I got a hit on something and shared it, that's all. You all did the real work. So," he said as he sat next to me. "Did you get a full confession?"

"He claims Melodie Rockman shot her husband and sister."

Bishop took over. "According to him, Melodie Rockman told him everything that happened with her sister and her husband before Melodie met Steve. She said Emily Hagerty continued to have a thing for Steve and that Mary Hagerty knew it, but she tried to push it aside, telling her daughter to do the same."

"Emily, not Melodie," I said.

Bishop nodded. "When Emily suggested the twins go on a vacation to work on their relationship, Mary Hagerty had to convince Melodie to go."

"She did it, but according to Haus, under duress," I added.

Jimmy laughed. "You two are like spouses telling a story. Neither lets the other tell it all from start to finish."

I glanced at Bishop. "Go on. I'll keep my mouth shut."

He smirked. "They went on the trip. One came back. Emily."

"And no one noticed she wasn't Melodie until her mother saw the scar," Bishop said.

"At least that part was true," I added.

"What happened to Melodie in Mexico?"

"Haus and Melodie met because he was transporting drugs from Mexico to the States. She was with a group of women being sold into sex trafficking. She escaped and eventually got to Haus," Kyle said.

"Right," Bishop said. "About a year after Emily returned as Melodie, Haus was on his last trip to Mexico. He'd been paying off a debt to the cartel. While there, one of his connections ran into a truck full of women. The truck tipped over and the door opened. All but three of the girls inside got out before it went up in flames. Melodie found a mule, said she had cash, and she needed to go back to Georgia. She didn't want to go anywhere else."

"The guy who found her knew Haus worked that route and hooked them up. She paid him for the drive, told him what happened and what she wanted to do," I said. "And they developed a plan. According to Haus, she didn't want to kill her family. She just wanted to get her son and manipulate her sister to tell everyone the truth."

"Where'd Melodie get money?" Jimmy asked.

"We don't know," I said. "But she paid Haus to establish a relationship with the mother, and he went beyond the call of duty."

"Gross," Ashley said.

I nodded. "Haus was screwing the real Emily and her mother and manipulating them to his benefit. That account with the money going in and seemingly not going out? Marshall knows people in the industry. Haus's brother hooked them up, and Marshall got a fee for setting up the fake account through his contact, but the money was never really in it. The bank rep created the dummy account in Haus's store name, but the real one"—I removed the bank account information from the file—"is here.

Both women put cash into the account, only Rockman didn't know her mother was adding to it, and Hagerty didn't know her daughter was."

"How'd he swing that?" Jimmy asked.

Bishop shrugged. "After sex talk, I'm assuming."

Ashley grimaced. "Gross."

"And the M. Hagerty account Emily Hagerty was depositing into, what was that?" Jimmy asked.

"What it was. Emily paying her mother to keep her mouth shut."

"What a great family," Bubba said. "Mine is so boring."

Bishop laughed. "The plan was for Haus to bring Melodie to Hagerty so she could tell her what happened. But Haus learned that Hagerty had confronted Emily shortly after she came back from Mexico. He said Emily claimed it was Melodie's idea, that Melodie wanted a less stressful life, that she'd met a guy in Mexico and decided to stay."

"Right," I said. "According to Haus, here's how the murders went down." I stood and mapped out the chain of events starting with the night of the killing. "Rockman and Haus go to the house. The deal, according to Haus, was that Melodie was going to call her sister out in front of the husband. At this point, Emily knows her sister is alive, and she thinks she's paying off Haus to keep quiet."

"Because he went to her and told her he'd met her in Mexico. That's why she was putting the money in the account," Bishop explained.

I pointed the dry erase marker at him. "Right. So, they arrive at the Rockmans' place. Melodie's asking where the kid is, but neither Emily nor Steve will say. She presses her husband. Wants to know how he can be with her sister for three years and not have a clue it wasn't her. Haus says Rockman told her he was in love with Emily throughout his entire marriage to Melodie and is glad to be with her. Haus thinks Steve knew from the beginning Emily wasn't Melodie."

"She lines them up against the wall," Bishop added. "Haus stands next to her, holds the gun aimed at the victims, and tells her to get the shit she needs and get out."

"Melodie wants the kid, but neither will say where the kid is," I said. "She loses it, pulls a gun from the back of her pants and shoots her husband, then aims it at her sister, and bang."

"She flips out," Bishop said. "She can't find the kid anywhere. Haus gets her out of the house and drops her at his place. He claims he's going to look for the kid, but he doesn't. Instead, he calls Mary Hagerty, who he knew was babysitting the kid. Hagerty rushes to the Rockmans' home, get the kid's suitcase and some clothes, and makes arrangements with the fired nanny to keep the kid."

"How did he know where the kid was, and why didn't Melodie?" Jimmy asked.

"We're getting there. Things got hot because Hagerty didn't expect the office manager to show up as early as she did. The plan, according to Haus, was for Hagerty to come to the house and find the Rockmans, not someone else."

"But that wasn't the original plan," Bishop said. "The original plan was for Hagerty to have the kid, Melodie to get the cash and things she wanted from the Rockmans, then get the kid from Hagerty. But according to Haus, Melodie was getting increasingly angry, and Hagerty worried she'd hurt the kid. So, she told Melodie that Emily decided not to leave the boy with her after all, letting Melodie think she didn't have the kid."

"Did Melodie know Emily was paying her mother to keep quiet?" Nikki asked.

"It doesn't appear so," I said.

"Does Haus know where the nanny is now?"

I shook my head. "Best we can determine is that Hagerty sensed Melodie thought she knew where the kid was and was coming for her, so Hagerty told the nanny to drop the kid somewhere and run. Melodie comes for Hagerty, can't find the kid, so she kills her."

"Jesus, this is a train wreck," Jimmy said. "We've got an MIA nanny, a missing psycho-murdering mother, and no idea where to find either of them."

"We think the nanny is in hiding, and I believe her cousin knows where she is," I said.

"We need to find them both," Jimmy said.

"Our biggest concern is the kid," Bishop said. "Melodie wants him, and she's not going to stop until she gets him."

"And that's why we're going to use him as bait."

∼

Juanita Flores sat on a faux leather recliner inside her small apartment. "I don't know where she is now. I swear." She made the sign of the cross over her heart and muttered what I thought was the Hail Mary in Spanish.

"Juanita," I said. "I need you to tell me the truth. Did you know your cousin had the boy?"

She nodded.

"Did she tell you who gave her the child?"

She shook her head. "I knew it was Ms. Hagerty."

"How did you know?"

"I think it."

"Did Ana tell you she was afraid? Did she think something was going to happen to her?"

"No, she just told me she was staying somewhere in the mountains. Someplace Ms. Hagerty gave her."

I looked at Bishop.

"Paid cash for a rental or something?" Bishop asked.

"Probably," I said. "When was the last time you spoke to your cousin?" I asked Juanita.

"Three days ago, I think?"

"And you haven't heard from her since?"

She shook her head. "I don't know where she is. I am very worried."

"Okay. It's very important that you contact us if you hear from your cousin. Very important. Do you understand?"

"I don't want to go back to Mexico."

"This isn't about Mexico," Bishop said. He handed her a card. "Don't let it become about it."

∼

"She's dead," I said. "Or Melodie's got her."

Bishop hit the button to start the vehicle. "You're probably right."

"She's going to get desperate. Her money's cut off, her mother's dead,

Haus and Marshall are both in jail. Everyone that's helped her is unavailable. She's going to have to hit up someone else for help."

"And we'll be there when she does."

We'd already set up a few patrol officers to watch Leah Marx, and after a verbal ass-kicking from our chief, someone finally did it right. We got the call that Marx was at a local big-box store, something she hadn't done in the few days we'd had people keeping tabs on her.

Big-box stores are popular for shoppers, but the patrol who called it in felt this was different enough to warrant assistance.

As we arrived at the Walmart on Windward Parkway, Bishop and I both stuffed our heads into baseball caps. I chose an Indiana University cap of Tommy's, and Bishop wore his University of Georgia one. Our not-matching pullover jackets hid our weapons.

"She's inside," the officer said.

I nodded, adjusted my hat, and headed toward the door.

"Wait," Bishop said, trailing behind me. "What're you going to do? Walk up to her and say hey?"

"Right. That's the plan." I shook my head. Sometimes my partner's small-town experience shined bright. "I'm going to watch her and the area around her. That's what we do in these situations, partner. We examine the area."

"Marx could recognize you."

I patted my hip. "Bet I'm a quicker draw than she is." I turned around and walked toward the store.

"Son of a bitch," he said and jogged up to me. "I don't like this."

"It's not my favorite way to spend the day either."

The store was crowded, but the location was always crowded. Bishop went to the customer service desk, and the next thing I knew, he was escorted into the back offices. I figured he planned to watch the cameras. Nothing like a little flash of the badge to get things done.

I followed the path Marx took inside the store, getting directions through my earpiece.

"She's in the dog food aisle," the officer said. "She's wearing a—"

I cut him off. "I know what she looks like." I stepped into the aisle, pulled my hat down low over my forehead, and pretended to examine the dog food options. Leah Marx stood there, her head hanging down, staring at the ground. She didn't look at me, but I watched as she shifted and peeked around the corners of the aisle. She checked her cell phone twice. She picked up a dog toy, fiddled with it, then set it back on the shelf. She checked her phone again.

I tossed a few items into my little basket, then walked casually toward the main aisle. As I turned, I watched her dart the opposite direction, heading toward the milk section. I flipped around, kept my pace, and walked that way as if I didn't have a care in the world. I kept my eyes on her as she tapped something into her phone and place it at her ear. "Where are you?" She asked. "I'm not waiting anymore. This is…it's wrong, okay?" She stuffed the phone into her pocket.

I walked over and tapped her on the back of the shoulder.

She yelped when she turned around and recognized me.

"The entire store is filled with cops," I said with a casual smile. "I need you to search inside the milk refrigerator, hand me some of the creamer and smile, then head to your car. There will be a car pulled out near yours. The driver will nod when he sees you. Follow that vehicle. We will have cars surrounding you, Ms. Marx, so if you do not follow my instructions, you will be arrested. Am I clear?"

She nodded and turned toward the refrigerator. She removed a creamer and handed it to me.

"Thank you," I said loudly. "I'm sorry to bother you. I just didn't see it." I winked at her, whispered, "Follow the directions," and walked away.

18

"I...I haven't seen her, I promise." Leah Marx twisted a ring around her right ring finger. "She called me. You...you have my cell phone. You can see that, right? But I...I haven't helped her. She just wanted to talk."

Bishop sighed. "Why didn't you contact the police?"

"I...she's my best friend, and she's been through so much. I felt I at least owed her a private conversation."

I stared at my thumb as I rubbed the tip of my fingernail with it. "Hope it's worth the jail time." I didn't bother looking at her as I spoke. "Because you'll do some, most definitely."

"What? Jail? For what? I...I didn't do anything."

"You aided a wanted suspect in a murder investigation," I said.

"I want an attorney, then. Don't I have the right to one?"

Bishop sighed again. He glanced at me with daggers shooting from his eyes.

I shrugged. "We're not going to arrest you. We just need to know what happened. What did Rockman ask you?"

"Nothing. She just wanted to meet."

"For what? To catch up on old times? Shoot the shit? She had to have a reason. What was it?"

"She said she needed to talk to someone she could trust."

"Did she ask you to bring anything?" Bishop asked. "Money? A burner phone? Clothing?"

"She asked if I could get her some cash, but I told her I couldn't."

"Ms. Marx, I have a best friend," I said. "I would do anything for her, so I understand where you're coming from. I really do. But if you want to walk out of here without any charges, we need you to tell us everything. Is that clear?"

She exhaled. "She said the person she was getting money from was gone, and she needs money so she can move forward with her plan."

"What's her plan?" Bishop asked.

"I...I don't know, and honestly, I didn't ask. I told her I didn't have any money, but she begged me to meet her anyway. She said she wanted to talk about Ryan. He's her son, and no matter what you think she might have done, she loves that boy."

"What do you think she might have done?" I asked.

"I've seen the news. I know you think she killed her family, but I just can't believe that. Maybe Emily, but not Melodie. She wouldn't do that."

"She would," Bishop said. "And she did. We have an eyewitness. The person who she was getting her money from."

"I don't believe it."

"We believe she killed her mother too."

"She's scared, okay? She knows you all think she killed Steve and...and her family, but she didn't. She promised me she didn't. That's the only reason I agreed to meet her. Do you think I'd meet with someone I thought was a murderer?"

"I think you need psychiatric treatment," I said. "Because she is a murderer, and if you can't accept that, you've got a problem."

"Ryder," Bishop said. His tone was tense.

I shrugged. "Truth hurts, partner."

"Ms. Marx," he said. "Did she say or allude to what she might do next?"

"She wants her son. She told me that. Can't you just let her see him again? Let her know he's okay? Maybe she'll...I don't know, turn herself in or something."

I laughed. "If she cared about her son, she wouldn't have put him through this."

"She didn't put him through this, her sister did."

There was no talking sense to a woman like Leah Marx. She whole-heartedly believed her best friend, and I knew she wouldn't help, but that didn't stop me from saying what needed to be said. "Ms. Marx, your best friend went through a terrible, traumatic event, I don't deny that, but instead of returning home and reporting it, she chose to enact her own murderous plan, kill three people, and put her child at great risk. No matter how much she says she loves her son, that isn't an appropriate expression of that love. We will find her, and she will be tried in a court of law, and it's very likely she will receive the death penalty. Do you know how Georgia executes death penalty cases?"

She stared at me as tears pooled in her eyes.

"Let me spell it out for you. Before she would have been given three drugs. One was used for sedation, much like an animal who's being put to sleep. Have you ever put an animal to sleep? They get a shot that calms them and knocks them out, and then the lethal injection of pentobarbital happens. It's the humane way of doing things, so the animal doesn't feel any pain, but we don't do that for people here in Georgia anymore. Now, we skip the sedative. When she's lying on that execution table, she'll be given one injection of pentobarbital, a one and done, if you will. Do you know what pentobarbital does to the body?"

She shook her head.

"It's ugly. Your best friend will feel everything. First, she'll struggle to breathe. She'll wheeze and feel like she's got a truck full of bricks sitting on her chest. Her heart will race. She'll feel like she's being squeezed hard, so hard, Leah, that she can't get air into her lungs. Her chest will hurt from the struggle. She'll become agitated, disoriented, and she'll have the most painful migraine she's ever had. And then, her lungs will stop working completely, and in a matter of moments, long, painful moments to her, her brain will shut down due to a lack of oxygen. For us, it's quick, for her, it's the longest, most painful thing she'll ever experience."

"Why are you telling me this? I've told you everything."

"Are you sure? Because if you haven't, maybe, just maybe, we can get to Melodie and stop her from causing any more harm, and maybe the district attorney will remove the death penalty option."

~

Bishop dragged his hand down his growing beard. "Was that necessary, Ryder? Really?" He paced the length of the investigation room. "That poor woman is a mess because of you."

"No, that poor woman is a mess because her best friend is a sociopath, Bishop. Come on, we needed to know what she knew, and I did what I had to do."

"You were out of line. She told us what she knew. You could have dropped it there."

"I didn't believe her."

"And yet she was being honest. Have a little fucking faith in people, Ryder. Jesus!"

I stared at him as anger filled my chest. I inhaled and pushed my chair back, then stood and charged over to him, my face millimeters from his. "Three hundred and seventy-five, Bishop. Three hundred and seventy-five fucking dead bodies! That's how many I've seen in under fifteen years as a cop. You know how many of those murders, and they were all murders, I've solved? Three hundred and twenty-eight. How many murder investigations have you solved? You don't know what I've seen or what I've had to deal with, so fucking forgive me if I don't do things your way. We have a triple murderer on the loose, and I'll do whatever the hell it takes to find her."

I turned around and walked out of the room and slammed the door behind me. I marched through the pit, refusing to make eye contact with any of the officers, who, I could tell, stopped what they were doing when I charged through the large room. I pushed open the exit and jogged to my Jeep. "Asshole," I shouted.

Maybe he was right. Maybe I didn't need to go into such dramatic detail with the woman, but I did what I had to do.

Kyle opened the door and walked over. He leaned against my Jeep and stared at the sky. "Smells like rain."

"He's an asshole."

"Won't be the last time." He kicked a rock on the ground. "Who're we talking about?"

I smiled despite my anger. "Bishop. He got on me for detailing the process of execution to Marx."

"Ouch. That's pretty rough."

"She was in contact with the suspect."

"No, I understand. God knows I've done worse."

"He doesn't have the experience I have."

"I just think the two of you have different ways of doing things, which is why you work so well together."

"He's an asshole."

"I believe you already mentioned that."

That damn smile creeped onto my face again.

"So, what did she tell you?"

"Nothing we didn't already know."

"No location?"

I shook my head.

"You letting her go?"

"Marx? Yeah, and she's been threatened jail time if she leaks anything, but I don't think Rockman knows she's here."

"She may try to contact her again."

"We've got her phone tapped, and Jimmy's putting an officer on her in twelve-hour shifts. She won't use the bathroom without us knowing."

Bishop stepped outside. He smiled at Kyle.

Kyle patted my shoulder. "I'll give y'all a minute."

As he walked away, Bishop walked up, leaned against my vehicle, and lit up a cigarette. I didn't want one, but at that moment I missed the ritual of smoking. I watched him go through the ritual with a little extra enthusiasm than necessary. "You're an asshole," I said.

"Goes both ways."

"Can't deny that."

"I just wouldn't have been so harsh." He inhaled smoke and blew it out his nose. "She crumbled. The paramedics had to come and deal with her."

I shrugged. I felt bad, sure, but I had a reason, and we were wasting time being all girly dramatic about it. "Listen, I get it, okay? And I'm sorry if I went overboard, but that's who I am, and if you don't know that by now, or you can't accept it or whatever, then you have to decide to either get over it or move on. Get a new partner."

He raised an eyebrow. "That's a little dramatic, don't you think? I was just asking you to be a little less intense and maybe a little more compassionate every once in a while, okay?"

"When someone deserves compassion, they get it."

He nodded once. "Okay, then. How about we table this drama until after we bring in Rockman?"

"How about we just table it completely?"

He smiled. "You're a good cop, Ryder, and the best partner I've ever had, but sometimes you're an asshole."

"Goes both ways."

Randy Rockman didn't understand the plan, though none of us had expected him to. "You want me to put my nephew in danger?" He flew out of his seat and tossed his hands in the air. "This is crazy!"

"Mr. Rockman," I said calmly. "That's not what we're asking. Ryan won't even be with you. We just need Melodie to *think* he is. He's already in a safe location with DFACS. They're not involved in this. They don't even know about it."

He stuffed his hands into his pocket. "Oh, okay. That's...that's...I understand." He exhaled. "Thank you for explaining. I guess I'm a little tense. I apologize."

Bishop said, "No need to apologize, sir. You've every right to be concerned for your nephew, but you have my word we will do everything in our power to apprehend Melodie Rockman and make sure Ryan is no longer in danger."

Rockman nodded. "Yeah...yeah, thanks. That's all I want." He sat down and ran his hand through his hair, then dipped his head down and sobbed. "I messed up. This was it, wasn't it? This was why Steve wanted to talk to me. He knew. He knew what was going on." He inhaled and blew out another breath. It hitched halfway through, and I knew he was going to cry again. "I could have helped him, but I didn't. He could still be alive."

The loss of a family member carries the weight of guilt for many. I understood that more than others. As law enforcement, there's a fine line between offering compassion and getting to work. We teetered on the edge of that line often. Wanting to pat the person on the back and tell them it'll get better—eventually—and smack them on the back and say, *We're going to get the bastard that did this to your loved one.*

In my experience, the living victims preferred the smack-on-the-back route.

"Mr. Rockman," Bishop said. "Looking back solves nothing."

"He's right," I quickly added. "Finding Melodie and making her pay for her crimes is the best we can do."

"And I want you to do that. How can I help?"

We gave him the rest of the specifics of our plan.

"Officer Emmett will be escorting you to your brother's home. We've already got eyes on the location in the form of a drone, by the way, but while you're getting Ryan's things, our officer will be installing cameras both around the home and inside." We already had a tech at Randy's home to install cameras. He'd arrived over an hour before under the guise of an air-conditioning repairman, which allowed him to work both inside and out also. It would be a little trickier for Emmett to do it outside, but we didn't doubt he'd be successful.

He smiled. "And what should I do?"

"Just get some of Ryan's things. We'll have a fake DFACS representative there. She'll introduce herself to you at the door and let you in. You'll get some of Ryan's things and then return to your house. The officer posing as DFACS will follow you in her vehicle.

"Once you arrive home, we'll have another officer posing as another DFACS representative. We want the appearance of your nephew being inside. We've created a recording of a child that we'll play when you enter and she exits, so if Rockman is close by, she'll hear it. We'll also set up life-like, child-sized dummies in two rooms. Once you're inside, we'll safely remove you from the location, in disguise, and replace you with someone dressed as you."

"How long is this going to take?"

"If your sister-in-law wants her son, which I'm assuming she does, not long."

"And when are we doing this?"

"Within the next hour."

"What should I do now?"

"We'd like you to wait in the reception area until we give you the all clear to go," I said.

"And we'll have undercover officers nearby through the entire situation," Bishop said.

Randy's emotionally drained expression morphed into an unyielding determination. His jaw stiffened, his eyes slitted into focused, determined specks, and his shoulders straightened. A man who had appeared defeated had taken back control of his emotions, and that was exactly what we needed. "And you think this will work?"

"It's our best shot," Bishop said.

We sat in my cubby waiting for word from the officers setting up the trap.

I removed my vest and belt, disconnected my radio from my shirt, and tried to relax. "Feels like I've had this stuff on since birth."

"I hear ya," Bishop said. He took off his radio and set it on my desk.

Though we couldn't see the sky through the ceiling or windowless walls of the pit, we felt the clouds looming over us, both figuratively and literally. The promise of rain filled the air, even inside, and I wondered if Bishop would grab his umbrella before we left. Bishop always carried his umbrella when it rained. I suspected if we were involved in a shootout in a downpour, he'd hold fire until he could pop his umbrella open to cover his everreceding hairline. Not really, but I did give him crap about it often.

"You know what I can't figure out," I said.

Bishop smiled. "Lately, most everything?"

"Good point, but no. Georgia rain. Why is there so much? Last I looked, we were inches above Portland, Oregon. Didn't think that was possible." I needed a distraction to pass the time.

"Beats me. Call Glen Burns. He might know."

"Maybe it's climate change?"

"Or maybe it's Mother Nature in menopause."

"Ouch. That's rough," I said. "Is this part of the reason you're divorced?"

He winced. "Probably, but I'm too old to change."

"And you shouldn't. You're near perfect as you are."

He smiled. "Wow. That's a big step for you, partner."

I shrugged. "What can I say? I'm growing."

"More like my amazingness is finally sinking in."

"That too."

"In all seriousness," he said. "You're the best detective I've met."

"You already said that."

"And I meant it."

"Nothing personal, but you're from small-town Georgia. I'm not sure that says much." I smiled and showed him my pearly whites.

"I know a good cop when I see one, Ryder." His tone turned serious. "I know you're frustrated, and you feel like—"

"A failure?"

"Like you could do better, more, maybe, but we wouldn't be where we are with this investigation without you."

I smiled. "I appreciate that, but let's be honest. We wouldn't be where we are in this investigation without us as partners."

He nodded. "I'll take that. You focused on the bigger picture, and I'm glad for that."

"Like Mary seeming ingenuine?"

"Like pushing that when I thought she couldn't be involved."

"But you were right. Sort of. She was involved, but she wanted to protect her grandson."

"In the end, maybe," Bishop said. "But her motivation was to hide the truth."

"Listen, I'm praising you for your rightness. Take it while it's hot."

"Done."

"So, the question remains," I said.

Bishop nodded. "Where's Melodie?"

"Where's Melodie. If she wants her kid, she can't be far."

"What if she's given up? Maybe she doesn't want the kid," Bishop said.

"I hate to think a mother could be that...that, I don't know, selfish, but we know it happens."

"I've seen worse." My department phone rang, and I answered.

The dispatcher said, "I have a call for you. Line one. She insists on speaking with only you, and she won't provide her name."

I glanced at Bishop and said to the dispatcher, "Get a trace on it, please."

"Will do. Sending through."

The call connected, and I said, "Detective Ryder."

"Do you know who this is?" the caller said. Even her voice sounded like a cloudy day.

I had a feeling I did. "Yes. Thanks for asking." I made eye contact with my partner. I didn't want to hit the speaker button, so I pointed to the phone against my ear. "It's her," I mouthed.

"Rockman?" he asked.

I nodded.

"This is a burner phone. You won't be able to trace it," Melodie Rockman said. "I am five minutes from your office at the biscuit place inside the Shell. I have a young woman with me. If you don't follow my instructions, she will die, do you understand?"

"What do you want?"

"I want you to come. I want to talk to you."

"Bishop is with me," I said. "He's coming."

"I assumed he would," she said. "But no one else. If I see anyone that looks like a cop, hear any cars that sound like cop cars, she's dead. Am I clear?"

"You're clear," I said.

"No one else," she said.

"Nobody but me and Bishop," I said.

"Do I have your word?"

"My word," I said.

"I know my brother-in-law is with you. Whatever you've planned with him, forget it. Five minutes or we're gone."

"The name," I said. "I need the woman's name."

"Ana Flores."

Shit.

I hung up. Bishop looked at me. "It was her," I said. "She wants to talk. Just us. Five minutes at the Shell station. She's got the nanny, and she knows Rockman's here."

"Shit."

I grabbed my vest and belt and said, "Let's go."

We left the station through the back exit. Bishop drove. I sat silently for the two-minute ride, wondering what the hell was going to happen. We were armed, and we'd take her in, but we had no time to assess the risk or secure backup. I hated not knowing what was coming and walking into a potential ambush.

The gas station lot was empty. The closed sign was flipped on the door, and the lights were out. If it was night, we wouldn't be able to see anything inside, but the grayness of the early evening made things inside visible.

A man walked through the door. We drew our weapons. He held up his hands automatically. "Don't shoot. I am the station owner."

I stepped forward, my weapon still pointed his direction.

"She...she sent me out to tell you no guns. She does not want guns." His hands shook. The man was old, probably seventy, and his accent was thick.

I lowered my gun slightly. "Does she have a weapon?"

He nodded.

"Is she alone?" Bishop asked.

"She's...a woman is with her."

At least she'd been honest about that.

"Is the woman okay?" I asked.

"She...I cannot tell. She is crying."

Given what she'd done to her sister, husband, and mother, Rockman was a decent shot. If we went in without weapons drawn, we risked head shots and probable death. Unfortunately, our Kevlar jackets only did so much. I had two weapons. The one in my hand, department issued, and my personal SIG Sauer in my boot. I also had a knife attached to the back of my belt, easily accessible and hidden under my light jacket. If she patted us down, she'd find my knife first. Things could go down from there. I knew she was watching even though I couldn't see her.

A vehicle pulled into the lot.

Bishop screamed, "Get lost!"

The driver did as told.

I set down my weapon, then made a big presentation of removing the knife from my belt and setting it next to the gun. I nodded and yelled toward the store, "That's it for me."

Bishop typically had one department-issued weapon, a small taser he kept in his pants pocket, and a knife in the back of his utility belt. He removed the knife and set it and the gun down.

Good. The taser would be helpful if she didn't check us and take it away.

"Leave," I whispered to the man as I walked toward him. "Run."

"No," he said. His entire body shook. "It is my store. I must stay."

"We can't guarantee your protection. Do you understand? Leave. Now!"

He shook his head vigorously. "She will shoot me."

I pointed toward the stack of used tires to his right. "There. Go there. Once we're inside, I need you to run. This is not a suggestion. Call 9-1-1 when you're across the street. Tell them Detectives Bishop and Ryder are with the suspect. Nod if you understand."

He nodded just as Ana Flores walked into the doorframe of the store with Melodie Rockman holding a gun to the side of her head. I stared at them for a moment then back at the man as he darted toward the pile of tires.

"Get inside. Now," Rockman said.

Bishop took the rear. We walked in, and Rockman closed and locked the door behind us. I had no idea if the owner ran, but I hoped he did. I couldn't risk looking outside, instead choosing to keep Rockman distracted with idle chatter. I needed to keep her calm, to devise at least a portion of a plan in case the man hadn't run and backup wasn't en route. And if it was, I hoped with all my heart they were quiet.

Once dispatch got the call from the owner, she'd know the call that came in for me was from Rockman, and hopefully, she'd send backup quietly. In situations like this, that was usually the way things went, but it didn't stop me from worrying things would go bad fast.

Balls to the wall would get us all killed.

I kept my hands visible to Rockman. I made eye contact with Ana Flores, whose face was swollen from crying. I looked at Rockman again. "I thought you wanted to talk. I didn't know you were holding the nanny hostage."

"She's my insurance."

"I gave you my word, and I've lived up to it. Now, I need something from you, Melodie." I took a cautious step forward. "Let her go."

Tears fell down Rockman's face. She shook her head. "No. I told you, she's my insurance."

"If you let her go, I'll do what I can to help you."

"No!"

"What do you want, then?"

"I want my son!" She pushed the gun barrel against Ana Flores's head. "And I want a way out of this, now!"

I ignored her request for her child. "You want a way out of here? The store?" I moved to the side. "You know where the door is."

"A way out of this shit! I want my freedom. I've waited a long time for it, and I deserve it!" She was sweating, and her eyes were bloodshot. Her hand shook as she held the gun. Maybe she wasn't as good a shot as I thought. Maybe it was just luck.

"Tell me what happened in Mexico, Melodie."

She pressed her lips together. Though her grip around Ana Flores was tight, she swayed back and forth. Her balance was off because she was emotional. If I could get the facts out of her while keeping her off-balance, we had a chance of getting our hands on the nanny. But there was a fine line between getting a suspect to talk and pushing them over the edge. I had to tread that line carefully, and I wasn't confident I could do it.

"You know what happened," she said. "Don't act like Haus didn't tell you!"

"I want to hear it from you." I stood with my legs hip-width apart and my hands in view. "It might help us help you. Do you understand?"

"My sister was a bitch. She wanted Steve. Did you know she fucked him for months claiming to be me?" She laughed, and it was filled with anger. "She told our pathetic excuse for a mother she wanted to make it all up to me, to reestablish our relationship." She shook her head. "Like we ever really had a fucking relationship!"

"You must have had some relationship because you decided to go with her to Mexico."

"Because of Steve! He wanted me to make amends. He thought it was a good idea. Bastard probably knew what she had planned." She held the nanny tight around her chest and kept the gun on the side of her head. "Do you know what he said the night I took back my life? He said, *I love you*, only, he was talking to Emily."

I exhaled. "I'm sorry."

"I shot the bastard then, and I made sure my whore of a sister sat next to him on the floor, and then I fucking shot her too!"

"Melodie," I said. "What did she do to you in Mexico?"

She laughed. "It was brilliant, really, and I spent three years devising a plan to be more brilliant than her. She sold me to the cartel. I stopped counting how many times I was raped after two hundred. I was their toy, their slave, and not just a sex slave. I...I..."

She was weakening. Her grip loosened on Flores.

"Melodie, did Charles Haus rescue you?"

She swallowed hard. "Only because I paid him to. He...he helped me get out of there, but he's a fucking traitor. He manipulated my mother and sucked money from her for himself. The bastard should fry for what he's done!" She pressed the gun harder against Ana Flores. "I want my son, and I want the fuck out of this!"

"How did you get money if you were a slave to the cartel?" I asked.

"How do you think? Fucked some idiot low-level cartel loser and stole it from him when he passed out." She pressed the gun harder into Ana's head. "I want my kid, and I want my freedom. I'm done talking."

"We can't make those kinds of promises," I said.

"You killed three people," Bishop added. "There's no way out of that. Even if we let you go, that'll stay with you the rest of your life."

"They betrayed me! They deserved to die. Don't you understand that? I don't give a fuck about them!"

"I understand," Bishop said. "But you've got to let Ana go."

"Not until I get my son."

"Listen," I said. "I know what it feels like to live inside this kind of pain. Really, I do. But holding Ana hostage won't get your son back."

She squeezed Ana Flores's shoulder. The young woman winced and cried harder.

She screamed, "You don't understand anything! Shut the fuck up!"

She was losing it, and we needed her to stay calm. One wrong move, and Flores was dead.

"Put down the gun, Melodie," I asked. "We'll work something out, okay? Just put down the gun and let her come this direction, and we'll talk."

"I need your word. I want my son." Her hand shook harder. "Or I'll kill her! You know I can do it! Give me your word!"

I nodded. I had no other option. Telling her what she wanted to hear was the only thing I could do. The clock was ticking, backup hadn't arrived, and we were in trouble. "You have my word."

The sound of a vehicle outside set things in motion.

Her eyes shifted to the door, then to Bishop, and then finally rested on me. "I told you no one but you."

"This is a gas station. Someone was bound to come here," I said. "What're you going to do, shoot them too?"

"I want a helicopter! I checked the roof of this place. They can land on it. I want out, do you hear me?"

Bishop spoke next. "How do you expect this to happen? You can't do this to your son, Melodie."

She gasped but controlled the cries escaping her mouth. "I did all of this for my son!"

Bishop's tone was strong and firm, even intimidating, like he was talking to a teenage girl. "You don't give a shit about your kid, Melodie. We all know it."

He pressed our luck.

"Not yet," I whispered.

Bishop stepped forward. "Fuck that!"

"Stay back!" Melodie screamed. "Or the bitch is dead! And get me my damn son!"

Just then Emmett busted through the door with his gun raised.

It all happened so fast. He screamed for her to drop her weapon, but instead she aimed it at Emmett and pulled the trigger. He went down.

"Shit!" I screamed. I dove down and rolled behind a display of magnets as Bishop did some miraculous karate moves to attempt to knock the weapon from Melodie's hands.

I crawled toward Emmett, grabbed his radio from his shoulder, and screamed, "Officer down," into it.

Someone responded, but I didn't listen. I checked Emmett's pulse. He had one.

"Bitch fucking shot me," he said. He grabbed his side.

"You asshole! What the fuck were you thinking?" I took off my jacket and threw it on him and said, "Hold this on the wound," then went to help my partner.

Bishop's right hand moved in for a neck cut. Melodie screamed but held tight onto Ana Flores. The gun was still in her hand, but then Bishop smacked it and it fell on the ground. Rockman dropped her left hand from around Ana Flores's neck. She was stunned, standing frozen for a second, probably in pain.

I made eye contact with Flores. "Move!" I screamed. "Now!

She dove to the side and crawled to the aisle on her left, then scooted behind it. Bishop kicked the gun further from Rockman. I jumped in, tackled her to the ground, and used the weight of my body to flip her onto her stomach and secure her there with my knees over her legs.

Bishop grabbed her gun and pointed it at her. "Make a move, Rockman. For the love of God, make a fucking move!"

I screamed, "Stay down!" I grabbed my handcuffs and looped them around each of her wrists, bent down and whispered in her ear, "I crossed my fingers each time I gave you my word."

"Fuck you!"

Bishop kept the gun aimed at her and hollered over to Emmett. "You okay?"

"I...I'll live, but son of a bitch, this hurts."

"I want my fucking son!" Melodie screamed.

"You have the right to remain silent. Anything you do or say can and will be used against you in a court of law. You have the right to an attorney. If you cannot afford an attorney, one will be provided for you. Do you understand these rights as I've read them to you?" I wished that she'd beg for kindness.

"Fuck you!"

"A helicopter," I said, laughing. "A fucking helicopter."

Bishop laughed too. He hustled his ninja butt over to Ana Flores, who'd crawled into a ball. As he helped her up, she fell into him, wrapped her arms around him, and rattled off something in Spanish too fast for me to understand.

Bishop patted her back. "There, there, honey. It's going to be okay."

He was such a dad cop.

"I...backup is here," Emmett said. "I need a medic!"

Kyle, Michels, the chief, and seven other squad cars had arrived. They had surrounded the place. Emmett gave the all clear over his radio and made sure the ambulance was there by saying, "I need a big-assed Band-Aid."

Bishop walked out with the nanny. He returned quickly with the rest of the team. Michels headed straight to Emmett.

"What the hell? You trying to be a vigilante or something?"

"I was...shit." He stared at his bloody shirt. "This hurts like hell!"

"That's what bullets do, man," Michels said.

I smiled.

I swung Rockman over onto her side and told her to get up. As I guided her out the door, I spoke softly into her ear. "You'll pay for your crimes. You have my word."

19

We processed Melodie Rockman quickly, then set her in an interrogation room and let her sit until she calmed down. She'd been screaming threats at everyone she could, starting with the officer who drove her to the station. He said he told her he *preferred his balls attached, ma'am*, when she threatened to bite them off. I cringed at the thought. Not of what he might feel, but the nastiness of the act itself.

Because of her iffy mental state, Jimmy held off on interrogation, choosing instead to wait for the district attorney to determine the process. In the meantime, her attorney arrived, and she was advised to calm down and shut up.

"Flores has an immigration attorney representing her, but she's willing to talk," Michels said.

"North Fulton Hospital, right?" Bishop asked.

He nodded.

"Let's go," I said to Bishop.

I leaned my head back on the headrest in Bishop's passenger seat. "This thing really is comfortable."

"Anything's more comfortable than your Jeep," he said.

According to Bishop, I was out seconds after that. He shoved me awake after parking at the hospital.

"Sorry," I said as my eyes flew open.

"Don't be," he said. "I'm exhausted too."

The receptionist gave us Ana Flores's room number.

She cried when we walked in. Her attorney shoved his hand toward my face. "I'm Hugo Santiago," he said. "I represent Ms. Flores. We are applying for amnesty. Her life is at risk in Mexico. She is fragile."

"More like lucky," I mumbled.

He eyed me suspiciously.

"Mr. Santiago, we don't care about your client's immigration status. All we care about is our investigation."

"Do I have your word?"

I eyed Bishop. "What's this word thing all of a sudden?"

He shrugged.

I nodded to the attorney. "You have my word." I smiled at Ana. "I bet things have been a little complicated for you recently, huh?"

She looked to her attorney for guidance. When he nodded, she said, "*Sí.* Where is Ryan? Is he okay?"

"He's someplace safe, and he's fine. Just fine."

She smiled as tears fell from her eyes. "That is good. I was worried. All I wanted was for the boy to be safe. I tried to help."

"You did good," I said. "Can you tell me what happened? Start from the beginning."

We arrived back at the department with a story that matched everything we already knew and filled in the blanks for what we didn't.

Bishop told the team Ana's story. "She laid out a near long list of events that would have put anyone on edge. Mary Hagerty came to her begging for help. She knew nothing about the pregnancy rumor and assured us she'd never slept with *the doctor*, as she called Steve Rockman.

"The woman she knew to be Melodie Rockman, a.k.a. Emily Hagerty, was cold and heartless, and not just to her but also to the boy and his father. Emily fired her when Ryan called Ana 'momma.' Mary showed up at her apartment in Cumming with the boy a few nights ago, begged her to keep him safe, and gave her the keys to a car and directions to a rental cabin. She was too shaken to recall how long she was there but was outside playing with Ryan when she received a text message from an unknown number that said, *Leave the boy at the nearest gas station and get out.* She immediately left with the kid and dropped him off at the nearest gas station, but instead of leaving, she went back to the house to get her things. Melodie showed up. Ana tried to run, but Melodie caught her and took her to wherever she kept her for at least a day. Ana didn't know the location. Melodie left and returned several times, each time wearing a wig and different clothing until she came back this last time and made Ana leave with her."

"And since we haven't been able to talk to Melodie, we can't determine her actions between those visits or what led her to calling me," I added. "But we'll find out eventually because her attorneys know she's looking at the death penalty."

"Her father hired the best attorney in the country, and he's second chair," Jimmy said.

I laughed. "He's not a criminal law attorney. He's just showing his balls."

Nikki laughed. "If he's got to show them, they're not very big."

I smiled, but the crowd of men in the room didn't find that all that funny. "I like you," I said to her. "You're going to do well here."

"Haus, Marshall, and Flores will testify against her," Bishop said. "The incidental women who helped Mary Hagerty will testify, but the DA doesn't think they'll offer anything to the case, and she's worried too many illegals going without deportation will ruffle feathers, so she's not willing to take the risk."

"She wants to be re-elected," Bishop said.

"Exactly," I said. I glanced at the clock. Another day had passed, and we were all going on no sleep. Just the thought of that made me yawn, and that came with a chain reaction.

"Go home and get some rest," Jimmy said. "All of you."

"I'm waiting to talk to Rockman," I said.

"Ditto," Bishop said.

"It's not happening. Not today," Jimmy said.

My jaw stiffened. "What? I thought we'd get the chance once her attorneys were finished with her?"

"They prefer to deal with the district attorney directly," Jimmy said.

"But we need answers. I...we..." Bishop smacked his hands on the table. "That's bullshit, Abernathy. Bullshit!"

"I know," Jimmy said. "But it's not my decision. But you're all going home now, and that's my decision. You've been working double duty for months now. If you don't get some rest, I'll put every one of you on desk duty."

"We just want five minutes with her," Bishop said.

"I'll talk to the DA," Jimmy said. "And if I get the go-ahead, I'll call you two back in, but for now, everyone's off. Forty-eight hours. Paid leave. No exceptions."

Michels popped up from his seat.

"Forty-eight hours paid?" Michels asked. "I'm in!"

Bishop groaned as he stood. "Not fighting that." He smiled at me. "You shouldn't either. You fell asleep on the way to the hospital."

"You're not helpful."

"Everyone meet at Dukes two days from now at nineteen hundred hours for Ashley's going-away party," Jimmy said.

"Going-away party?" I asked. "She's not leaving yet. It's not even been two weeks since she gave notice." I looked at Ashley. "What's going on?"

"I've got my first investigation with the DEA," she said. "It starts in three days."

"And we're going to send her off with a bang," Jimmy said. "Now, get out of here. All of you." He smiled and walked out.

The rest of the team followed, leaving just Kyle and me in the room.

"I'll follow you home," he said.

I stood and studied him. He was attractive. Tommy was attractive too, but in a different way. Tommy's looks were more boy next door with a hint of toughness. Kyle was all-out military dressed in tight-fitting civilian clothing. He looked like an Army Ranger or Special Forces, and he wore it really, really well.

"Rachel?"

I shook my head. "Oh, sorry. I, uh...I need to get something from my cubby." I ran out of that room so fast I nearly tripped.

Jimmy tapped on my cubby wall. "Listen, I know I just ordered you home, but I just talked to Savannah, and she would like to see you. Would you be willing to stop by the house?"

"I would love to stop by the house." I stared at Kyle standing behind him and said to Jimmy, "Give me a minute, and I'll head out, okay?"

"I'll see you there."

Jimmy turned and bumped into Kyle. "Oh, sorry, man. Hey, we're heading over to my place to see Savannah. Why don't you come?"

Kyle looked at me. I shrugged.

"Sounds like a plan," he said.

Savannah sat on the couch in their den, propped up on a pile of pillows with a bottle of water filled with an assortment of fruits covering the bottom. She wore a Georgia sweatshirt and a pair of black leggings, her long hair was tossed in a bun on the top of her head, and she was completely free of makeup. I'd seen her makeup-free once in our years as friends. She was stunning. Glowing like a pregnant woman should.

"Hey, girl!" She patted the empty spot by her feet. "Come cop a squat next to me."

I smiled. "How're you feeling?"

Jimmy kissed his wife on the forehead. She smiled at Kyle. He smiled back and asked her how she felt.

"Fresh as a daisy," she said. "Go on and get yourselves a beer. I bet you need 'em."

The men walked into the kitchen.

"Did you see how that man looked at you? Honey, he is *all in*."

"Can we talk about you, Sav? Just for five minutes?"

She waved her hand at me. "I am fine. Between us, I thought I'd hate this bed rest, but so far, I'm kind of enjoying it. Jimmy does everything! Well, he's paying someone to do a lot of it because people keep dropping dead in this town, but you get my point."

I laughed. "I'll try to help him more at work. But seriously, how are you?"

Her smile faded a little. "Scared, praying a lot, but I have faith." She patted her very firm, still very flat belly. "This little one is going to make it just fine."

I wished I had the faith in things Savannah had. "You'll be fine too."

"I'm not the least bit worried about me, but I am worried about you."

"I'm tired."

"Obviously," she said. She pointed to my eyes. "I've got some cover-up that'll make those dark circles disappear."

"I've literally worked my ass off with very little sleep. I earned those dark circles."

"Meh, you're right. Kyle doesn't seem to care. If he can tolerate your smell, I'm sure he can tolerate your pale face and dark circles."

I sniffed myself. "I don't smell?"

She laughed. "Honey, God is kind. If we had to sit in our own foulness, we'd lose our minds. He saves that for our friends."

My eyes widened. "Do I really smell?"

She tilted her head to the left. "Pregnant women have superpower noses. Ask Jimmy."

"I'll take the risk," I said.

She laughed. "How are things going?"

"There are no things going, really. We've been working too hard for things to be going."

"But he's here. What's that mean?"

A smile pushed across my lips. "He was going to follow me home, but Jimmy asked me to come here."

"Oh, yes! That one-night stand gets a re-do!"

"Savannah!"

"Oh, be honest. You were drunk, he was drunk. Do you really think it was as good as you remember? We know men like to claim they're great in bed when they're drunk, but us women all know the truth."

I laughed. "I honestly haven't thought about it." That was the truth. I probably would have thought about it, but I didn't have the time because I was busy chasing down a triple-murder suspect.

"Well, here's your chance to throw that rope and lasso that man in."

"You've really got a way with words, don't you?"

"Hell yes." She yawned and rubbed her belly. "This baby is wearing me out."

I couldn't bear the thought of losing Savannah or the baby I'd yet to meet. "Sav, honestly, is everything okay?" Jimmy barely provided any details, and I suspected it was because he didn't want to jinx his baby's and wife's health.

"We're good. This is nothing we can't get through, Rach, I promise. Trust me, this baby isn't ready for its godmother to raise it, not yet." She poked my arm. "Not that you'd do a bad job of it."

"I'm the godmother?"

"Did you think I'd ask someone else?"

Kyle stood at my kitchen counter with a beer in hand. He swallowed a sip back and leaned against the counter. "Good work, Detective."

I clicked my beer bottle to his. "Right back atcha, Agent Olsen."

"You're tired. I won't stay. I just wanted to make sure you got home safely."

"I appreciate that."

He set the beer down and turned to leave.

"Wait," I said.

He turned back around.

"I'm...I need to chill out a bit before I sleep. Would you like to stay awhile?"

"Very much so."

"Great," I said with a little more excitement than I'd expected. "But I need to shower first. I'll be quick."

"I'll feed Herman."

"Herman! Oh my God! Please. He's starving, I'm sure." I pulled off my boots and headed to shower. As I got to my bedroom door, I spotted the picture of me and Tommy on my nightstand. I stepped into the room and closed the door behind me, then I walked over to the photo and picked it up while I sat on the bed.

Tommy's eyes sparkled when he smiled, and that sparkle was forever memorialized in that photo. "I like him," I whispered. "I think I'm ready." I set the photo back on the nightstand, blew Tommy a kiss, and headed to the shower.

Kyle didn't stay the night. I offered him the guest room, but he had an early meeting in Atlanta and knew I needed the sleep. I appreciated him gracefully bowing out before I chickened out on what I was afraid might happen had he stayed.

Baby steps, he'd said.

I visited Emmett in the hospital. He'd had surgery to remove the bullet, and the doctor wouldn't release him until he had a few days to recover.

He was not pleased. "I'm fine. I don't even have any pain. Why won't they let me go home?"

I laughed. "You don't have any pain because you're drugged up on painkillers."

He furrowed his brow. "No, I'm not. I haven't had any pills since I got here."

I pointed to his hand and the tube running from it to the medicine. "Have you ever had surgery before?"

He shook his head. "Well, unless you consider when the dentist took out my wisdom teeth."

"Nope. That's not real surgery. That tube is pumping all kinds of stuff into your veins. I can't believe the nurse didn't explain that to you."

"She said I was getting something, but I was pretty out of it when she explained it all to me. I guess I forgot."

I chuckled. "Shocker."

"Is Chief pissed?"

"He's not thrilled, but I think you'll be okay."

He looked relieved. "How'd the interrogation with Rockman go?"

"It hasn't. Her attorneys won't allow her to talk. They want to work a deal with the DA."

"Man, that sucks."

"Yup."

I ended up back at the department an hour after visiting Emmett. Jimmy looked frustrated, but I wanted to talk with the DA. After some convincing, he understood.

"They want to plead her down due to insanity," she said.

I exhaled. "I knew that was coming."

"She's been through a lot."

"You're not going to let that happen, are you?"

"She's a white woman who was trapped in Mexico and held as a sex slave to the cartel, all at the hands of her sister. A jury of her peers, especially women, will feel compassion. They'll put themselves in her place."

I shook my head. "She killed three people, kidnapped a woman, damaged her kid for...for life. I don't care what happens to a person, nothing is cause for that kind of revenge."

"You're right, but the defense is already playing her as a victim. Her father's been all over the news this morning. Honestly, I'm not sure she's even capable of standing trial."

"Let me talk to her."

"Not going to happen, Ryder. And she's not here, anyway."

"What? Where is she?"

"The psych ward at Northside. Per her father's suggestion."

"Shit."

She shrugged. "It's still a win. She's not going to be released."

"You don't know that."

"I'll make it part of the negotiation." She sipped a coffee she'd been holding. "Listen, I'm not happy either, but this is the least risky route to take, and it's my decision. You don't have to like it."

I didn't like it, but she was right. It was her decision.

EPILOGUE

December 22, 2022

The man stood over her. She was still—distant, even. Her eyes no longer begged for help, they shed no more tears. She was asking for release, he thought. Release from the torture. Release from the pain.

He crouched down and brushed a blond hair away from her face. "It'll all be over soon." He smiled. "Close your eyes."

She did as she was told, and the man walked out of the barn.

He stood just outside the door, smiled again, and then dropped a match onto the gas-soaked ground.

BODY COUNT
Rachel Ryder Book 5

A serial killer is leaving numbers as his only clues...but nothing seems to add up.

When the fire department discovers a body near the scene of a suspicious blaze, Detective Rachel Ryder and her partner Rob Bishop are called to investigate. A set of numbers has been deliberately left near the body, and an autopsy reveals that the victim was killed before the fire.

This death was no accident.

When the investigation turns up few clues and no previous references to the killer's calling card, Rachel and Rob turn to the media for help, eliciting contact from an unexpected source. It seems a killer from the past is back in the game...and the body count is growing.

Rachel and Bishop must solve a seemingly impossible case to stop the murders—and they don't have much time.

Facing off against a cold-blooded mastermind who leaves nothing to chance, what will it take for Rachel to beat the serial killer at their own game...before another victim's number is up?

Get your copy today at
severnriverbooks.com

ACKNOWLEDGMENTS

A lot of work goes into writing a book, and much of that work is done by others. I owe a great deal of thanks to the publishing team at Severn River Publishing for the complicated and detailed job they do each day to make sure my books are the best they can be. They also handle every minor detail of the publishing process which allows me to spend my time tapping away on my keyboard. I am forever grateful for and in awe of their hard work.

A special thanks to Randall Klein, my concept editor for his support and detailed notes on my mental musings. I may write the outline, but he picks through it with a fine-toothed comb and offers insight that makes the story much better than I ever could.

An equally special thanks to my copyeditor Kate Schomaker for the wonderful work she put into tightening my long-winded sentences, a few fragments, and a lot of run ons, too! She polished the manuscript to a shine, and trust me, it's much better from her expertise.

As always, a shout out to my friend and local expert, Major Ara Baronian for his knowledge and understanding of the law in Georgia. He is always a gold mine of material, and my books would not be what they are without him.

Of course, to my readers, thank you! I'm still kind of shocked that people read my stories!

And last but certainly not least, a big thank you to my biggest fan, my husband, who has supported my career from the day I decided to write my first book. He is also my sales rep, selling my books via Amazon to everyone he speaks to daily. He's the best.

ABOUT CAROLYN

USA Today Bestselling author Carolyn Ridder Aspenson writes cozy mysteries, thrillers, and paranormal women's fiction featuring strong female leads. Her stories shine through her dialogue, which readers have praised for being realistic and compelling.

Her first novel, *Unfinished Business,* was a Reader's Favorite and reached the top 100 books sold on Amazon. In 2021 she introduced readers to detective Rachel Ryder in *Damaging Secrets. Overkill,* the third book in the Rachel Ryder series was one of Thrillerfix's best thrillers of 2021.

Prior to publishing, she worked as a journalist in the suburbs of Atlanta where her work appeared in multiple newspapers and magazines.

Writing is only one of Carolyn's passions. She is an avid dog lover and currently babies two pit bull boxer mixes. She lives in the mountains of North Georgia as an empty nester with her husband, a cantankerous cat, and those two spoiled dogs. You can chat with Carolyn on Facebook at Carolyn Ridder Aspenson Books.

Sign up for Carolyn's reader list at
severnriverbooks.com

Printed in the United States
by Baker & Taylor Publisher Services